SUPPER CLUB

SUPPER CLUB

A Novel

 LARA WILLIAMS

G. P. PUTNAM'S SONS
NEW YORK

PUTNAM

G. P. Putnam's Sons
Publishers Since 1838
An imprint of Penguin Random House LLC
penguinrandomhouse.com

Library of Congress Cataloging-in-Publication Data

Names: Williams, Lara (Writer of Treats), author.
Title: Supper club : a novel / Lara Williams.
Description: New York, New York : G. P. Putnam's Sons,
an imprint of Penguin Random House LLC, [2019]
Identifiers: LCCN 2018046714 | ISBN 9780525539582 (hardcover) |
ISBN 9780525539605 (epub)
Classification: LCC PR6123.I55254 S87 2019 | DDC 823/.92—dc23
LC record available at https://lccn.loc.gov/2018046714

First published in the United Kingdom in 2019 by Hamish Hamilton,
an imprint of Penguin Books Ltd.

First US edition published in 2019 by G. P. Putnam's Sons,
an imprint of Penguin Random House (LLC)

International edition ISBN: 9780593085806

Printed in the United States of America
1   3   5   7   9   10   8   6   4   2

Book design by Kristin del Rosario

This is a work of fiction. Names, characters, places, and incidents either are the product of the author's imagination or are used fictitiously, and any resemblance to actual persons, living or dead, businesses, companies, events, or locales is entirely coincidental.

For Celina

Eat me. Eat me up like cream pudding.
Take me in.
Take me.
Take.

—ANNE SEXTON, "ANNA WHO WAS MAD"

The Fearful Are Caught

Lina was the first. We met her in a café with cloudy gray furnishings and a needless accumulation of potted plants. The tables were piled with magazines that had titles like *Wheatsheaf* and *Gardenia*, their covers featuring tanned girls with ribbony limbs, all pigtails and peasant dresses. One by one, Stevie turned them upside down. Lina messaged us from outside, and we watched her do it, crinkling her nose at the beginnings of rain.

I'm outside.

Shall I come inside?

I mean, shall I meet you inside?

Where are you sat?

Sorry, I just hate not knowing where to sit.

Are you near the back window? I think I can see you.

Okay, I can see you. I'm heading in now.

Sorry.

Sorry.

Lina had blond hair knotted over her shoulder. She wore a navy cord suit and a white silk shirt. Her bulky trainers were incongruous to her outfit. She explained she wears them to and from work but in the office is required to wear heels.

She worked as an office manager at an expensive hotel. It was reasonably paid; she'd get a discounted Caesar salad in the hotel bistro for lunch, plus use of the steam room and sauna. But she worked a fifty-hour week and once got docked pay for having chipped her nail varnish on the tram. And watching all the rooms being used for affairs and, worse, for ordering sex workers, had made her paranoid about her husband's fidelity.

"At first it was the middle-aged couples leering over the counter. Drunk and conspicuous, like we couldn't believe their audacity."

She wore a thin gold bracelet, which she rolled between her fingers. Spinning it in circles against her skin until it left a faint red mark.

"Then it was the younger ones. Women asking which lift would take them to Room Thirty-three. Their eyes never really leaving the floor. Walking out of the hotel still adjusting their clothes."

Stevie and I made notes: me scribbling into a notepad, Stevie tapping at her phone. We didn't know what we were collating at that point, but the data felt urgent and indispensable. Lina's round face turning pink.

"But it was the sex workers who got to me. And the men who use them. These completely ordinary-looking men."

Lina's obsession began with the women: eyeing the sizes of their waists, scrutinizing their faces—wondering whether he might find them attractive. She'd think about the way they dressed, whether her husband might want her to dress like that. The women, of course, mostly weren't sex workers, but to her they might as well all have been. These other women, with their lipstick and their lacquered hair. All offering something else, something new, something she never could—being in possession of just the one human body—and trying to make a penny off it, too. She wondered whether she hated these women or if she was afraid of them. Whether there was a difference.

She became fixated on the idea that her husband must be having an affair or using sex workers—or that he eventually would. She'd follow him home from work, leaving her own work early, making up doctors' appointments or dentist checkups, taking Ubers across town. She'd sit on the other side of the square outside the recruitment agency where he worked, having already taken note of the colors he was wearing that morning in order to better spot him. She'd follow him on the opposite side of the street, a few feet behind, her gaze fixed on him diagonally across the road. She'd trail him into shops on the way home from work, ducking behind the bread counter in Tesco. Once she held an especially large watermelon out in front of her head so she could walk past him undetected and check the contents of his basket (Jazz apples, cooked ham, Ritz crackers). She would trace him all the way to the train station, where he would sometimes stop for a drink at the station pub, not telling her, saying he had to work late; and if he was lying about this, then what else was he lying about? Dishonesty, she felt, was a spectrum; you might be on the less dangerous end, but you were still on it, prone to slip up, slide further along, depending on the circumstances.

She wouldn't stop until she had followed him all the way to their door, and then she would crouch down, sometimes crawl on her hands and knees, hiding behind the brick wall that fronted their home. She would wait there for thirty minutes, sometimes an hour, until she was sure, until she was absolutely certain, he wasn't going back out.

Once he had gone to bed, she would stay up late to devour his Internet activity: scrolling through his history after he'd fallen asleep. She installed a keystroke logger on their downstairs desktop, finding out all his passwords and accounts. When her husband used the bathroom or showered in the morning, or popped out to buy a pint of milk, she would check his phone, reading his texts, looking at his photos, reviewing his outgoing calls. She learned what kind of pornography he liked and that sometimes he looked up his old girlfriends on Facebook. But no sex workers. Never sex workers. She began feeling almost resentful at his inactivity, thinking about all the well-dressed businessmen who ordered champagne and chateaubriand who wouldn't patch through their wives' telephone calls—did he really think he was better than them?

It became a routine of sorts. The following. The checking up. The phone. One Saturday afternoon he went to watch the football, and she noticed his phone left behind on the kitchen counter. She didn't even think about it, it was instinctive. Perched against the oven, she opened his messages: a text from an unknown number. Thanks for last night, let's do it again soon, how much do I owe you for the room—punctuated by an image of lips, clavicle, rib cage, and breasts. She stared at the message for a while, worrying she had imagined it, that she had literally willed it into existence. She waited for the anger, the disappointment, the betrayal she had anticipated to course through her veins, surprised when all she felt—all she actually felt—was relief. It was over. It had happened. And it didn't hurt that bad.

"That's why I'm here," she told us. "That's why I want to do this."

Stevie and I could not contain ourselves. We squeezed hands underneath the table. She grinned back at us.

"You're in," Stevie said.

"We've not got a date for the first one yet," I added. "Or a venue. But we're looking. Probably something next month."

We finished our drinks and told her more about our vision for Supper Club. We told her about the ethos. About what we hoped the events would look like. The sort of women we were hoping to recruit.

"So your husband," Stevie said. "Did you leave him after you found out?"

"Oh, no," she replied, perhaps a little dreamily. "We stayed together. We're kind of happier than we've ever been. It's weird to think," she added. "It was just one year. Just one really peculiar year. But it transformed my life forever."

Stevie's face changed. "That's ridiculous," she said, forever teetering on the precipice of hostility, never afraid to speak her mind.

"Don't you think that's ridiculous, Roberta?" She turned to me. "To put an emphasis on one arbitrary stretch of time that's . . . you know, a total construct? I mean, we are all just these giant accumulations of stuff and experiences and talking and things happening to us. You can't break a human life down into years and say that one of them in particular really means something."

Lina looked embarrassed. She began fiddling with her bracelet again.

"Roberta?" Stevie said. "Roberta, don't you agree?"

I half smiled—out of generosity or discomfort, it was often hard to know. And I didn't say that I didn't agree, but I didn't say that I did.

Expectations

The September I left for university, color clung to the branches. There is something particularly unbearable about being sad in the heat: the terrible knapsack of it, carrying it around like a heavy load. Something between melancholy and nerves, a blank no-man's-land, lousy with the lethargy of hot weather. Who can be bothered?

On my last morning at home, I looked out at the cemetery that backed onto my bedroom window. I hooked open the latch and pushed forward the glass pane, swinging my legs over the ledge, lighting a cigarette, and exhaling thin curls of smoke toward the graves. Growing up next to a cemetery had made me flippant about death. It was as perfunctory as chopping cabbage beside my mum: Van Morrison on the radio, the dog expectant beside our legs, flipping scraps of veg to the floor. Hearses dragged slowly past our house, but so did garbage trucks and milk vans. Families sobbed and howled, we turned up the TV. Sometimes I liked to pretend my own dad was dead: imagining the funeral, what I might say, what hymns might be sung. Whether there would be any readings or speeches. I got a strange satisfaction from thinking about it.

He wasn't dead, of course. Just gone—he'd left when I was seven. And though my mum encouraged me to stay in touch with him, eventually I stopped replying to his letters, wouldn't answer his phone calls. So I was used to the vagaries of loss, the spaces left behind, my dad's absence apparent in the most peculiar ways. The suite of friends' husbands that swung by, each offering a particular trade or service: fixing a clog in the gutter, ringing the council about streetlights. Not that my mum was incapable. She was a problem solver, resourceful in a way I've never since witnessed.

"Some things come better from a man," she would tell me, wearily. Though I could barely remember my dad, I was acutely aware of a lack in my life: missing something I'd never really known.

I sat on the windowsill and thought about death, my dad, and whether or not I'd get a good room in halls, while downstairs my aunt Hetty loaded up the van.

My aunt was a woman who drove a van. It was an olive-green Toyota HiAce, and she drove it in sleeveless shirts and khaki shorts, a carton of orange juice wedged in the cup holder to be slugged back noisily at traffic lights. On the weekends she'd go to watch Arsenal wherever they were playing, traveling all over the country, the continent, with the large group of men who were her friends. She'd tell me stories about cutting them down to size, drinking them under the table. "I know men." She tapped her index finger to the side of her head. "I know how their brains work." She was a woman who'd lived a very glamorous life.

I stubbed out my cigarette against the exterior wall and went downstairs. My aunt was throwing in suitcases and canvas bags, landing each with a loud thump.

"Careful!" I yelled.

"You know, you might have helped," she responded, and I wondered why it hadn't even occurred to me to offer.

Joan of Arc snapped at our feet. She was a usually stoic French bulldog. The rescue trust we'd adopted her from told us she'd been abandoned, found whimpering beneath a cooling bonfire. She must have crawled there for warmth. The name was obvious. We called her Joa for short; appropriate, as that was the shape of her bark. *Joa! Joa!* she would yap, as if with an accent.

"She knows you're going," my mum offered solemnly. I picked Joa up, snuggling her loosely in my arms. We had been a triad: her, me, and my mum.

"Can she come with us?" I asked.

My mum leveled her gaze on me, and I took Joa inside, scooping up her face. "I'll be home soon," I said, kissing her good-bye.

My mum had taken the passenger seat while my aunt switched on the engine. The van hummed a low vibrato. I got in the back.

"Right," my aunt said, revving the engine. "Let's get you moved out."

I pulled the lap strap across my waist as tight as it would go.

I was not unaccustomed to the trappings of an urban environment: once a year we'd take a trip to the city for shoes. We'd eat sushi off rubber conveyor belts, dinging the bell for more sparkling water. I'd drag my mum to vintage stores and buy oversize sweatshirts and buttoned dresses. She'd marvel at their cost and scrutinize stains, rubbing the fabric between her fingers. "You'll get that out with vinegar," she'd concede, shaking her head in seasoned disbelief. We'd finish with a trip to the cinema, a rare opportunity to see something foreign. But I was always happy to come home. There was a sense of order there. Everything closed at five, so you knew where you were.

Now I was moving to a much bigger city. A city in which the train station contained more enterprise than my entire hometown. "It's like an international airport!" I'd exclaimed on my first visit, coming to look round the university. My mum eyed me warily: my callow gait and habit of tripping.

The roads were wider and more hazardous than I was used to. Everything felt immediate and perilous. The buildings slowly increased in size and density. I pressed my face against the glass. We passed Turkish sweet shops and Chinese bakers. Snooker halls and shisha cafés. Organic grocery stores and newsagents with bars across their windows. Newspaper boards warned of gang crime and fraud, reported stabbings and rape. Back home we'd passed just two: BEE INFESTATION CLOSES SCHOOL and LAKE ALGAE: KILLER? The traffic wound sluggishly through the city center, backdropped by an orchestra of car horns and emergency services.

As we neared the campus, everything began to space out. We circled its glassy modern structures for a full hour, trying to find my accommodation. My mum and aunt bickered in the front. *They are like an old married couple,* I thought. *They are literally like an old married couple.* A map was produced, and we realized that my new home was set just outside the city, not quite suburbia but almost. "Here," my aunt said as we approached rows of dilapidated three-story town houses surrounded by a somewhat bleak industrial landscape. It was a world away from the grassy slopes and induction activities I'd imagined. On the website the halls had been photographed capped in snow. They'd looked a lot nicer that way.

Across from the student blocks were low rows of shops and businesses. A tiny vegetarian café. A semiderelict laundrette. A chip shop. There was an unmarked plot of land that contained a single abandoned supermarket trolley. We unloaded.

My assigned flat was located on the top floor. I was the first to arrive. My mum relayed a strategy while I stood, guileless and dismayed, at the center of the communal kitchen: historic smears of bean juice on the counters, the walls stained and cracking. My aunt put her arm around me. "The good news is, you get first pick of the cupboards and drawers."

I chose the smallest ones. Once unpacked, I saw my family downstairs. Each step released something spidery inside me: the sick-making terror of need. Needing the accumulative, impervious love of being forced to eat all your broccoli even when it is making you retch and gag to put it in your mouth. The love of the TV being turned off past eleven. The love of being asked to say hello to the dog over the telephone. I'd always seen my mum and aunt from knee height, never quite managed to meet them as equals. It occurred to me how ludicrous it was that families slept in separate bedrooms, not piled on top of one another like lazily sunbathing lions.

My aunt blew kisses as I stood in the damp landing of what was now my home. I heard the van's engine start, turned to go back upstairs. There was a tap at the door, and I looked back to see my mum on the other side of the glass, holding her coat: a thick waterproof affair she took everywhere. I let her in. "Here," she said, handing me the impossibly middle-aged item, two sizes too big. "Because you don't have anything decent for when it gets cold." She kissed my forehead and left.

I went back to my room, threw the coat I knew I would never wear on to my bed. I lay beside it and cried.

I thought leaving home would be a liberation. I thought university would be a dance party. I thought I would live in a room vined with fairy lights; hang arabesque tapestries up on the wall. I thought scattered beneath my bed would be a combination of Kafka, coffee grounds, and a lover's old boxer shorts. I thought I would spend my evenings drinking cheap red wine and talking about the Middle East. I thought on weekends we might go to Cassavetes marathons at the independent cinema. I thought I would know all the good Korean places in town. I thought I would know a person who was into healing crystals and another person who could teach me how to sew. I thought I might get into yoga. I thought going for frozen yogurt was something you would just do. I thought there would be red cups at parties.

And I thought I would be different. I thought it would be like coming home, circling back to my essential and inevitable self. I imagined myself more relaxed—less hung up on things. I thought I would find it easy to speak to strangers. I thought I would be funny, even, make people laugh with my warm, wry, and only slightly self-deprecating sense of humor. I thought I would develop the easy confidence of a head girl, the light patter of an artist. I imagined myself dancing in a smoky nightclub, spinning slackly while my arms floated like laundry loose on the breeze. I imagined others watching me, thinking, *Wow, she is so free.*

I'd had friends before. I had a group to check in with at lunch. We'd go on cinema trips and talk about boys at sleepovers. We'd go to bars and horrible clubs, and on birthdays we'd go bowling. But we never really connected; standing side by side like soldiers, we were just marching through. It was sort of understood we wouldn't stay in touch beyond the last summer of school. We were stand-ins for the people we were eventually supposed to meet. They would meet their sporty friends, their religious friends, their studious friends; I would meet my arty friends, my pleasingly weird friends. In those first few weeks, I would meet people, thinking, *Is it you? Are you the person I am supposed to find?* But most people didn't fit that frame. These were not the sorts of people I'd left home for. And if they were, I couldn't quite recalibrate myself to be the sort of person they would want to spend time with. No matter how much I shifted and shrugged, I was still right there.

The first night at university, someone told me everyone congregated in this one pub. I went down alone. Grating techno blared from the speakers, and the whole room smelled of perfume and sugar. But there was a thick sense of anticipation in the air, a sense of the invisible membrane that separated us from our future selves. If you could just worm your way through it, a plentiful and rewarding existence awaited. I ordered a drink at the bar, my heart rattling at my throat. I looked around. The girls were all tanned, hair grazing the curves of their bottoms. The boys wore open shirts buttoned down far below their sternums. I felt the bloom of a hand on my shoulder.

"My name's Natasha," the girl said. "But everyone calls me Nidz."

I stared up into her eyes, unable to make my mouth into the shape it needed to be, to say my name.

"This is Becca." She gestured toward the tall blonde by her side. "But everyone calls her Becks."

I extended my hand to shake theirs. They looked down at it: my damp, floppy palm.

"Okay, well, nice to meet you!" she said, then hurried her friend on, giggling. I finished my drink and went home.

When class started, our tutor asked us to turn to the person next to us and talk to them about our favorite writers. I watched as the room naturally turned inward—looking first to the girl to my right, whose back was to me, and then to the boy to my left.

"No," he said, reaching for his iPod and headphones, listening to music while staring straight ahead.

My flatmates were equally resistant. There were five of them. Across the hall a girl called June: Home Counties, law, embarrassed by her obvious wealth, every bit as fussy and rigid as the obsolescence of her name implied. Next door was a boy called Samuel, a little snarky and vague, though I very much liked his boyfriend, Robert, for his soft-faced handsomeness and manner of gently closing the door. Next door to June was Mei-Ling, spirited and friendly, though with a habit of looking right through you. She'd ask you questions about your day, but you got the impression she wasn't listening to a word you were saying, just formulating an agreeably benign response: "That sounds bad" or "Is it really?" At the end of the hall, two boys, Adnan and Nadeem, on the same course cluster. Adnan was confident and a flirt, even with me, though I suspected mostly out of kindness. One morning I got up to pour a bowl of cereal, the bloated blush of my stomach protruding above my pajama bottoms, my hair a slick mess. Adnan was at the kitchen table, tinkering on his laptop. "How am I supposed to get any work done with beautiful girls slinking about . . . ?" he began, then, looking up from his laptop, corpsed, and carried on typing. Nadeem was skinny and shy unless drunk, in which case he was an absolute nuisance: inviting his seemingly masses of friends around, playing dance music until the early hours of the morning.

Other flats had formed rowdy gangs, mutually supportive units. Everyone I lived with seemed to have a vivacious social life, complete with emotionally cohesive bonds, strictly outside the confines of our flat. June knocked around with other posh girls who had impossibly voluminous hair and lax personal hygiene. Samuel hung out exclusively with Robert. They had a decidedly domestic arrangement for two nineteen-year-olds, but they seemed happy: washing up side by side, getting takeaways. Mei-Ling's friends were mostly from her fashion marketing course, aloof but essentially nice. They'd go to a Vietnamese noodle place just off campus, then out dancing dressed in immaculately conceptual outfits: crinoline skirts and heels like works of art. Adnan hung out with an eclectic bunch of varying ethnicity, nationality, sexuality, and gender; the only thing they all seemed to have in common was being exceptionally good-looking. Nadeem's friends were a large group of boys who liked playing sports. I'd not met anyone. I sipped tea and stared out of my grimy window, my heart winding tentacles around the city, clutching blindly in the dark.

M y room was reassuringly small, a modest unit of space. I'd spent a lot of time harmonizing the light. The issued lampshade produced a pallid glow that looked like the color of depression, so I purchased a brass reading lamp and lined LED candles along the floor. I wasn't allowed to hang pictures, but I could Blu-Tack postcards to the walls. I found a crocheted throw to put on top of my bed and began a small collection of vintage ashtrays. And although it wasn't the space I imagined—one in which friends would drop by to see me, in which I would entertain slim-shouldered theater grads—it was my space: my first snug space.

In lieu of a life, I settled on an existence. I spent most of my time in bed, eating noodles and doodling crosswords, listening to music. Sometimes I'd just lie there with the window open, breathing in the steel smell of the rain. I'd blow huge chunks of my student loan buying clothes no one would ever see me in or hop from web page to web page, researching conspiracy theories, reading about serial killers. Occasionally I would write an essay or attempt some required reading.

I'd started smoking roll-ups because they were cheaper and killed more time. I'd take myself out on trips to art galleries because they were free, go on walks around town. I'd check out films from the library. One morning it occurred to me that a good way to spend the day might be cooking. My days were punctuated only by meals, with so little in the spaces between them. People could spend hours in the kitchen: thickening risotto or browning meat. It was something to do.

My mum had already taught me the basics: how to cook rice, scramble eggs, how to boil pasta. But that was eating to survive. The more I experimented, the more I wanted to discover flavor, texture, scent. Gently toasting spices. Mixing herbs.

My immediate instincts were toward anything like comfort food, the hallmarks of which were a moderate warmth and a sloppy, squelching quality: soups, stews, casseroles, tagines, goulashes. I glazed cauliflower with honey and mustard, roasted it alongside garlic and onions to a sweet gold crisp, then whizzed it up in a blender. I graduated to more complicated soups: Cuban black bean required slow cooking with a full leg of ham, the meat falling almost erotically away from the bone, swirled up in a thick, savory goo. Italian wedding soup was a favorite, because it looked so fundamentally wrong—the egg stringy and half cooked, swimming alongside thoughtlessly tossed-in stale bread and not-quite-melted strips of Parmesan. But it was delicious, the peculiar consistency and salty heartiness of it. Casseroles were an exercise in patience. I'd season with sprigs of herbs and leave them ticking over, checking up every half hour or so, thrilled by the steamy waves of roasting tomatoes and stewed celery when I opened up the oven. Seafood excited me, but I felt I had too much to learn. The proximity of Polish stores resulted in a weeklong obsession with bigos—a hunter's stew made with cabbage and meat and garnished with anything from caraway seeds to juniper berries.

I started baking bread. My first was an unadventurous granary loaf, which came out sort of armadillo-shaped and a little too brown in the crust but had a gorgeous graininess and was definitely tasty. I'd never thought bread could have any sort of complexity or depth of flavor, but now I found there were so many notes to be savored: yeast, sea salt, pepper, rosemary, charcoal, butter, olive oil. I was mad on bread. I baked rolls before class, leaving them to cool, then cracking them open for lunch, dunking them into beer and cheese stews, curried lentils. The space beneath my bed, next to the radiator, became the perfect proving spot, and I took particular comfort in taking a nap above whatever dough was lethargically rising at the time.

I'd match meals to books and films. Requisite reading for my Southern Gothic seminar was accompanied by waffles and grits. New French Extreme called for steak tartare (I threw up for hours). Hot dogs and curly fries for a Friday beneath the duvet with *National Lampoon's*. Earl Grey and scones during a late-Wednesday-night rewatch of *Brief Encounter*. One especially bleak Saturday afternoon, *Kiki's Delivery Service* and some unmemorable Pixar: ramen and diet lemonade. It needed work.

I never made anything sweet. No cakes or desserts. Pies were filled with kidneys and game. Loaves were picnic, zucchini. Though

I liked the idea of creating my own ice creams or pastries, it seemed sort of frivolous. What I need was sustenance. Fortification.

The act of cooking imposed a kind of dignity on hunger, which had become terrifying. I couldn't remember how I had managed hunger, the animal wildness of it, before. At home we gobbled, we were a family who ate. You could sit in front of the television and shove handfuls of crisps into your mouth, you could smother ripped-up pieces of bread with margarine over the kitchen sink. There was a bravado in it: leftovers were for losers, and if you didn't have a hearty appetite, there was something wrong with you. But the eating always had a kind of context: in my mum's house, with its flotsam of dressing gowns and stupid shows on the television, it felt reasonable and normal and right. Now my eating, my bottomless, yearning hunger, was a horror. I felt monstrous, shoveling in the amount of food I wanted to, more anxious with every bite. Cooking became the buffer: an act of civility before the carnage ensued.

And more importantly, it was a singular respite from academic life. Lectures and seminars were charged with nervous energy. Class felt like sitting at the bottom of a well: I could never raise my voice loud enough to be heard. On the rare occasions that tutors would try to engage me, their almost immediate regret was plain: registering wild panic in my eyes, beating a hasty retreat. I was terrified of being asked for my opinion, and yet I also longed to be—staring hard at the text in front of me, trying to conceive an original thought. When we took turns reading aloud, some piece of short fiction or theory, I'd restlessly anticipate which bit would be mine, running and rerunning the numbers, making sure I didn't mess it up. Once, when the moment finally came, my section was only a paragraph long, seven sentences at that, before our lecturer instructed "Next" and the guy to my left, some scruffy doofus in a baseball cap and a ROCK AGAINST RACISM shirt, took over. I had the feeling I might cry. Another tile in the mosaic of tiny injustices that had become my life.

When I didn't have any classes or seminars, I could sometimes go up to forty-eight hours without using my voice. I'd contrive ways of saying things just to make sure I still could. "This bloody thing," I'd announce, booting up my laptop. "Ouch," if I tripped. The actual word of it. Ouch.

I still spoke to my mum once a week, usually on Mondays. "I'm busy," I'd tell her. "I've got so much going on."

"I know," she would reply wearily. "I know."

Isolation was a strange thing. Sometimes the lack felt like a blank page, like a possibility. I'd spend a lot of time daydreaming. Long, convoluted narratives—picking at my dreams like I was choosing a movie. Lying on top of my duvet staring at the small expanse of my ceiling, I'd relay the humble fantasy of my choosing. What about the one where I meet that guy from Critical Theory, we hit it off, and he goes down on me in the library? Or the one where I buddy up with Mei-Ling? Do we go to the Vietnamese place and gossip? Or out meeting boys? But I was always tripping up. My fantasies were rooted in a tangible reality. Mei-Ling works at Bella Italia on Thursdays! We'd have to rearrange! And as for the sex in the library—would he be able to tell I hadn't done it before? Would there need to be a conversation about that?

My virginity was an issue. It had never bothered me before. Back home, sleeping next to Joan of Arc, my mother's faint snores just audible in the next room, I almost never had sex on my mind. Now it was everywhere. Nadeem's pouting poster girls on the kitchen walls. The squeaky groans from June and whichever anti-Israel guerrilla club promoter she was hooking up with that week. Almost all the books and films I studied. NHS posters pasted across the union walls. Even Mei-Ling had occasionally been known to take two cups of coffee back to her room. I'd always thought she'd have been above it. I came to imagine my own genitals as unusable and impenetrable— as smooth as a doll's.

Like sex, friendship seemed at once possible and impossible. Tiny rivulets intermittently seeped through. Sometimes I'd be washing up late and make conversation with whoever was in the kitchen past twelve, gathering scraps by veil of night. "Can I make you a cup of tea?" I'd offer, say, June, her silk halter tear-stained and sweaty from deep house and an ecstasy comedown. I'd produce stew and soft rolls. We'd chat about workloads, homesickness. I'd pretend to understand what it was like to be called back by a boy. Sometimes I'd talk about my dad, listen to stories of bickering or divorced parents in return. We were still so close to the child part of our timeline. But those conversations were just a small space of intimacy in the pale blue dim of the communal area, always dissolved come daylight.

A Vacant Space

S ourdough begins with a starter, which is also known as a leaven, a chief, a head, a pre-ferment, or my favorite—a mother. There are several different types of starter, depending on the ratio of water to flour, so you may have a loose and sticky starter or a stiff and heavy starter. What I am trying to say is: there is more than one way to begin.

If you're planning to make sourdough, you are going to need some time—anywhere between one week and six months, depending on your patience. And you are going to need a lot of patience. Begin by identifying a time of day when you will be consistently free. Many people choose first thing in the morning or last thing at night. You also need to be available twelve hours after this time, so do take that into account. To create the starter, combine flour and water—roughly half as much water as flour—and stir until they have become a single sticky ball. Seal the ball in an airtight container and leave it somewhere warm. Twelve hours later the feeding begins.

Feeding the starter involves adding more of the mixture to the mixture. And so you make another ball of flour and water and stir it into the existing ball of flour and water, which at this point should be crusty and a little lackluster. You will do this again twelve hours later, this time increasing the volume of water, and then twelve hours later again. At the third feeding, start throwing away some of the starter. It is alive, and it is growing, and half of it needs to go. Carry on like this for two more days.

Now we need to talk about bubbles. A few days into nurturing your starter, you should notice bubbles and perhaps a funny smell. It is only going to get worse. Bacteria have invaded your starter, and they are releasing gas. Keep to the twelve-hour feeds. When the starter starts to smell sour and double in size between feeds, you are ready for the next step. Begin by clearing some space in your refrigerator.

You should now feed the sourdough only once a week, each time halving it and throwing one half away. When you retrieve your sourdough from its new home in the fridge, it may be topped by a thin, brown fluid. This is called hooch. It is alcoholic, but you cannot drink it. If you have a lot of hooch, pour it off. If you have only a little, stir it into the starter. Remember, the starter determines the flavor.

After a while you might want to start thinking about baking it. You will need more flour and water, plus butter, salt, honey, and, of course, the starter. Mix a cup of starter with the other wet ingredients. Mix the dry ingredients separately and combine the two. Knead the dough until your wrists hurt. You're doing a great job. Let the dough rise somewhere warm for anywhere between twelve and twenty-four hours.

The dough will be enormous now, and you will need to punch it down with your hands. Once the air is knocked out, shape it into a smooth, leathery dome and put it into the oven. If you want a hard crust, put a bowl of water in the oven next to it. If you want a really hard crust, brush the dough with egg yolk. Bake for twenty-five minutes.

With the leftover starter, you have a few options. You can keep feeding it and throwing away the excess, baking bread whenever the feeling takes you. You can keep feeding it and give the excess to your friends. Or you can just throw it away because you've had enough. It's not for everyone, and it may not be for you.

One more thing to remember: it is messy work, and the dough gets everywhere.

Not long after my twenty-eighth birthday, I stopped in a café on the way home from work. I was hungry, and I didn't want to wait until dinner. It was cramped and hot, with a large queue snaking around the tables, occupied mostly by men wearing beards and flannel shirts, staring despairingly at their MacBook Pros.

I joined the back of the queue and tried to slow my breathing from outdoors. I patted at my forehead, which had begun to sweat. I felt a little anxious, as I do in small spaces. I craned my neck to see where everyone had found the menus they were all thumbing, spotting an empty menu holder in the same brown/bronze color scheme as the rest of the room. The queue moved slowly forward. I started thinking about what I might like. When I could see the pastries and muffins, I squinted my eyes to see what was in them. I hate walnuts and sultanas, and that makes buying baked goods more challenging than it needs to be. There was a banana-and-salted-caramel muffin that looked big, bulbous, and satisfying, and a cinnamon swirl enthusiastically smeared with frosting, but I couldn't see what was inside it.

Another person departed the front of the queue, coffee and brown paper bag in hand. My stomach started to rumble.

People began joining the queue behind me. One lady bumped into me, and I apologized to her. She apologized to me. But I apologized again, out-apologizing her, as a kind of reverence.

"I should have been moving with the queue," I said.

"I wasn't looking where I was going," she insisted.

"I'm an idiot," I said.

"No, I am," she said, and then again, with some gravity: "I am the idiot."

I was only two people away from the front of the queue. I started rehearsing what I was going to say—trying to think of the most efficient and economical way of asking whether the muffin contained walnuts, whether the swirl disguised sultanas. How I would make my decision depending on the outcome of those two variables. How I would then quickly make my order and ask for a coffee, too—with hazelnut syrup. I worried about that last bit. An irritating addendum.

"Does the muffin have walnuts?" I would ask, and then wait for an answer.

"And does the cinnamon swirl have currants or similar?" I would follow up.

Then, depending on the outcome of those two questions, I would say, "Please may I have a banana-and-salted-caramel muffin?" [or] "Please may I have a cinnamon swirl?"

Then, "And please may I also have a latte with hazelnut syrup?" which I quickly amended to, "And please may I have a tall latte with hazelnut syrup?" adhering to the available lexicon of the establishment, visible on the overhead blackboard. I mentally whizzed up the speed at which I would say "hazelnut syrup," and hoped I could do the same when the moment arrived.

Another person left with a coffee and a brown paper bag. It was almost my turn. The man in front of me walked up to the service area of the counter. He leaned back and put his hands in his pockets. He stared up at the blackboard. He stared at it for a long time, making the sorts of little sounds you make when you are trying to decide something. He sucked air through his teeth. He clucked his tongue.

"What nondairy milks do you have?" he asked the lady behind the counter.

"Soya and almond," she replied. "I think."

"Okay," he said. "Okay."

He looked up at the blackboard a little longer.

"No rice milk?" he asked.

"I don't think so," she said. "But let me check."

She turned and dropped down onto the backs of her heels and had a good root around the fridge. There was only soya and almond milk. Everyone could see. She kept looking, though. Moving things around.

"I'm afraid not," she said, on her feet again and planting a carton of soya milk and a carton of almond milk down on the tabletop to show the man she was doing her best.

"Hmmm," he said, and resumed looking up at the blackboard.

"What herbal teas have you got?" he asked.

She turned around and looked at the board that all of us, every one of us in the queue, including him, could see.

"We've got English Breakfast. Earl Grey. Mint. Green. Lemon and ginger. Lemongrass. Chai. And raspberry."

"Right," the man said. "Okay."

He took his hands out of his pockets for a bit and flexed them by his sides.

"I think I'll have a lemongrass," he said, walking through each syllable of every word very carefully.

The lady opened one of the glass pots filled with tea bags behind her. She riffled through them for a long time.

"I'm afraid," she said, "we're out of lemongrass."

"Ah, man," he said. "Oh, dude."

She raised her arms and displayed the flats of her upturned palms, an evolutionary gesture: I mean you no harm.

"Have you got any in the back?" he followed up.

"I'll just check," she said, and then she disappeared into the back for a small while.

"No, I'm afraid not," she said when she had returned. She looked a little pink and dewy.

"Okay," he said. "Right."

He was leaning back, staring at the blackboard again, with his hands in his pockets.

"In that case," he said, "I'll have a flat white with . . . almond. No—with soya. No—with almond milk."

"Great," she said. "A flat white with soya milk!" she called out to the man behind her.

"Almond!" the man corrected her.

"Oh, yes!" she said. "A flat white with *almond* milk."

"Anything else?" she asked the man.

"Hmmm," he said. "What are the croissants like?"

"I don't know," the lady replied. "I've never tried one."

"Okay," the man said. "No problem. What about the brownies?"

"They're pretty good," the lady replied. "Actually, they're great."

"Okay," the man said. "Then I'll have a brownie."

The woman removed a brownie from the display tray with a pair of silver tongs and packaged it up in a brown paper bag. There was a moment when you could see a sense of relief wash across her face, the tiny muscles around her mouth, eyes, and nose all relax.

"Anything else?" she asked.

"Let me have a think," the man said.

"The sandwiches are nice," the lady said. "If you're in the mood for something savory."

"Just let me have a think," the man said. "Just let me have a think about that."

"Flat white with almond milk!" the man behind the lady shouted.

"That's me!" the man said, and was handed his coffee. He took a long sip from it. He nodded at the man behind the counter, demonstrating his approval.

"Okay," he said, staring down at the premade sandwiches. "Now, what have we got here? Do any of them come with cucumber? I hate cucumber."

"I can find out," the lady said, and from beneath the counter she removed a large folder, which she flicked through.

"I'm sorry," she said, having looked at it for a while. "It doesn't say whether they come with cucumber. Just whether they have gluten or dairy or monosodium glutamate."

"Okay," the man said again. "All right."

He was still staring at the sandwiches.

"Do you think you could have a little look inside?" he asked. "Just to check."

"Of course," the lady replied. She administered a pair of white latex gloves and began peeling back the tops of the sandwiches.

"This one doesn't have any cucumber," she said.

"What's in that one?" the man asked.

"Cheese and pickle," the woman said.

"I don't think so," the man said. "What about the one next to it?"

The lady peeled back the top of another sandwich.

"Ham and cucumber. Sorry!"

"What about the one next to that one?"

"Hummus and avocado. No cucumber!"

Triumphant.

"Okay," the man said. "I'll have that."

"Great," she replied, and packaged up the sandwich. "That will be twelve pounds thirty."

"Twelve pounds thirty?" the man said. "That's an absolute rip-off."

The lady lowered her eyes to the floor, authentically ashamed of the steep prices of the coffee shop in which she worked only part-time.

The man removed a twenty-pound note and handed it to the woman. The jaw of the machine jutted out, and her eyes searched the tiny cash compartments in total despair. She gathered the change into her hand.

"I'm afraid," she said, "we've run out of five-pound notes. So I'll have to give you your change in pound coins."

She dropped the change into the man's hand. She looked about ready to die.

"It's fine," the man said graciously, though from the half smile he dispensed, you could tell that it was not. He counted and then pocketed the change. He took a moment to look around him to make sure he had gotten everything he needed, and then he left.

"What can I get you?" the woman asked me. But I had forgotten everything I'd been practicing and couldn't think what I was supposed to say.

"Just a coffee," I said. "Just a filter coffee, please."

A few weeks later, I met Stevie.

I work at a fashion website. Some people think it is a very glamorous job.

The job was advertised as writer, and I was attracted to the absoluteness of the phrase. Though the writing experience I had was writing emails, writing essays, and writing texts to my mum, I applied anyway. When I didn't hear back, I kept ringing them and emailing. Persistence in the face of indifference was something I was familiar with. Eventually they invited me to an interview, where I was presented with a pair of boots and asked to describe them. I regarded them as objectively as I could, writing down a brief and very literal description. I was offered the job.

"Everyone else wrote the description with loads of color and character," my future boss told me. "But you just described it. I mean, you just very accurately described it. There is absolutely no color—no flourish whatsoever. It's just the thing. Just the unadulterated thing. And that's exactly what we're looking for."

My job was writing product descriptions. I would describe thirty near-identical pairs of trousers, all with slightly different pocket detailing. I would spend full weeks characterizing brogues. I would spend days only on ear cuffs or Samsung phone cases. There was a meditative quality to it, like a tap I could switch off and on. I actually sort of loved it. I'd listen to radio plays and podcasts. I'd have months where I'd commit to hearing every Nina Simone studio album, where I'd listen to hours-long documentaries about the Holocaust. I'd do all this while completing the strangely satisfying job of rendering an object exactly as it was.

The job was based in a large contemporary office with rows of desks lined up one after another like pews. Everyone had an Apple Mac with two monitors, their eyes darting from one screen to the other. I sometimes wondered about the space between the screens. Did they ever look at that, and, if so, what did they see? At lunch I would read in the cafeteria or the park, and at three thirty on the dot, I would make a cup of chamomile tea. On Fridays they would bring around a drinks trolley, and we stirred sickly-sweet cocktails while staring at our screens. Sometimes they played music, gauche dance or hip-hop, and one of my colleagues would invariably address us collectively as "ladies." *Who's in a party mood, ladies? Who's out tonight, ladies?* The answer was, *Not me*, because I liked to go straight home, sometimes straight to bed, sometimes without even taking off my coat.

I did this job for four years. One morning as I peeled a banana and stared at the blandly comforting view of a reclaimed-brick façade, my boss interrupted me for a quick meeting. I stepped into his office and seated myself unobtrusively at the edge of the room.

"Roberta," he said, folding his hands in an avuncular fashion. "We've got some bad news and some good news."

I was told they were making cutbacks and were outsourcing all product descriptions to external copywriters. I was being moved to the studios to assist the stylists and photographers. I would help out in the accessories closet. I would fold stuff. "It is less of a brain job," my boss said, "and more of a body job."

So I had a new role, and that was fine, too. I enjoyed the locomotion of it. I liked how every day had different textures. Some days I would be handling reams of crinoline and chiffon. Other days I would push a felt cloth across the smooth surfaces of the studios. I would spend full afternoons sitting cross-legged on the floor, detangling a box of necklaces. I would steam blouses for hours. I would fetch cigarettes and Diet Cokes for the models. I would look through portfolios and decide which models would be best for beachwear and which would make the most attractive brides. I once spent three hours looking at photographs of wrists, determining which wrist was the most appropriate for displaying our new line of bangles. I had very few friends and spent most weekends with my mum and my aunt.

Sometimes my mum asked me how I felt about spending so much

time with models, whether it made me feel inadequate, and the truth was it didn't. It was like working with clouds or cats. Their lives were such an opaque abstraction that I felt somehow superior to them, facilitating their movements in ordinary human existence. This is how you book a train. This is how you file an invoice. This is how you throw away an apple core. Sometimes I would look the models up on Instagram and marvel at their world. They would be in Berlin slouched against some graffiti. They would be in New York hashtagging #avotoast. They would be in Ibiza sipping spritzers on the hulls of yachts, wearing swimsuits cut to the navel, their hair immaculate in the breeze. They had boyfriends with the sorts of bodies I found intimidating. Or they had spry, lithesome girlfriends who were very often models themselves. They were almost never single—and why would they be?

I'd gotten quite good at my job—that is, I had gotten good at making myself look busy. I walked across the room, striding with industry and intent. I had perfected a sort of brow flex when asked to complete a task, evidencing my arrangement of this task among the presumably hundreds of other things I was supposed to be doing. I was left to my own devices a lot. I very rarely had to work as part of a team or collaborate on anything. I had my own jobs to do, and I just did them, and I was fine with that.

One morning I was asked to refold all the fabrics in the design studio. It was the sort of small job I enjoyed, left alone in a room all day, playing music and putting things in order. Midmorning there was a tap at the door. I paused my YouTube tutorial on different types of folding patterns, looked up from where I was watching it, hunched on the floor. My boss entered, her chandelier earrings jingling cartoonishly, the tassels of her caftan tickling the ground. "This is

Stevie," she said, gesturing to the person next to her. "She's going to be your intern."

I looked at the girl. She had dark hair piled onto her head like an animal folding in on itself to sleep. She had enormous green eyes lined with kohl. She wore a red cheesecloth skirt and a zebra-print coat at least two sizes too big for her. She was shifting her weight from side to side.

"Hey," she said, a barely decipherable hint of upward inflection incongruous with the bravado of her look.

"Stevie's going to be with you for the summer, so if you can show her the ropes, tell her how you like your tea, or rather, my tea . . . ha-ha."

I delivered a thin smile, staring at this thing that had ruined my thing. An intern? She was no more than two years younger than me. And my job was scarcely senior to intern. The situation was absurd.

"Sure," I said. "When does she start?"

"She starts now," my boss said, staring vacantly at her phone while flicking her wrist in my direction. "Like, right now."

Stevie joined me on the floor, contemplating the tangle of formal scarves that lay in front of me, as the studio manager wafted out of the room.

"So," she ventured. "This is, like. Your job?"

It didn't take long to explain how to separate the scarves and fold them according to weaving pattern and yarn type. We sat side by side, slotting them into filing cabinets like vertically shelved documents.

"This is nice," Stevie said. "I get why you like this."

"Do you want to listen to something?" I asked. "Music? Podcast?"

"You choose," she said, and so I resumed the Dusty Springfield album I'd paused earlier.

"*Dusty in Memphis*," she said. "That's the best one."

We caught eyes. A shared nod of affirmation.

"She was bipolar, you know?" Stevie said. "And a cutter."

I made a noise of acknowledgment, trying to ignore the blood rising behind my cheeks.

"Also bisexual. Dusty was cool. How about you? Boys or girls? Or both?"

"Me?" I asked. "Um, straight I guess. Boys."

"That's cute," she said. "I don't get it, but it's fine."

There is something socially accelerating about a shared, repetitive task. We jumped immediately into the kind of candid conversation women our age could have. We discussed our menstrual cycles and our favorite films and our most hated male writers. We shared our theories on David Lynch's problem with women and our favorite episodes of *Twin Peaks*. We dispensed full biographies in which we detailed run-ins with school bullies and absentee fathers, dwindling career ambitions and would-be side hustles.

Stevie was interning at the website because her mum was friends with one of the directors. She had been trying to make it as an artist—experiencing a limited sort of success for a while—but had been out of work and living at home for over a year. She'd left art school thinking she wanted to be a painter, feeling the sort of scorn for all other practices and forms that painters allegedly feel, before trying out sculpture and installation. She was interested in time- and site-specific works and for a while used to make mechanical pieces with the pendulums and gears taken from watches and clocks that would morph and rotate, displaying a different shape depending on what time you viewed them. "Total bullshit," she said. "Embarrassing." She went back to painting for a while ("ironically") and was invited to rejoin her old university as a lecturer. "That's when I knew

I was doing something wrong," she said. She ditched the art to go traveling for a while, backpacking around East Asia, then moving "on a whim" to New York, where she lived and worked in a cat café in Brooklyn Heights. "It was a pretty cool job," she said. "I'd feed and groom them. Clean out their shit and piss."

I giggled while trying to suppress the spike of energy I'd felt at her mention of New York—but couldn't. I wanted to hasten our intimacy, to cut straight to the chase.

"My dad lives in New York," I said—a fact I had recently happened upon and had not been able to share with anyone. "What I mean is, I haven't spoken to him, like, ever. Then about a year ago, he emailed me out of the blue saying he's living in New York."

"Wow," Stevie said. Her parents were still together, she told me, and, more surprisingly, they were still happy. They went on dates to the cinema, took romantic holidays, and called each other unusual pet names like "Fruit Loop" and "Old Ham." I got the impression Stevie craved instability, that she yearned to come from a broken home.

"What did you do?" she asked. Her green eyes got wide. The opacity of her gaze, I would soon learn, prompted me to amp up whatever I was telling her, to write checks I couldn't cash.

"I didn't reply. I haven't. He just keeps emailing me. Once a month. Telling me about his cats. What he's watching on Netflix."

"And your mum?"

"I haven't told her."

"Sheesh."

My mum had once described living with my dad as like living with an unstable whoopie cushion. How an ill-timed look or gesture could set him off, sending him careening around the room. She often told me about the time he abandoned her at a restaurant when she asked him if he might keep his voice down while referring to their waitress as "that old horse face." That once at the supermarket checkout she had commented on how much she liked a particular brand of pizza, watching it move on the conveyor belt in front of her, and he'd grabbed her arms from behind and punched them into the air, yelling "P! I! Z! Z! A!" and she'd had no choice but to go limp and let him do it.

I had little recollection of the time when my dad had lived at home. He'd vanished so abruptly, informing my mum he was going to Blockbuster to get something "Swedish and sexy" and never coming back— and somehow I could never imagine my family home with him in it. Or with any man in it, for that matter. The punnets of blueberries next to pots of cold cream in the fridge. The bath salts lined up on the landing. *Sex and the City* perennially on the TV. It was all so female.

I felt suddenly embarrassed for telling Stevie about my life so readily. I changed the topic, asking about her art. "So what are you planning on doing with it?"

"I don't know," she said after a while—and I could tell she really didn't, and that was making her sad. "Being at art school felt so vital and ripe. It felt like I was on the edge of something, you know? Now I've no idea. I still want to do it, but I don't know what I even have to say." She sighed. "How about you? Make any art-with-a-capital-*A*?"

"Oh, no," I replied. "Absolutely not."

I watched my hands working, folding cloth and shelving it away.

"But, you know, I cook."

"How retro."

"Fuck off. It's important to me. And I'm pretty good. Maybe I'll cook for you sometime."

"Yeah? I'd like that."

"Okay," I said.

"Okay," Stevie replied.

When we left the room, a few hours later, it was like emerging into the daylight after an afternoon trip to the cinema, leaving behind the mythical for reality, the feeling of being quietly but fundamentally changed.

I liked Stevie so much I felt embarrassed. I'd giggle at her jokes too hard or listen to her stories too intently. I wanted to jump up and down at the feeling of our connection. When we'd had a long talk or spent the day comfortably not talking at all, I wanted to clap and shout, *Look at this! This is happening!* It was like falling in love. I'd imagine conversations with her on the walk to work, in the shower, before I fell asleep. I'd narrativize my day for her, collating observations and thoughts I'd hope to share with her later. Sometimes I felt I was performing for her when she wasn't even there. I'd put on music I thought she might approve of while cooking my dinner. I'd dress for her even when we weren't meeting up. I'd hyperarticulate the parts of my personality I sensed she liked. I wanted to lean into the person she was influencing me to be. It was like the beginning of a new relationship, one where you're confident the other person really likes you—or at least how I'd imagined that might be. I could reply to her messages within seconds of receiving them. I could call her late at night. I didn't feel weird asking her to do stuff three days running. I felt like I'd been enrolled into a club I'd never known anything about—and it was wonderful.

After work I would watch how she sipped her cocktail, all sass and sophistication, a Pink Lady snapping gum. I was ready to be taken anywhere she wanted, and I felt that she knew it. We'd have dinner in Ethiopian restaurants hidden above takeaways, drink in secret bars at the back of taxi ranks. We'd walk down the canals at night. We'd go to midnight screenings of comic-book films and buy enormous boxes of popcorn. She'd taken to sleeping over at my place most nights, to the point that the couch was always made up into a bed and she had her own drawer. It was nice to have someone.

Pretty soon it made sense that we get a place together, and so we started looking for flats. Everyone at work thought we were mad. "Do you two not get sick of each other?" my manager would ask— and we would grin gaily, go out in the rain to smoke, ignoring the sense of a collective eye roll happening around us.

After weeks of pinging emails to agents, viewing flats in re-claimed mills and terraces not too far from town, we settled on a town house in the suburbs.

"I like it," Stevie said, signing the lease. "It's as if we're settling down. We should get a Volvo."

We had an agreement: she would take care of making the place look nice, and I would cook all our meals. She'd never learned to cook, and when her mum hadn't made her dinner, she'd lived off freeze-dried ramen broken up into chunks, eaten dry and hard, or entire packets of Rich Tea biscuits.

"What are you going to make me tonight?" she'd ask, standing demurely in the kitchen like an expectant child.

Having somebody to cook for was like having something slot into place. I wanted to show off for her, cooking all my favorite dishes. I'd come home from work and cook for up to two or three hours. Stevie would sit in the living room, wrapped in a blanket on the couch, reading or flicking through Netflix, calling, "It smells *delicious*" or "Is that bacon? What are you making with bacon?!" I would present her meal at our small dining table—a table with just enough space for two. She would set it with a candle or sometimes a flower plucked from the alley behind our home, arranged in a plain glass vase, and we would talk and talk, despite having talked all day.

We slipped quickly into a matrimonial dynamic. We would walk home from work together, stopping in at the supermarket, discussing how we might spend our evening. If we came home separately, which we rarely did, we would check in with each other, text to let the other know we'd got home. If I were spending the evening with my mum and aunt, I'd usually plan ahead, leave her something she could heat up in the oven. Six weeks into living together, she came hammering on my door while I was getting ready for work.

"My God, woman!" I called out in mock exasperation. "What?!"

She threw open the door and walked in. Her jeans were pulled up to her hips but gaping open at the fly. She struggled to make the button meet the buttonhole.

"Look at this!" she said, prodding her belly. "This is your work!"

"Would you like me to sign it?" I asked. She told me she would, and I grabbed a felt-tipped eyeliner, wrote "Roberta" in swirly, slanted handwriting.

"My finest piece!" I exclaimed, adding a black kiss.

"It's not funny," she said. "I only bought these last month."

Around that time Stevie began reconnecting with some old art-college friends. She found them on Facebook one afternoon, peering over her computer and hissing at me.

"This is Sarah," she said, swiveling the screen around. "She was such a hack bitch. But look at her now. She's doing a load of installation work around pregnancy and play."

She clicked through an image gallery of a tall girl in a pussy-bow blouse sitting in a cage full of enormous pastel-colored wombs, big bouncy things you could curl up in.

"Look!" Stevie said. "It's actually *good*."

A few minutes later, she was hissing at me again.

"Tamira's curating a conversation program about death!" she said, her eyes wide and desperate. "She's got Arts Council funding!"

Her art friends had invited her out to an exhibition launch, which she'd asked me to attend with her. "You're weird," she'd said. "They'll like you." But I declined.

Sometimes I felt like an impostor beside her. Or I thought of myself comparatively tiny: a borrower peering above the curvature of her foot. But then she would reach over and move my hair, tell me my makeup looked amazing, and I'd feel grateful, so stupidly grateful: a turkey graced the president's pardon. The idea of attending one of the gallery things with her artist friends made me feel sick. I had nothing to offer them. Nothing beyond tips on coring lettuce. Methods for mincing garlic.

So she went alone. The following Friday we were eating dinner at the dining table: spaghetti with mascarpone and spinach, one of Stevie's favorites. I wound pasta around my fork between sips of white wine while we talked about recently memorable incidents of street harassment and how much we hated men.

"One time I was coming home from a party with flecks of vomit and cigarette ash in my hair," Stevie said. "And this guy drives past and shouts, 'Gimme a blowie!' And I just thought, 'Wow, you must have really low self-esteem.'"

"After the first and only time I ever tried therapy," I offered, "I stepped outside the counselor's office and this guy across the street immediately yells, 'Smile!' So you know, I had to."

We giggled and chewed, got a little drunk. Stevie played Elvis Costello on her laptop.

"Hey," she said. "I'm thinking of getting a studio. You know. Where I can *make my art.*"

"Wow," I said. "Okay. I didn't realize you were thinking of getting back into it."

I was careful to cleanse any traces of resentment and inadequacy from my intonation. I studied the spiral of pasta clinging to my fork.

"Where?" I added. "Also, how will you afford to? You're on what, twelve grand?"

"My mum and dad are going to pay for it," she said. "How else do you think I pay rent?"

"I suspected."

"Anyway, I've been thinking. You should do something, too. Do you really want to work at that website forever?"

"Yes, I want to label footwear and reorganize cupboards of bras. It is my heart's song."

"Come on."

"I don't care. I'm not ambitious, I guess. I don't even know what I would be ambitious about, if I were."

"That doesn't matter. Listen. You should be doing cooking. I mean, why isn't that what you do? It's madness."

"I couldn't."

"You could."

"I don't know if I'd want to. I like cooking for me. I like cooking for people who I love." I gestured toward her. "I don't want to make money out of it. I just want to do it."

I stopped talking because I knew if I continued I was going to cry. But then I was crying anyway. I wasn't sure why. I wiped the tears away in an exaggerated manner, beginning with the heel of my palm and ending at the tip of the elbow, trying to regain control. Then I gave up, covered my face in my hands, and wailed.

"Hey," Stevie said, rushing around and plonking herself on my knee to hug me. She wiped my cheek and held my head to her breasts, stroking my hair. I limply hugged her back, embarrassed at the pool of damp I was leaking onto her T-shirt.

"I'm okay," I said, sniffling. "Sorry, I'm fine."

She placed her hand to my cheek, rubbing it with her thumb.

"Come on," Stevie said. "Let's put on something daft."

She selected a film about a policewoman who has to go undercover as a stripper. There's a slow shower scene where she has to shave off all her body hair. It turns out she's a natural on the pole and becomes one of the most sought-after private dancers at the strip club. She meets a handsome and wealthy businessman who isn't sure about dating her because she's a pole dancer, but when he finds out she's a policewoman only posing as a pole dancer, he takes her out for dinner. At the end she jacks in the police work and the pole dancing and marries the wealthy businessman. "You're glowing," her friend tells her when she hears the news. "You know how you looked when you were a cop? You looked tired."

Roberta, hello.

How are you? I hope you are very well. The cats say hello. They're trying to steal my grapes. They keep swatting at them with their paws. Can cats eat grapes? Hang on, I'm going to look it up.

Grapes are apparently TOXIC to cats and can possibly even cause kidney failure. Uh-oh. Well, they've only had one or two, so they'll hopefully survive. Also, I'm sure they've eaten worse. Once Mildew ate an entire latex glove. He was doing this weird meow and kept squatting and stuff, so I took him to the vet's, and the vet (who is an amazing big Russian woman with a foul sense of humor) pulled the full thing out of his anus, this brown latex glove, while laughing like a total maniac.

I'm sorry. That's a disgusting story.

I just watched that film *Panic in Needle Park*, and now I'm quite depressed. Not in an actually depressed way, no need to worry (!), just feeling a bit mopey. I might go for a walk around the block. It's really sunny out, and there's this new waffle bodega that sells these amazing doughy waffles with crème fraîche and salted caramel. They're delicious. I'm getting completely fat from waffles, crème fraîche, and salted caramel, and it is completely worth it.

I got a small pay rise at work this week, so that's nice. It works out at about $150 a month more, and that's not nothing. I'm not going to spend it all on baked goods, I promise (I don't). Everyone's freaking out at work 'cause one of the windows won't properly close. You would think we were living in some sort of nuclear winter the way they're carrying on, bringing blankets and filling up hot-water bottles. It's not even that cold. One of the women in my office, this lady called Judy, said she'd make me a crochet shawl cause I sit nearest the window. I think she likes me. I said that would be very nice, but now I'm completely dreading her bringing in this bloody crochet shawl and having to wrap it round my shoulders like I'm the flipping matchstick girl.

This weekend I'm going to actually do something cultured, if you can believe it, and visit the Frank Lloyd Wright exhibition at the Met—which I've been meaning to do every weekend for the past six months, and now it's the last weekend, so it will be packed, but that really is typical me. Leaving everything till the last minute. Anyway, it looks like a cool exhibition, with some of his original sketches and models. I'm at an age where that sort of stuff appeals. Have you ever seen the documentary about him? It's worth a watch, if you have the chance. You can even get it on YouTube. I just checked, and you definitely can. So if you're not too busy with all your love affairs and dinner parties and shopping sprees (that's what you girls do, right?), then do check it out.

Hey, you know what Jianjun next door told me? He told me that since his boys have moved out to Iowa with their mother, to this big farmhouse in the middle of nowhere—well, in the evenings they go out with their mates and go, wait for it, COW TIPPING!! Have you ever heard of such a thing! They wait till the cows have gone to sleep, and then they tip them over. To what end I did not ask. Jianjun's happy they're no longer in Queens, but he really didn't know what to make of that. And why would he? Americans really are strange sometimes. Honestly, the more you know, the less you understand. Great waffles, though. Really can't fault those waffles.

Anyway I've rambled on, or should I say waffled on (sorry), enough now, and I'm sure you're adequately bored/sleepy at this point. Like I say, I do hope you're very well. I think about you often. If you ever wanted to reply, well, that would be fantastic. But if not, I'll just keep sending you these completely fascinating updates from my whirlwind of a life.

All best,

Jim (Dad)

X

S tevie wanted us to have some of her new studio friends over for dinner, a couple called André and Emmeline. André made sculptures out of metal and twine and also ran an art label, though I wasn't sure what that meant, and I'm convinced neither did Stevie. Emmeline was completing her PhD on West African sculpture. They'd just spent six months living in Berlin. I was sort of dreading meeting them, but Stevie was very excited.

"They are going to *love* you!" she kept saying—though as she said this, she preened me, smoothing the hair across my face or running a thumb under my eye. I suspected what she meant was, *They are going to love the version of you I will be presenting.*

The evening of the dinner, Stevie perched on my windowsill, blowing smoke out of the inches-wide crack the window would actually open to, kicking the backs of her feet against the wall. I did my makeup wrapped in a bath towel. The breeze was making my skin prickle. I'd been slow-cooking lamb for five hours, and the whole house smelled of meat. Stevie stubbed her cigarette out against the dirt-streaked glass and threw it into the backyard, hopping down to rummage through the metal rack that I kept my best clothes on. She pulled out a bottle-green dress with a large lace collar, draped it over the bed, and wordlessly left the room.

In the kitchen I chopped cilantro while Stevie drank wine and fussed with the playlist, occasionally yelling things like, "Warren Zevon? Yes? No?" or "Does anyone actually like Tropicália, or do we just have to say we do?" When I poked my head around the door, she was swaying in front of the laptop while watching herself in the mirror.

André and Emmeline arrived carrying paper bags filled with

elegant-looking beers, and a box of mint Matchmakers, which they found improbably funny. André had long dark hair pulled into a bun and wore slacks with a short-sleeved silk shirt. Emmeline had wavy blond hair that tumbled down her back and shoulders, and she was big. Tall and heavyset. For some reason I wasn't expecting that. I thought artists were supposed to be lithe and spiky.

We had to eat cross-legged on the floor, as our tiny table wouldn't fit everyone. Instead I set it up like a small buffet counter: big pot of curry, steamer of rice, fresh chilies, coriander, raita, and chutney.

"What sort of curry is this?" André asked, raising his eyebrow.

"Kashmiri," I replied, and then couldn't think of anything else to say. I looked urgently toward Stevie in the way I'd seen children looking at their mothers, when asked a question they were too embarrassed to answer.

"Roberta's an *amazing* cook," she offered, patting her belly exaggeratedly. "I'm getting so *fat* living with her."

I cautiously shot Emmeline a look, but she hadn't seemed to notice. I felt attuned to the fact that her presence was making me a little uncomfortable. I kept shifting my weight. I wanted to position my body toward her, to make my soft parts visible, my own vulnerability apparent. Equally, I wanted to position my body away from her, to act as though she weren't even in the room.

"Emmeline's a great cook, too," André said, pulling at a tendril of her hair. "Aren't you, honey?"

Emmeline patiently allowed him to play with her hair, idly twisting it around in his fingers and studying her split ends. I felt annoyed on her behalf, like how dare he manipulate a part of her body while she was trying to answer a question? She watched him with an expression I couldn't quite decode, somewhere between resignation and gratitude. She waited for him to grow bored with it before turning to me and saying that she was also interested in cooking. It seemed bold, but I couldn't understand why. My interest in food had always felt like something that could be spoken about but not made visible. I worked hard at keeping my weight within pleasing parameters. It seemed so crass, so unacceptable, to be a woman who liked and was interested in food, and who dared to look like she did.

"I just took a sugarcraft course, actually," she said. "Where I learned to pipe icing and make sugar flowers and stuff. It was great."

The image of her piping sugar onto a thin biscuit arrived uninvited into my mind. I wrangled with the delicacy of the act. She put down her bowl and slipped out her phone, scooching over to show me some of her creations. Stevie and André, I noticed, scooched together, too.

"I love it," Emmeline said. "It's like my meditation. Like when I make my masks and hats. André thinks it's daft." She looked over at André, who was leaning to whisper something into Stevie's ear; Stevie had her shoulder half hunched and looked silly and pleased. Emmeline watched them for long enough that I started feeling uneasy.

"Are you seeing anyone?" she asked eventually, turning round.

I thought of the last time I'd had sex. Some guy I'd met at a work thing, who didn't want to actually have sex with me, just run the tip of his penis along the opening of my vagina while I looked on with a bemused sort of curiosity. I had a sudden urge to relay the encounter in microscopic detail. To wonder aloud, What was that about? I sensed I probably should not and instead replied, "No, not at the moment." I paused for a moment, then added, "I haven't had a boyfriend in nine years." I was perversely enjoying the amount of time that had elapsed since I was last in a relationship. Like peeling back a piece of dead skin and watching with a not-unerotic horror at how long it can go.

"André and I are thinking of getting married," Emmeline said. "Do you think that's a good idea?"

Behind her, Stevie was fanning out her fingers, placing the tips across various points on André's face while he grinned like an idiot. I heard her say something about facial chakras and wondered where she'd picked that up. She pressed her thumb against the dip between André's eyes, and Emmeline twisted round to see what was going on. I had to break the tension. "Stevie has a theory that the women who get married and have babies quickly are the smart ones," I said. "They've lassoed the beast, she thinks. And now they're working on taming it."

"That's true," Stevie said, interjecting. "Me and her. We're the idiots." She was gesturing toward me. "We're just lingering in the crowds. Waiting for it to break free. We'll end up pinned or in its jaw, too tired and damaged to fight. Do it now. Do it while you still have the strength."

I watched Emmeline strain toward André, trying to read the softly elliptical expression on his face. Even though I sort of hated Stevie for her shamelessness, I also sort of adored her. I loved her fluid confidence. How she spoke. I imagined how I would feel as her partner, so proud of my beautiful, articulate girlfriend.

"Here's to marriage!" Stevie said, lifting her glass. "Here's to settling down! Here's to curry!"

We lifted our glasses in the air, wine spilling sloppily over the side.

After talking about things we were watching on Netflix, Dadaism, and what you can do with softened tomatoes, we decided it would be a good idea to dance. We pushed back the table and sofa to make a space in the middle of the room. Stevie put on "Cut Your Hair" and turned the volume right up. Stevie, Emmeline, and I sang the lyric "Darlin', don't you go and cut your hair, DO YOU THINK IT'S GONNA MAKE HIM CHANGE?" extra loud, and André looked confused, because of course he didn't understand.

We took turns selecting songs and danced on the carpet and on the sofas, arms swimming and legs jumping up and down. Every now and then, I would catch André staring at Stevie in a greedy way, and I noticed Emmeline watching him, too, how he'd follow her hips and breasts as they bobbed around. I grabbed Emmeline's hands and tried to pull her away from the scene, but even when her back was turned, I could tell she was still looking.

They left in the early hours of the morning. By that point we were all slumped on the floor, lazily crunching through Matchmakers and commenting that they were actually really good and we'd probably start buying them regularly now. After the door clicked shut, I asked Stevie if she was sleeping with André, and she said "Yes" like she was answering the most obvious question in the world. She asked if she could sleep in my bed that night, and I said she could, even though I sleep much better alone.

In bed I blinked at the dark while Stevie shuddered to sleep. I thought back on the evening. How perfect and imperfect it had been, both in equal measure. How nourishing it was to cook for people I actually liked. I thought of the mountain of washing-up I had to do. The removal of a Matchmaker that had been trodden into the carpet. I wanted more evenings like that. In the morning I woke up, and the idea was already in my head.

"That's what I want to do," I told Stevie, grabbing and shaking her shoulder.

"What?" she asked hazily. "Is it make me a coffee?"

"No," I replied. "It's much more exciting than that."

"What could possibly be more exciting than wanting to make me a coffee?"

"I think I want to start, like, a supper club?" I said, and she half rolled over, mascara smeared both down her face and across my pillow. "But kind of a wild one."

"Yeah," she said, sleepily turning away. "I think that's a pretty good idea."

The thought of a supper club was somehow strange, a formalization of something personal and already strangely weighted. Eating and love had been, throughout my life, irrevocably connected. Fantasies of cooking for a partner. Promises of takeaways ensconced on the couch. My mum fussing in the kitchen while Joan of Arc whined at our feet. Sunday dinner with my aunt. I once heard a big girl in my philosophy class announce that she was starving. "I could eat the world!" she said, prompting exchanged glances from my peers. But I didn't think she had a big appetite; I thought she had a big heart. Watching programs on cannibalism, reading horror stories about lovers devoured, reports of people searching the Internet for someone to eat them, I'd think: *I get it.* My whole life was the push/pull of appetite: wanting to consume but also to be consumed.

And though I enjoyed cooking for Stevie, there was always a sense of deeply private communion to it. I liked the option to eat feverishly alone. But the thought of gathering people together and cooking for them felt plump with potential. A clan of my own that I could feed and nurture. An image of us, wild and hungry—and still expanding. The weight gain was Stevie's idea. She wanted us to be living art projects.

So we started planning. One of the more obvious tenets of a secret society is, you know, secrecy. Other common elements: the violation of social convention, the pursuit of a slippery and elusive truth. Well, what could violate social convention more than women coming together to indulge their hunger and take up space? And the pursuit of truth definitely fit with what we were trying to achieve: living an experience to see what knowledge it might bring us. We wanted to expand and to be nourished—we wanted to know how that felt. To be full up, instead of hungry and wanting, all the time. Finally, an element of cryptography is found in most secret societies—and we absolutely adored the sound of that. Stevie designed a symbol for us: the coupling of two parentheses, like a pair of eyelashes facing inward. It felt right: cyclical, contained, vaginal, incomplete.

Those evenings, sitting on the living-room floor, laptops to our sides and an array of paper scattered across the floor, drinking wine and listening to music, were suffused with a warmth like nothing else I'd ever felt. I thought of it as the same feeling people get when planning their wedding. It felt enormous and essential and transitory: this papier-mâché beast that we were trying to carve into form.

A job had come up at work, managing the social media, covering maternity leave. I'd applied, not expecting anything to come from it, but in the end they offered it to me. It meant a lot more money and considerably longer hours. I was spending my days imploring our customers to get pool-ready, to get beach-ready, to get winter-ready, to get bank-holiday-ready. I put together photo galleries of sandals. I reported on how many people were asking about swimwear. I replied "Please address this to our customer-service account" approximately two hundred times a day. Once every few weeks, I got to interview a mildly famous soap-opera actress or former reality-TV star and ask her questions like "What is the secret of your skin-care regime?" and "Will you be braving the culotte trend this spring?" To which they would offer painfully earnest and detailed replies.

It also meant I was sat next to a girl called Kate, whom I despised.

Kate had black hair cut into a bob with a heavy blunt fringe, like Uma Thurman in *Pulp Fiction*. I didn't hate her because she was objectively very attractive, although that certainly didn't help. I'd sometimes catch myself staring sideways, admiring her perfect profile, thinking, *Imagine having that, imagine going out into the world with that, with those big, watery eyes and those cheekbones, imagine what that does to a person.* I thought that some people had the compassion and intelligence to become fundamentally decent people while also being very beautiful, but that Kate wasn't one of them. She reapplied her lipstick thirty times a day. She took a selfie every morning and afternoon—not to post or send to anyone, just to look at. She got anxious when she ate carbs. She rearranged her hair and asked for feedback on her posture every few hours. We were once in midconversation about an annoying meeting we had to attend, and she veered off to state "I've never had a brown coat," to no one in particular. I found her a peculiarly oppressive presence—just being near her made me feel anxious. Being beautiful, I suspected, had ruined her life. Sitting next to her, I thought about how exhausting it must be to settle for nothing less than perfection because you had the capacity to obtain it. I felt grateful for my own average looks. My wide and unyielding forehead. My slightly crooked nose. It made me feel like what I was doing was very important and that it could maybe even help people. I started thinking I would work on initiating Kate into the Supper Club as a sort of end goal. If we could get her, we could get anyone.

One night Stevie and I were at our little table talking about the project while dunking chunks of bread into hummus. Stevie was telling me about Breton's surrealist manifestos; she wondered whether we should incorporate surrealist aesthetics into the Supper Club. We were stuck on surrealism's relationship with women, how few women engaged with the movement.

"We've got no skin in the game," Stevie protested. "Everything was formalized by men." We had taken to rolling our eyes at the invocation of "men." "Why would we subvert something we haven't even had the opportunity to create?"

"But that's precisely why we would!" I argued. "Build this thing from the ground up."

Stevie rose from the table and walked to the other side of the room, staring out our small window. It was dark and clear, the moon large and yellow.

"I'm fed up with talking about this," she said. "We need to do something to make it real. We need to do something now."

She went upstairs, and I could hear her stomping around her room and throwing open her drawers. After a few minutes, she railed back down the stairs, hollering, "Yes! Yes! Yes!" She walked into the living room holding four cans of black spray paint, her fingers wrapped around them like she was bringing drinks back from the bar. She landed them on the table.

"We're doing this," she said. "Tonight. We're going around town and we're making our mark."

We crept out of the house past one, both dressed ridiculously, and necessarily, in head-to-toe black, looping scarves around our necks in case we needed to hide our faces. It took us a while to get there, and our initial zeal somewhat dissipated along the way. We went to the part of town with large and glassy buildings, containing bankers and financiers, bottomed with pricey coffee shops and sandwich outlets. We looked around for security guards and couldn't see any. We pulled our scarves up around the bottom halves of our faces, and Stevie sprayed a closed parenthesis on the pavement in front of a Pret A Manger. She looked up at me, glossy-eyed and almost stupid with pride.

"Here," she said. "Now you do one."

I held out the can and hunted around for a good target. I settled on the front of the NatWest offices and sprayed three large Supper Club symbols across the entrance, my eyes watering and my heart thumping in my chest. I stepped back, presented it to Stevie like I was displaying a potato painting, a contender for the front of the fridge.

"I did it!" I cried. "I did it!"

Stevie made a few more on the sidewalk and on the sides of the offices. I sprayed the sides of some bars and restaurants. We were jumping up and down, hugging and only intermittently suppressing squeals. At one point a couple in long woolen coats holding briefcases approached from the distance, and we yelped and ran off. We ran past the art gallery and got its side. We sprayed Supper Club signs on the doors of the Town Hall and on the steps of the library. We got a couple more restaurants and shops. We must have made a hundred Supper Club signs all over the city. When our cans ran out, we dropped them in a bin behind a stationery shop, then headed home, holding our scarves in our hands and talking about what we'd done. It was a cold night, but we were hot and sweaty. At one point we held hands, swinging them like objects between us. It was happening.

When we finally got home, we were ravenous. I made us some scrambled eggs, and we sat side by side on the countertop, scooping them up with slices of brown toast. That night Stevie slept in my bed again. At that point she was sleeping in my bed most nights.

We'd put up cryptic messages in arts collectives and women's centers, using our landline, asking women to leave a voice mail. After a couple of weeks, we had fourteen messages in total, only five of which were from genuinely interested women. The first person we found was Lina. The second was Andrea.

We met Andrea in her flat, which smelled very strongly of cigarettes. She began smoking almost as soon as she sat us down, offering us each a cigarette, which we both accepted. It felt weird and transgressive to be smoking indoors, in the home of a person we'd only just met. She held out a luminous pink lighter, and when we leaned in, I noticed her hand was very lightly shaking. We asked her if we were able to record the conversation, and she said we could. I set my phone down on the coffee table in front of us, and Stevie asked the question we'd decided we would ask all the women. "What are you afraid of?"

Andrea told us she'd been living in London for ten years. She was the chief strategy officer at a company that offered corporate training days, where middle-aged CEOs would learn how to build boats out of scrap metal and talk about their feelings. She went to a lot of meetings and was periodically asked to wear more obviously expensive suits. But she liked it. She enjoyed having a seat at the table and once spent eight hundred pounds on a shirt. She went to Michelin-starred restaurants at the weekends and played netball on Thursdays with some old university friends. She and her then boyfriend were talking about adopting an older child. They liked children but didn't want to have a baby. One morning she woke up and her boyfriend had made her favorite breakfast: boiled eggs and soldiers. When she lifted the lid off the egg, she found a little engagement ring inside, all slimy and covered in yolk. She thought it was a pretty funny way to propose. A few months after getting engaged, she was out jogging before work. She tried to jog three or four circuits around the periphery of the park a couple of times a week. She noticed a jogger running in the opposite direction and prepared to offer a smile of early-morning solidarity, but as he jogged nearer, she saw there was something wrong with his face, and when she was right up in front of him, he lifted his left fist to his chest and hit her once, to the right side of her nose. She said that her first thought was of old cartoons where the dog or the duck gets punched and sees tweety-birds and stars bobbing around them. She said it wasn't the thought that made her laugh so much as the thought of the thought. She just stood there in the far corner of the park, laughing, watching the other jogger make his way around the track. She ran home feeling blood trickling from her nose, and it wasn't until she had showered, eaten some cereal, got dressed, and answered three emails flagged as "important" that she cried.

After that she was a different person. She'd have her boyfriend drop her off and pick her up from work. She didn't want to go to restaurants because of the crowds. She'd tried playing netball just once but kept throwing up her hands whenever anyone passed her the ball. She started having panic attacks in meetings and would spend hours staring passively at her screen. HR asked if she'd consider taking some time off, and she said that she would. She decided to stay with her dad for a while, sleeping in her old single bed, staring up at the glow-in-the-dark planets and crescent moons still stuck to the ceiling. She and her fiancé were still technically together, though she was certain he was sleeping with a woman in his office, someone called Diane.

"What I'm scared of," she said, "is everything."

We took out a loan to pay for the first Supper Club. We just needed enough to cover the venue, having decided we'd dumpster-dive for food. Stevie's new friend Erin, who I was only a little bit threatened by, was a regular dumpster diver. Even better, she had access to a car, and she'd agreed to drive us around some of the riper supermarkets ahead of the first dinner. We found out about a small Persian restaurant that was soon to close down, and they allowed us to rent out the premises for four nights running. One night so I could learn how to use a professional kitchen. Another to do prep work. Another to host the actual Supper Club. Finally, one more to clean up.

A few days before the club, Stevie and Erin produced the wares of their dumpster dives. New potatoes, udon noodles, shiitake mushrooms, raspberry doughnuts, baked meringues, feta cheese, frozen peas, farfalle pasta, tomato puree, tinned salmon, plus a load of day-old radishes.

"The most important part of any dumpster dive," Erin said, moving her hand expansively over the food, "is showing off what you have found."

I processed the food as she'd taught me: cleaning the packaging with diluted bleach and soaking the vegetables in a vinegar-water solution. In the large chrome restaurant kitchen, I spread it all out across the counter and thought about what I'd make. We had bought just one extra ingredient: enormous cuts of T-bone steak. We thought red meat should be a prerequisite for all Supper Clubs. An element of spontaneity had also been agreed on, with no set menu, no dietary requirements—just eat whatever's in front of you and be sure to eat it all. The plan was to spend all night at the restaurant, waiting hours between courses.

I made grilled potatoes and spiced salmon for the first course. I roasted radishes and topped them with crumbled feta for the second. Cold noodle salad with shiitake mushrooms and peas for the third, and T-bone steaks cooked rare, with a side of garlic-tomato pasta, for the main course. For dessert I made a strange sort of Eton mess, with chunks of torn doughnuts and smashed meringue covered in cream and sugar. Lina mixed the cocktails for the evening. She bought some crystal jugs from a charity shop and filled them with Kir Royale and Espresso Martini. And we stocked up on red wine and prosecco, too, just to be on the safe side.

There was an awkward energy when everyone arrived: me, Stevie, Erin, Andrea, Lina, and Emmeline. No one was quite sure what to expect. Stevie had thrown herself into the occasion, wearing an insane multicolored metallic poncho she'd made herself, strips of shiny fabric stitched together and touching the floor like the plumage of a magnificent exotic bird. She invited everyone in, wrapping her arms around them all and kissing them hard on the cheek. I longed to feel loose and free, but in a room full of people I hardly knew, I was instantly shy. I busied myself in the kitchen until Stevie dragged me out, demanding everyone do three shots of lit sambuca, which helped with the air of discomfort.

We sat down to eat with a feeling of timidity, very carefully cutting up our food into modest portions, anxiously eyeing one another, seeing who was eating what. No one spoke much. During the second course, I watched Andrea push all her radishes to the side of her plate, feeling disappointed I had made something she couldn't bring herself to actually eat. I began worrying that my cooking was terrible, that that was why everyone was chewing with such trepidation. It was my fault. After the third course, Andrea and Emmeline complained of feeling full, not being hungry enough for their steak. "Fuck this!" Stevie shouted, banging her fork against the table. "This is bullshit. This isn't some bloody canapé party. We're meant to be reclaiming our appetites here."

She threw her fork to the floor, wrapping her hands around the lump of meat and eating it like a bear in a river tearing at the belly of a still-wriggling fish. There was a pause as we watched her, giving us permission, assuming her status as leader of the pack. When I picked up my own steak, self-conscious yet exhilarated, I felt acutely attuned to the animal nature of what I was devouring, the fact of flesh in my hand, perhaps for the first time in my life. Around me everyone else began doing the same, eating with hands, running index fingers around the lip of the dish to gather sauce, tearing meat into chunks and knocking them back like M&M's. Lina was the first to throw the steak bone over her shoulder. Stevie shook up a bottle of prosecco and sprayed it on the table. It was a slightly forced gesture of debauchery, but we all whooped nonetheless. We picked at the Eton mess more cautiously but managed to eat about half of it. After we'd cleared the plates into the kitchen, Andrea produced a small bag of white powder from her purse.

"I don't know if it's this kind of party," she said. "But I do have some coke."

"It is *definitely* that kind of party," Stevie said. We crowded around the table, and soon I noticed the hammed-up animation with which we started to talk. Andrea began telling an incredibly long story about the time her grandma had yelled at someone in the supermarket and they'd knocked over some eggs. And even though it seemed like nobody was actually listening to her, we all managed to laugh at the right moments. After about an hour, we did some more.

"I've a weird idea," Erin said a little later on. "I think we should all take our tops off. I did it as part of a cleansing ritual when I was living in Madrid a couple years ago. It was sort of amazing."

"Let's do it," Stevie said, immediately liberating herself from her poncho. "Free the nipple!"

Stevie and Erin both threw off their bras with a gusto the rest of us couldn't quite summon. The others followed much more gingerly. "Tops *off!*" Lina screamed, though she was rather warily unbuttoning her blouse.

Quickly I was the only one in the room still clothed from the waist up. And even though it was the last thing in the world that I wanted to do, to show my bare breasts to a roomful of virtual strangers, I took my top off and unhooked my bra, throwing them into the corner with everyone else's. I looked around the room at all these wonderful women and their proudly bared breasts—and it felt good.

We left the restaurant around five, after a feeble attempt to dance. We all took taxis home, leaving the place a total disaster. I was not looking forward to cleaning up the following night.

When Stevie and I got home, we went straight to the bathroom to be sick, me hunched over the toilet, Stevie in the bath, crouched on all fours, throwing up directly into the plughole. At one point we turned to look at each other between retches, and grinned.

Human Restaurant

The first term of university was unseasonably warm, the sun maintaining a chirpy glow, not a cloud in the sky. The heat was oppressive, straining to break too late in the year. The library was the source of a particular unpleasantness. Condensation dripped from the windows, and the lack of ventilation resulted in a sweet-and-sour smell that was at once comforting and repulsive. Recently occupied seats bore buttock-shaped sweat stains. I once witnessed one of the shelf stackers idly wipe her brow with the pages of a Zola, just slip it beneath her fringe and blot.

And yet everyone had colds. We were permanently sniffling. As one virus ebbed, another was on call. Dirty tissues spilled from our pockets and bulged beneath our sleeves. Waves of menthol and eucalyptus drifted alternately through the halls. Our voices croaked and our noses were pink and dripping. We were ill people, but it failed to unite us, just made us cautious and resentful, patient zero always on our minds. Ever since I've associated Indian summers with illness—illness and anguish. I get antsy for the weather to change. On waking to clear skies and early-morning warmth, my heart sinks.

When autumn finally came, it was like jumping into a swimming pool on a long hot day. I languished in the breeze, the chill exhilarating, the damp zesty and refreshing like a citrus wet wipe after a curry. *Autumn!* I would think, kicking up the leaves that pirouetted to the ground. It didn't last for long. Eventually they piled in a wet slop, the wind was angry/calm/angry/calm, the sky a plain and uncompromising gray. It rained for weeks and I spent most of my time in bed, shivering, surrounded by a confetti of Kleenex. I'd caught the flu from the tail end of Samuel's: proper flu that tints your skin green, where turning over in bed exhausts you. I felt wretched, and my days passed in a delirious blur. I'd wake to a darkening sky and have no idea what time it was, what day it was. I extended my legs out of the bed to cool them, horrified to see they'd grown dense with hair. My skin was thick with oil and I smelled rotten. I pined to be home, to be looked after. *I'm ill,* I'd imagine telling my mum, the singular weight of it commanding some launch into a protocol of tea and television. *I'm ill.*

I'd drag myself out of bed a glass of water, waiting until I was certain none of my flatmates were in, too embarrassed to let them see me like that. On the eighth day of being too ill to leave my bed for more than about five minutes, I just cried. Outside, the rain kept falling, hammering against the window like it wanted to be let in. My room had the aura of disease.

Most of all I missed food. My appetite had vanished, replaced with a keen revulsion for anything edible. I'd nibble a water biscuit and feel immediately sick, like lie-down-on-the-floor nauseous. I was somebody who ate for comfort, for pleasure, and the absence of mealtimes left me feeling weak and evacuated, loose skin and old brittle bones.

I felt more alienated than ever from my flatmates, ignoring their hesitant tappings on my door, sincere offers to pop out if I needed anything. One night Mei-Ling's friends came round and began playing loud music, which was abruptly turned off. Mei-Ling irritably exclaiming, "Fuck sake, she's really ill!" It was sweet, but I'd never felt more removed. I thought of them as an unswerving monolithic unit, healthy and happy and a million miles away.

By November my cold had dried up, but I was smoking fifteen cigarettes a day. The neat arrangement of my room had devolved to a small chaos. One of the bulbs in my fairy lights had gone, so of course they had all gone, but I left them hanging, white plastic vines serving no purpose at all. I'd stopped opening the window when I smoked, had moved the ashtray to beside my bed. The walls were already yellowing and stained. I still cooked but admired the spike of my hipbones, the slink of my legs, gifted from the flu, and so rationed myself to just one meal a day.

I found myself slumping to more obvious levels of mental collapse. Walking down the street, I'd mutter to myself, little conversational tidbits, my face emoting whatever notion passed through my brain. I'd gnaw at my fingernails with an industrious precision, chewing torn pieces of dead skin and swallowing, to the disgust and bewilderment of anyone happening to catch sight. I'd begun liking things to divide comfortably by five, mouthing numbers at streetlamps or tiling, my brow furrowed to check that things fit the pattern. But I was all right. I went to classes. Took myself around the city. Went to the cinema alone. It wasn't so bad. I could be my own caretaker, nurturer, boyfriend; that was a revelation in and of itself.

My favorite date was to wander around the art gallery, the heels of my shoes delivering a pleasing clip-clop as I took in the soothing watercolors, the pre-Raphaelite girls looking spaced out and wan, before drifting over to Chinatown. I found Chinatown both impossibly sophisticated and unbearably out of vogue. Chinese restaurants were a guilty pleasure of mine. I loved how they evoked the living world—either the Walden-like sense of individualism of the Ocean or Happy Garden, or something more candid ("Yummies!"). Back home they had been a preserve of birthdays and special celebrations: a lazy Susan packed with ribs and Peking duck, rhapsodically spun to the sound of Fleetwood Mac or the Police, with banana fritters drenched in syrup and a round of flowering tea to finish. It felt as cosmopolitan a dining experience as I would ever encounter. Contextualized amid the big-city landscape of politicized microbreweries and sushi, a hearty table of MSG and marinated pork felt at best crass, at worst obscurely racist. But there was something about the gloop and the sugar that I couldn't resist. And Chinatown was peculiarly untouched by my contemporaries, so I could happily nibble at plates of salt and chili squid or crispy Szechuan beef while leafing through the pages of a magazine in peace.

My favorite was Hunan Restaurant, the sign outside smudged so it read "Human Restaurant," which seemed inclusive if not unambitious. There was something grandmotherly about it—the carefully starched table linen, the mannered seating and decor. It had few of the usual semiotics—lanterns kept to a comforting minimum, just the one metallic dragon—plus, they did an excellent hot-and-sour soup, and the portion sizes were enormous. The waitstaff had a demure tenderness, and I frequented the place so often I'd occasionally spot them in town, buying groceries or trying on cardigans. In these moments I would want to hurry over to say hello, before recalling the thin lines within which our unity was drawn.

On one visit I took my usual table, nestled behind the fish tank, with equal view of the bar and the corner TV, and had begun flipping through a feature about Jennifer Aniston's weight gain while noisily crunching wontons, when I noticed to my immediate horror the face of a boy I recognized from my degree. A crisp shard of dumpling found its way down the wrong side of my throat, and I began spluttering, so of course the boy looked around and clocked me. I stood to go outside for a cigarette, feeling his eyes on me as I made for the door.

Stepping back inside, I saw he'd taken the vacant seat opposite mine. I wondered whether I could just leave, abandoning my bag, my phone and keys, and come back for them later. Though I was also intrigued, presented with a rare opportunity for interaction, and with a man no less. I walked over to him.

"My date just canceled," he said, watching me sit down. "And by the looks of it, so did yours."

I removed my jacket and idly pushed a wonton around my plate.

"No date," I replied. "I come here alone."

I watched both the conscious and subconscious reshifting of his expression, from surprise through to pity, hovering around distaste, landing eventually at a light curiosity.

"Ah," he said. "So you know what's good."

"The beef," I dryly offered. "The beef with green peppers."

"Then that's what I'll have."

He reached over and ate a dumpling from my plate. The invasion of my space, the presumption of entitlement to my food, was thrilling—alluring, actually. I crossed my legs and wondered if I could excuse myself to the bathroom to put on makeup. I briefly imagined pinning myself to him like a pentangle, the scratch of his stubble on my face. He ordered us some beers.

"So . . . what?" he said. "You just eat here alone?"

I instinctively giggled, tried not to feel panicked or embarrassed by my weird, private behavior, my unstoppable hunger. I suddenly noticed his wrist, a tiny cross semiobscured by the sleeve of his sweater.

"What's that?" I asked, railroading the conversation.

"Oh, this?" he said. "It's stupid. I got it on my last birthday. I wanted to articulate my faith or something. I wish I hadn't done it."

He tugged his sleeve over his hand, the sinews and solidity of his arm now annoyingly unavailable.

"It's not stupid," I said. "Let me see it."

He placed his hand palm upward on the table, and we studied his arm together. The gesture seemed uncharacteristically submissive: here are my veins, this is my religion. *A Christian,* I thought. *Huh.* I punctured a strip of chicken with my fork. Took a moment to consider his face. His narrow nose. His square mouth and jaw.

"So what do you do here alone?" he asked.

"I sit. Eat food. Read." I nodded at my magazine, ignoring the swell of tears rising unannounced, as happened from time to time. I felt my cheeks flush and full. I held my breath.

"Reading, eh? Well, you're doing better than me. I know you from Contemporary American Fiction, right?"

"You do."

"So how come you always sit alone? Like, deliberately on the opposite side of the room?"

I shrugged my shoulders, splayed and pinned. I thought it was impolite to interrogate a person's obvious insecurities. "I dunno," I replied. And I didn't. I didn't know.

Our drinks arrived. We clinked glasses.

"I'm Michael," he said.

"I'm Roberta."

After Hunan Restaurant we went to a bar that had long shared tables and drank wine from globular glasses. I realized I was drunk for the first time in what must have been a while, sloppy and sentimental, pink-faced and slow, with a bright mania just behind my eyes. Languishing ecstatically in his full attention.

He was from Wolverhampton, where he lived with his dad and sisters. He was funny, with a dry but not unpleasant laugh. His parents were divorced. He was studying English and film, but he wanted to be a programmer. He liked pizza, graphic novels, eighties action films, and Suede. He had a small crease between his eyes and a pit on his left cheek, which made him look unusually weathered for such an otherwise clean boy.

At some point it was determined he lived not far away from me, and before parting ways we would swing by his place to watch *Annie Hall*.

His accommodation was much nicer than mine; it looked like an exceptionally plush youth hostel, with lots of pale green and orange papering, wood furnishings and breakout areas.

Walking through the atrium, we passed a bunch of students hammering away at the small computer lab to the side of the entrance door.

"Conscientious," I commented.

"Facebook and porn," he dismissed. "C'mon. I'm on the seventh floor."

As the lift doors shut, he suddenly pressed himself against me. We kissed but couldn't quite reach a groove, working at different rhythms, different angles. It had been over a year since I'd kissed anyone. The bristle of facial hair against my cheeks and the slightly soured smell of his body were attractive but also dissonant, giving me the strange sense of the whole thing happening to someone else, as if I were very far away. We fumbled hopelessly for no more than a few seconds. As the lift door opened, the mood dissipated and the notion seemed somewhat absurd.

His room was tidy, a pile of balled socks from where he'd been folding laundry to the left of his desk, upon which everything was carefully arranged and ordered. A small stack of paperbacks rested on his bedside table, and the white walls displayed a restrained selection of posters: *Shogun Assassin* and Brett Anderson, Kylie Minogue over the bed, wearing a baby-doll dress, holding on to a lolly.

I perched on the edge of the mattress while he switched on his computer, positioned it on his bedside table, arranged his pillows vertically against the wall. He sat back on the bed, and I moved in beside him. Sometime into the film, he began creeping his arm behind my back. "Don't knock masturbation," Woody Allen told Diane Keaton. "It's sex with somebody I love." Michael rested his hand against my shoulder, gently stroking my biceps in a soft circular motion. It wasn't a charged gesture, more comforting: I felt cool waves of relaxation flow through my body, which, coupled with the soupy red-wine lull I was coasting, made me sleepy. I rested my head against him. I thought how magical it was, how truly enchanting to be lying there, happily exhausted, half watching a film with a boy who seemed to like me. I closed my eyes, the dialogue of the film tuning in and out.

I woke up scared, but I didn't know why. It was not a wild terror or panic, more a low-key fear, the sick knowledge that something bad was happening. I registered the heft of a body on top of my own. The absence of my underwear. Something moving in and out of my vagina. *I am having sex*, I thought. *Oh God, I am having sex*. His hand pushed up my shirt and forced itself beneath my bra, squeezing my breast and crushing my nipple. *This is it*, I thought. *This is the one*. I wondered whether I should be making a sound, some husky moan or breathy gasp, some indication of desire, but I didn't have any. *I don't want this,* I thought, or rather the thought emerged. *I don't want this.*

The not-wanting presented itself as an objective idea, something to be viewed from all angles. I walked around it as I might a sculpture in a gallery. Getting up close and then moving farther away. No matter how hard I stared at it, it would not change shape, only becoming more insistent under observation. *I don't want this. I don't want this. I don't want this.*

It occurred to me I could scream. *I am going to scream,* I thought. *I am going to scream now.* But when I imagined myself doing it, it seemed daft and histrionic. I tried pushing him, not hard but enough. When he went to kiss me, I turned my head like a reluctant child at dinnertime. I was aware of my extraordinary lack of physical strength. He was industrious. He was a man on a mission. Moving in and out of me urgently, like he was doing push-ups. I started to wriggle. I wasn't strong, I couldn't overpower him, but I could wriggle. "Hold still," he said, clasping his hand around my throat. The room was dark and smelled of the cigarettes I'd smoked earlier. His hand on my throat formed a line, my brain separate from my body. Below the hand was something I had no control over, but above the hand was still mine. Lack of oxygen started making me foggy. I coughed, feeling little specks of saliva land around my lips. "Stop it," he said. I coughed more, coughing deliberately. It was the smallest gesture of control, this last space of my own: my breath. I could cough and splutter. I could rip open my insides and spill out the terrible things inside me. I coughed myself hoarse. His penis inside my vagina. My phlegm on his neck. *This is the worst thing,* I thought. *This is the worst thing, and this is still happening.* I wriggled again, coughing and wriggling at the same time. He grabbed a fistful of my hair and butted his head against my lip. I felt blood trickle into my mouth. I was an extraterrestrial thing. I was white bone and slime, a high-pitched scream. Beyond that I felt *rude*. I was offending him. I sobbed as he pulled out and came on my stomach, rolling onto his side. I stared at the wall, naked from the waist down. He leaned over and pulled a roll of tissue from his bedside table and began wiping himself clean. He put on his clothes and went to the bathroom. I could hear the stuttering sound of him pissing.

I remained there half naked. I didn't want to put on my underwear. It would have been a full stop on the encounter, and I was still inside the moment. I looked over at the computer; the film had finished, and the screen was on standby, a tiny red dot of light letting me know it was still on. I studied the insistent little nubs of my hip bones, flat beaks or the snouts of rodents, pressing against my skin. I knocked one with my fist. Since I'd lost weight, my tummy was unrecognizably flat, my skin and belly button pulled taut across it. His ejaculate had left a slick sheen below my waist that, even when I rubbed with tissues, still would not go. I reached down to my brutalized vagina. It was wet. I wondered whether that was from him or from me. Later, when I went to the toilet, I would find small spots of blood on the tissue paper, which made sense. I was a virgin. I wondered whether all sex felt this horrible. As I heard him switch on the shower I counted to twenty, then I got dressed.

When he finally emerged, he was clothed, random splotches of damp disturbing the pattern of his T-shirt, rubbing his head with a towel.

"Now," he said. "Shall I walk you home?"

I heard myself say, "Yes please."

The Spaces Between Things

In the run-up to a Supper Club, we'd need to go dumpster-diving most nights for a week. Sometimes we'd go as a group—taking a few cars, visiting different supermarkets, delis, and grocery stores. Otherwise we'd go out separately, sharing our haul on the group chat.

The first time I went I felt wild. Erin and Stevie advised me to wear thick gloves and waterproof trousers, which I tucked into my socks. There was certainly something subversive about the act, lifting the lid of a filthy and unwanted space, rifling around inside. We started with the giant Asda just outside town. The dumpsters were around the back, about forty of them all lined up, floodlit but unguarded. There was a gap in the fencing we could dip through. I felt a thrilling audacity, striding beneath the bright lights and making for the bins.

Stevie and Erin went straight in, while I sort of lingered behind, watching them. They lifted the lids and reached in, tossing aside bin liners and large pieces of cardboard. Stevie lifted her gloved hand, covered in gloop.

"Gross," she said.

"It's just egg yolk," Erin replied. "Get over it."

Erin showed me which bin bags to watch out for, the ones that looked vaguely clean and plump with goods. She prodded them with the litter picker she'd bought off eBay.

"You sort of get an instinct for it," she explained. She poked a liner filled with boxy shapes. "Like this one. This is going to be a good one."

She tore open the bag, and inside were boxes of Double-Stuf Oreos and white-chocolate fingers. The bag was a little damp, but the biscuits were dry. We pulled them out and put them aside.

"Vegetables!" Stevie called from a dumpster a few rows down. She lifted a head of broccoli still wrapped in its plastic and a couple packets of spinach. I rifled through a few more bins, gingerly at first, though it quickly became normalized. The smell and the dirt, which I found disheartening initially, actually spurred me on, and I was giddy with my capacity to get arm-deep in waste, to be hoisted fully into a bin, ignoring the squelch of long-gone bananas or torn-apart tubs of yogurt. I managed to find only one bag of pretzel crisps and a packet of cooked ham, but Erin insisted we'd chosen a bad night and should come back at the weekend.

After Asda we visited a smaller Tesco and a fancy foodie store. At the Tesco we found a few tins of tomatoes and some frozen green beans. At the fancy foodie place, we found four packs of really good feta. It wasn't a bad night.

At home we lined up all our found food on the kitchen floor, industriously treating and processing it. Some of it wouldn't last until Supper Club, but most of it would. We'd need to make a few more trips. After Stevie had gone to bed, I looked at our fridge, ripe with unwanted food, and started imagining all the things I might cook. Feta baked with oregano and tomatoes. Sautéed green beans and ham. Oreo chocolate concrete. And suddenly I was overwhelmed by a sense of the porousness of the world, its gaps and chinks. These meals that would never have existed, like secret passageways beneath the city.

In later months that sensation only grew. I'd see a chair abandoned on the side of the street and think, *I'll have that*. We'd drive past a river or lake, and I'd think, *I can swim in that*. Everything felt a little more liquid. I became aware of the rank fabrication of things, these strange rules to follow.

Erin first went dumpster-diving while squatting with straight-edge anarchists in Madrid. She moved to the city to be with her then girlfriend, Valeria; up until that point their relationship had been conducted mostly online. They'd met at a Kathleen Hanna concert in London, bonding over their shared hate of global capitalism, their shared hate of the meat and dairy industry, their shared hate of commercial visual art. Erin did not think it possible to fall in love with a person online, and yet she would gaze at her computer screen after having read one of Valeria's composed attacks on toxic masculinity or European neoliberalism with the sort of dopey expression she had seen only on American sitcoms. They would visit each other every few months, and afterward she would feel every cell in her body singing. She moved to Madrid a year later.

The squat was an abandoned bookstore, littered with old bikes, white men who wore their hair in dreadlocks, and cats who belonged to no one but who were apparently taken care of. Valeria and Erin shared a room containing a lumpy mattress without a frame, a vintage gramophone that no longer worked, and a steel rail on which they hung their clothes. The cats wove in and out of the different rooms, and Erin enjoyed waking up late in the morning to find one of them invariably curled at the bottom of the bed. The squat was home to between twenty and thirty people at any given time, and they mostly did things as a group: they went to protest heteropatriarchy as a group, they went dancing to dubstep in fecund fields as a group, they went dumpster-diving around all the local supermarkets as a group. It sometimes felt like they were a single multifaceted organism, something that existed at the bottom of the sea, beautiful and evolved. But very often it also felt suffocating, and sometimes Erin would spend a full hour sitting on the toilet in their dilapidated bathroom, just to be alone for a while.

They made very little money. Valeria led yoga in the old storeroom every weekend morning. Erin started teaching bass guitar to teenage girls who lived in the neighborhood. Most of their food was foraged from bins. They had no hot water. In the evenings Valeria would light candles and line them up around their mattress, and they would lie inside the loop, enshrined by fire. They would talk about all the things they hated. Erin had thought falling in love and moving to Spain might make her hate things less, but instead she found that her hatred for the world and its wretched systems was only getting more severe. Lying in bed, she imagined her hate as a sort of reverse radar, the line of detection moving inward, a circle looping tighter and tighter. It began in distant places all across the world— corrupt regimes in West Africa, the oppression of women in Iran. Then the circle would tighten a notch: the proliferation of far-right politics in Poland, rampant Islamophobia in France. It would tighten again: cuts to education spending in the city, a local library shut down. And again: Juan-from-upstairs' insistence on calling her and Valeria "girls," the way Jonno would slip dishes into the sink while Erin was doing the washing-up, the implication loud and clear. It tightened so much that Erin felt that the only expanse of space in which she didn't feel a visceral, burning hatred for was within the circle of tea lights on their bedroom floor. It was no longer a romantic affectation but an absolute necessity: the only place where she could let herself breathe.

Stevie met Erin over Christmas. She had come home to visit her family—and had decided to stay. Stevie found her sitting alone at a photography preview, thumbing through the guide. She sat down next to her, hoping to have someone to talk to, and they chatted a little bit about the art. Then they talked about their lives, Erin launching into all the things she thought she despised and how, staying with her family over Christmas, she had realized she probably didn't despise them after all—which was truly news to her. She said that she was thinking of staying in the country, finding somewhere to live, and that this meant she was staring down the barrel of ending a relationship with someone she was very much in love with via text. They went to a bar, and then she came back to our house and slept on the couch. In the morning I woke up to find an incredibly tanned stranger making coffee in the kitchen. Stevie appeared a few minutes later. The three of us sat in the living room, and I felt jealous—immediately, predictably—jealous of all the experiences Erin could talk about and draw from, the enormous red balloon of her life.

One evening not long after that, she came round to watch *Flatliners* and eat cauliflower cheese, and we told her about Supper Club. She wasn't sure she wanted to be part of anything anymore, other than her family. But one evening she and Stevie went out without me, and in the morning Stevie told me Erin was going to join. I didn't ask any questions. I knew Stevie could be convincing in a way I didn't feel compelled to deconstruct.

We thought gold would make an appropriate theme, obscene and dripping gold.

We'd started giving each Supper Club a theme. Once the theme was literary heroines, and we all read passages from our favorite female writers, standing on the table as if it were a stage. Another time it was princesses, and everything was gauche and pink. A favorite was brides—Stevie and I found wedding dresses from charity shops, and Lina wore her actual wedding dress from her actual wedding, though she had to have it taken out because it no longer fit.

But the gold theme was good. We papered the room with gold lamé, so it looked both Etruscan and sort of space-age. We draped gold fabric over the chairs to make them thrones. We hung gold ribbons from the ceiling. We spray-painted roses and tossed them across the floor. We filled bowls with chocolate coins, gaudy and bright in their foil shells. We placed gold church candles around the room. We threw handfuls of glitter over the table.

And we all wore gold. Stevie wore a gold brocade suit with nothing underneath it. I wore gold hot pants and a black shirt. Andrea wore a gold T-shirt and jeans. Erin wore a gold tinsel wig. We all painted our faces gold. We looked completely insane.

On arrival we served Bloody Marys, though we couldn't in all good conscience garnish with sticks of celery, so we finished with bacon and shrimp. I no longer did all the cooking; instead we each brought a dish. The first course was one of Stevie's specialties, macaroni and cheese. There was something vaguely hacky and antiquated about it, which fit the gold theme perfectly; she always made it very rich and dense, crisp on top and silky underneath. Her trick was to use "twice the recommended amount of butter and three times the cheese." After the pasta we had ham hock with whipped peas, the ham stringy and salty, the peas fresh and slightly minted.

We took a break for a couple of hours, and Stevie poured us all shots of vodka, the hot nothingness of it making the edges of the room sharper and softer at the same time. I looked around at all the female faces. Our gold face paint was starting to run or sweat off, and everyone looked sort of patchy and faded, bronzed statues when the metal starts to oxidize. Erin's wig was askew. Emmeline had dripped peas down her dress. Andrea's teeth were covered in lipstick. I thought, *Look at this brilliant mess, isn't it marvelous?*

"Fuck shots," Stevie said, and had us all tilt back our heads and open our mouths, like baby birds, while she walked around the table pouring vodka directly down our throats.

We started getting hungry again, and some of the women started chanting, "MEAT, MEAT, MEAT!"

We were having steak tartare. It was the only appropriate main course we could think of, for such a graceless theme, and seeing as nobody in the club was confident making it, we had to order it in. I made chips to serve with it, though. I deep-fried them in beef fat.

The steak was served in little roulades, raw and minced, like horsemeat. It was topped with a raw egg yolk, chopped onions, pickled beetroot, and capers. I had wanted to use the Wisconsin version, which is served on cocktail bread and dubbed "cannibal sandwich," but Stevie insisted we go classic. Not everyone could stomach theirs with the raw egg yolk, too, and so, unusually for a Supper Club, there was quite a lot left over.

We took another break to drink and move about the room. Some of us took MDMA. Emmeline had brought a box of French macarons, tiny pastel-colored things, which we threw over the table, trying to get them into one another's mouth, invariably missing.

For our proper dessert, we had a crepe cake: a stack of pancakes bound together with melted chocolate. We ate it with homemade ice cream, which was becoming a real staple. Afterward there were more cocktails, Singapore slings this time, and then coffee.

Stevie had elected herself master of ceremonies, hustling all the women into getting drunker, announcing toasts and speeches. She reveled in the role, and we spent a lot of time listening to her stories, to her thoughts on Mary Wollstonecraft. Sometimes I would think, *She's performing,* and it would annoy me, and other times I would think, *Let her perform.* Mostly I felt a deep pride and sororal love. I would throw my arms around her and declare, "I *adore* you!"

Once our stomachs settled, we started dancing to chart pop and nineties R&B. We danced up on the chairs and on the table. Later we thought it would be funny to kiss each other, and we made our way around the room conscientiously, looking for women we hadn't yet kissed.

As the sun came up, Stevie and Andrea scoured their dating apps for people to hook up with. Erin and her girlfriend were loudly having sex in the bathroom. We final few stayed up dancing, pulling down the shutters as people outside made their way to work. Come eleven there were only three of us remaining, and we lay on the floor drifting in and out of sleep. The others got taxis, but I decided to walk, the midsummer sun heating the oil on my face, still partially covered in gold. It took me an hour to get home, where I fell asleep on the couch immediately.

Waking in the early evening, I drank three pints of water over the

kitchen sink. Stevie was still not home. I washed my face and showered, then took a taxi back to the restaurant. The gold lamé was
hanging from the walls, like skin peeling from sunburn. The candles
were burned down into flat little puddles. There were chunks of raw
meat on the floor and powdery patches of crushed macarons. Somebody had thrown up in the corner. My head felt ready to explode.
I found the mop in the supply cupboard and went about cleaning it
all up.

I'd put on about thirty pounds since the start of Supper Club. My
thighs rubbed when I went on walks, and I had to wear anti-
chafing bands or balms in the heat. Sometimes even my head felt
bigger, as if the orb of my skull had been inflated. I'd imagined
being larger to be an effort—lugging the weight of myself through
my life's days—but instead I felt grounded, no longer drifting or
liable to float away. It is something special to go from being small
to being big by your own choice. To be in your late twenties and still
able to grow.

Most of the others had gained weight, too, or were maintaining
what might be termed chubby or fat bodies. There was liberation in
the fact of our bodies being more or less the same, a neutrality to it,
even a democratization. I didn't wonder whether Emmeline thought
I'd put on weight. I didn't think Erin was staring at the folds of my
stomach. The parity in our bodies allowed us to bond. But there was
also a sadness that perhaps, under different circumstances, we might
not have. And the liberty of this sameness was felt only within Supper Club. Beyond our group, we still had to deal with the same old
stuff. Unwanted and unsolicited advice came regularly. *You shouldn't*

be wearing that. Could you try eating this? Perhaps if you cut out carbs. Doctors presumed any ailment or illness was on account of our weight gain. And then the caustic looks from strangers. Eyes on us when we took the bus or went shopping, feasting on our bodies as on a meal. The sometime tutting as we squeezed past them or the staring in the supermarket, rolling their eyes to demonstrate their condemnation should we buy biscuits or bread. If we dared wear something fitted or tight, we would be gazed at with open horror, as if these strangers were personally aggrieved we weren't shrouded in linen. It was as if we'd been entitled to a specific mass, and anything beyond that became public property. It was oppressive. It was upsetting. It was a total fucking drag.

Sometimes I would wake up in the morning confronted by the fleshy expanse of my stomach and feel a momentary panic—the lurching anxiety of remembering that you have missed the deadline for renewing your passport or that you are alive and will one day die. I would remind myself that it was completely fine, that I was accepted and I was loved. But it was a position I had to breathe into, like assuming a stretch in yoga. I would force myself to think of Supper Club, the glorious spectacle of it.

It helped having something to structure my life around. I started noticing how others did the same with their own hobbies, like a strange approximation of church: finding meaning where you could. My mum and her herb garden. My aunt with the football. "Living art projects," Stevie would whisper into my ear as I stirred a curry after work. Catching my eye across a room, she would mouth it: *Living art*. Sometimes the phrase would arrive in my mind and I would shiver. It was the closest I'd ever felt to divine.

I'd taken up running to compensate for a slight drop in energy. I'd tried running before, but it had always felt like punishment. I'd run until I could cough up blood, until my lungs might have exploded. It was a self-brutalizing thing, pounding out the bad feelings that slithered like leeches just beneath my skin. I suppose I believed on some level that if I could run fast enough, or for long enough, I might cease to exist: an object turning to dust on breaking the sound barrier. I hated every second of it, but still I would run, propelled by thoughts of smooth thighs, by the calories I was burning, by the blank promise of oblivion. But now I found that running could be exhilarating. It could exist on the same spectrum as Supper Club, a means of elevation. I'd run in the sunshine, and I'd run in the rain. I'd run before or after work. I'd play music that made me want to dance and revel in the extraordinary fact of my functioning human body.

It helped to have something to let me destress, because my job had recently become chaotic and demanding: the website had become popular overnight, after a Hollywood actress had said it was the only place where she bought her tights. Suddenly there were editorials that featured our lines and articles about how it was the best online budget brand in the country. Managing the social media, I no longer filtered questions about shipping and tracking numbers, instead sending gushing responses to people tweeting about how much they had always liked us and how our new Bardot tops were great. It made me feel strangely good, like I was being personally praised.

But it did make it harder to balance work with my life. Stevie and I still emailed each other about Supper Club and a million other things, all day, but we rarely had time to meet for lunch. Or we'd come home late and separately, be too tired to cook or to spend proper time together. I felt I was missing out on huge chunks of her life, that she didn't know enough about how I was feeling day to day.

"You see," Stevie would say. "This is how capitalism kills love."

I could no longer spend full afternoons reading *New Yorker* articles about racism in the US. There weren't periods where I had so little to do that I could just watch *The Office* on one of my two screens. I was requested to promote looks on our Facebook. The Chanel Look, the Amelia Earhart Look, the Boadicea Look, the Heidi Look. "Heidi!" I yelped, unable to gulp my coffee. "Heidi was an entitled piece of shit." On Fridays when the drinks trolley was wheeled around, we would pounce on it, sipping designer beer at our desks. Sometimes my manager would produce a bottle of wine from her shopping.

My manager was called Margaret. She had recently shown an interest in me, asking if I wanted to take any training or if I'd like to have coffee and pick her brains. Margaret did not look like she worked for a fashion website. She would wear hiking boots and waterproofs. At the weekends she and her husband went fishing. Fishing might seem like a whimsical pastime but of course it is lousy with horror. The fish often die of shock; they swallow the hooks, and the fishers have to shove their fingers down their throats to retrieve them. Sometimes they rip the fish's jaw out with the hook, sometimes its guts, too. I would find myself chitchatting with Margaret, getting on with her quite well, and I'd have to remind myself of the senseless violence of which she was capable.

One afternoon Margaret called me into her office. She asked me to take a seat, and I did. Her office had a sweet citrus smell that I later attributed to the curls of tangerine peel sitting in her wastepaper bin and a single scented candle beside her computer. She had Post-it notes on the walls and on the peripheries of her monitor with inspirational phrases like "Let the smile change your world, but don't let the world change your smile" and that Marilyn Monroe one about being selfish and insecure. She offered me a Ferrero Rocher, which I politely declined.

"How old are you, Roberta?" she said. "If you don't mind me asking."

I told her I did not and confirmed my age: twenty-nine. She looked kindly at me, sighed, and said, "It comes for us all."

I looked at my feet. I said that I did fancy a Ferrero Rocher after all, unpeeling its wrinkled gold skin and feeling the tiny studs of nut across its rubbled surface, the chocolate already melting in my hand.

"You know, I see a lot of myself in you," she said. "I see someone with potential."

I smiled a thin-lipped smile, all flesh and no teeth. I told her that was very nice of her to say so.

"But what I can't work out is," she added, "what it is you actually want to do. Because every time I walk past you, you look abjectly miserable."

I was taken aback by this information. In a meeting a few days earlier, I had called the new content strategy nonsense, delivered a passionate case for switching digital agencies. I'd pointed out two typos in the minutes. I'd thought I was putting on a real show.

"I'm not miserable," I replied, feeling my voice stupidly shudder at the final syllable. "I'm not."

"Well, maybe you are and maybe you're not," Margaret said. "But what do you actually want to *do*? Do you want to work in fashion? Do you have an actual interest in social media? What about a boyfriend? Or girlfriend?"

I looked around her office: the inspirational quotes and photographs of her son, the printed-out spreadsheets and small pewter desk lamp. I thought of her in here, running analytics and making calls, then fishing at the weekend, her and her husband complicit in their small private sadism, something that made them feel calm. How she had once invited me along. How she had said all I needed to bring was a decent pair of boots and my sense of adventure. I didn't want it, but I didn't not want it. Thinking about what I might want from my future felt like learning about an additional sense: I had no frame of reference to go by. I had never really wanted anything, certainly had no idea how it felt to get something that I wanted. I just barreled around on a second-to-second basis.

"I like my job," I said. Margaret remained silent, like some sneaky interrogation trick. I just had to wait it out, but of course I could not.

"I always look like I'm on the verge of walking out on something," I said. "I mean, I *am* a little bit always on the verge of walking out on something. But I very rarely actually do it. You don't have to worry about me."

Margaret inched her gaze at me from across the room, like I was something she was grazing with the tips of her fingers but couldn't quite grab.

"I guess I just always look miserable," I said. "But that does not necessarily mean I actually am."

Margaret stared at me with a tolerant kind of sympathy. "That's really not the point at all," she said.

And I had to agree it was not.

The Flaw in the Flesh

D on't believe vegetarians who tell you that meat has no flavor, that it comes from the spices or the marinade. The flavor is already there: earth and metal, salt and fat, blood.

My favorite meat is chicken. I can eat a whole bird standing up in the kitchen, straight from the oven, burning my bare hands on its flesh. Anyone can roast a chicken, it is a good animal to cook. Lamb, on the other hand, is much harder to get right. You have to lock in the flavor, rubbing it with sea salt like you are exfoliating your own drying skin, tenderly basting it in its own juices, hour after hour. You have to make small slits across the surface of the leg, through which you can insert sprigs of rosemary, or cloves of garlic, or both. These incisions should run against the grain, in the opposite direction to which the muscle fibers lie. You can tell the direction better when the meat is still uncooked, when it is marbled and raw. It is worth running your finger along those fibers, all the way from one end to the other. This doesn't help with anything. It won't change how you cook it. But it is good to come to terms with things as they are.

Preparing meat is always an act of physical labor. Whacking rib eye with a rolling pin. Snapping apart an arc of pork crackling. And there is something inescapably candid about it, too. If you've ever spatchcocked a goose—if you've pressed your weight down on its breastbone, felt it flatten and give, its bones rearranging under your hands—you will know what I am talking about. We are all capable of cruelty. Sometimes I imagine the feeling of a sliver of roast beef on my tongue: the pink flesh of my own body cradling the flesh of something else's. It makes sense to me that there is a market for a vegetarian burger that bleeds.

As I left Michael's building, I thought about all the advice I had received on walking home alone at night: walking in the center of the road, pretending to talk to someone on the phone. But I was not alone tonight. I was being conscientiously escorted to my door by Michael. I don't know whether I felt safe or not, whether safety was something I even had the capacity to register.

Arriving at my flat, I went straight to the bathroom, staring at my reflection in the mirror for a long time. Watching myself, I had that feeling of realization that there is something disgusting on you—a spider, perhaps—and you shake your hand so violently you cannot see it move, until the thing is off you, until it has gone. Except I had that feeling one million times over, coupled with the most lurching, stomach-deep nausea. Sickness beyond describing. My whole body trembled, but it was not enough to get the disgusting thing off me, the thing that seemed to be everywhere. *My whole body is different,* I thought. *It is an animal's body. It is the body of a wounded animal that should be put down. Take me to the doctor's and give me the injection.* As I sat there, I knew I was not going to tell anyone. I knew I did not have the words.

I showered, scrubbing myself with the hard side of a washing-up sponge, later using my nails, scratching fat red lines across my legs. After the shower I returned to the mirror, studying my lip. It had swollen up already. *When my lip is healed,* I thought, *I will feel better. It will just be a thing that happened that is now in the past.*

I told my flatmates I'd fallen over drunk. They raised their eyebrows and attempted to laugh but couldn't really get there. In class people looked at me like I was a disease. Every day I studied my swollen lip, the slick pink snail of it. Freshly remade flesh, my newly alien self. I pulled back the skin and studied the inside, sometimes mashed my hand against my face to feel the teeth my lip would have split against. After around a week, it had gone down, leaving the smallest crease where the skin was still healing. I felt panicked at the thought of its not being there—this visible trace. I closed my eyes and balled my hand up into a fist, punching myself where it had split, reopening the wound. It became a routine, week on week, growing bolder in strength. There was a satisfaction in what I could do.

Christmas evoked a sense of cheer: a bleat of camaraderie among our mostly insular flat. June and Samuel, who had struck up an unprecedented but otherwise highly functioning friendship since Sam and Robert split up, decided we were going to have a festive dinner.

I'd always found Christmas a little unnerving, an affront to my low-key countenance. Everything turned up a notch. The colors brighter, the sounds bolstered by jangles and chimes. It wasn't so much the pressure to have a good time or being surrounded by people seemingly constantly having a good time. It was the precarious summit that the good time balanced on: one topple, one popped balloon, and it could all end in tears. The thought made me tense, walking on smashed baubles.

Though I had to admit June had done an admirable job of jollying up the flat. The table, usually buried under pizza boxes and flyers, was clean and crisp with a white paper tablecloth bought from the corner shop and an enjoyable mishmash of crockery and silverware. Bottles of wine and ceramic bowls of nibbles centered the arrangement, and the day was soundtracked by sixties girl bands and the Pogues. My contribution was an ambitious sprouted-grain stuffing, with port-marinated cranberries and pistachio nuts—though I couldn't quite get it right, and by the third attempt it was still a little blackened on the outside and wet in the middle.

By early evening the flat was steamy with cooking and bustling with chatter, and I sat on the sofa watching the condensation trickle against the windows. June had insisted nobody bring guests, it was a chance for us to get to know each other, and of that I was relieved. Adnan, it seemed, had claimed the responsibility of looking after me, my resentment at being pitied overridden by a base need to be taken care of.

"There she is," he called from across the room, and made his way over toward me. "Sneaky, sneaky."

I smiled, unsure how to respond appropriately. I was just happy he was talking to me, wary of not becoming too attached and sticking to him like a limpet. Adnan was generous with his confidence, something I hated and admired about him in equal measure. Some people squirreled away their confidence or commanded it like an army, but Adnan's was an accessible confidence, a buffet to be shared with the room.

"Dark horse," he'd occasionally tease; it was a kindness, making out that my total isolation, my fundamental lack of anything interesting to do, was some kind of glamorous enigma. I was happy to play it up, raising my eyebrow and cocking my head. Sometimes tapping a finger to my nose.

The more I drank, the more I began to relax. It started feeling not exactly like home but something a little like, something adjacent to home. We moved from the sofas to the kitchen, idling comfortably around the room. By my third glass of wine, I was talking about the books I'd been reading, the films I'd recently seen. Samuel told me about his breakup. Nadeem outlined the merits of Formula One. Mei-Ling asked where I'd bought my shoes. It was nice. I was enjoying myself, though stray thoughts kept popping intrusively into my head. Thoughts like, *I want to die.*

We sat down for dinner, June slipping effortlessly into a maternal role, explaining the dishes, the varying allergens ("There's gluten in the stuffing") and nutritional benefits ("Sweet potatoes are a superfood!"). She spooned up hearty portions, thick dollops of creamed leeks, cheesy mash, and smashed carrots. The centerpiece was pork, a white-strung shoulder, glazed with honey and mustard, strips of crackling on the side. She patted it with a knife, looking touchingly delighted, and we made the requisite sounds and sighs before she sliced off chunks and passed them around the table. We toasted our efforts and wished each other a merry Christmas, and then it was time to eat.

I stared at my plate. Around me everyone was squishing vegetables up against hunks of meat, dipping into cranberry jelly and devouring. The tougher pieces of pork were wrestled with before being chewed off satisfactorily. Crisp domes of Yorkshire pudding were slopped over with gravy. Green beans were bitten elegantly like long, edible cigars. The metallic clatter of cutlery and the wet smacking of mastication surrounded me—but I couldn't bring myself to eat even a mouthful. The plate before me suddenly represented a problem to be solved.

I had always believed that the very best food contains something elementally repugnant. That its innate grotesquerie is what makes it so perversely alluring. My own favorite foods tended toward a certain sludgy, muddy texture. And from the most expensive and genteel through to the indulgently crass, the appeal of slop abides: caviar, escargots, foie gras or hamburgers, kebabs, macaroni and cheese. Even vegetable soup forms a membrane. Apples begin rotting from the very first bite. No matter which end of the spectrum, there lies something fundamentally and yet delectably disgusting, some squirmy, sinewy, oozing, greasy, sticky, glutinous, mushy, fatty, chewy, viscous *thing* that compels. The line between pleasure and revulsion can seem so very thin, if it even exists at all.

But staring at the plate of roasted vegetables and meat, the gravy thick as treacle, the potatoes yellow with oil—I couldn't do it. It was like looking at something that was not food. Like looking at a plate of fancied-up dog shit. I pushed things around with my fork. I knew I was being difficult.

June looked over at my still-full plate. "Don't you like it?" she asked.

"It's not . . . ," I began. "It's just that I'm not really hungry."

She seemed offended. I could tell she was resisting a shared look of "Tuh!" with Samuel, and I stared at my plate, hoping to miss it. A coolness entered the room. The chatter died down.

"She's just watching her weight!" Adnan announced, cutting through the quiet, the goofiness of his voice, the sheer charm of his persona dragging the party back, almost, to its former joviality. "Aren't you, princess?"

I forced a smile.

In the end I managed a couple bits of pork, one brussels sprout, and some leeks, honestly surprised I kept them down. Afterward we hung around at the table, drinking, smoking—though we knew we weren't allowed—and then I offered to do the washing-up, while the others put away the table and married around the room. Mei-Ling and June turned up the music and started dancing, and soon they were all on their feet. I retreated to the sofa, shyly refusing invitations to join them, just enjoying watching their silly moves and exaggerated routines. I was happy and drunk. I felt like I had friends.

"Christmas Wrapping" came on the playlist, and Mei-Ling knew all the words. We clapped her along as she breathlessly bellowed them, drunker than any of us.

I leaned back into the sofa thinking it was the best university day I'd had so far.

Sometime around two we began winding down. Mei-Ling had passed out on the sofa, and Adnan carried her back to her room. Half an hour later, the sound of violent retching could be heard from the bathroom. I started on the last of the tidying, but June shooed me away.

"Go to bed," she said, hugging me, and I did.

A couple of hours later, I woke up and went to use the bathroom. I could hear the soft murmurs of a late-night conversation, a conspiratorial whisper. Something snaked from my heart to my brain, and I crept further toward the door, lurking outside to hear what they were saying.

"Did you see how much she ate? Like nothing."

"She's lost loads of weight, too. Have you noticed?"

"Yeah. She looks gross. At least when she was fat, she was pretty."

"She wasn't fat."

"Okay—fatter."

"It's weird, 'cause she used to be, like, obsessed with cooking."

"Well, at least now some of us get to actually use the kitchen."

"You reckon she's got any friends? Like, any friends at all?"

"I doubt it."

"Adnan insists she's dead nice, just a bit of an oddball."

"Do you think he fancies her?"

I padded back to my room, retreating from their muted titters, lying in bed and squeezing my legs shut.

Idiot, I reprimanded myself. *Stupid idiot bitch. Idiot fucking cunt.*

I rolled onto my side, feeling my bones press into the mattress, my horrid knees clack together.

The morning after the party was washed out with the chilly normality of a comedown, a stony and somber *oh*.

Mei-Ling remained in her room, emerging just once to collect a takeaway. Adnan went to lunch with his friends. June and Samuel stationed themselves on the sofa watching Disney films under a shared duvet, laughing and complaining that their heads hurt. I lay in bed staring at the ceiling, the small expanse of space I knew so well. I didn't want to cry anymore, just to languish in the white noise that followed.

A few days after classes had finished, they were all gone, vanishing to their unusual-sounding villages and market towns. I stayed in halls right up until Christmas Eve. I was terrified at the thought of being left alone, but I couldn't bring myself to go home.

The campus was dreamily vacant, and I drifted through it on a zephyr of my fluctuating sadness, strung out and thinning. My pelvis pressed against the pale skin of my middle, a flash of bone white beneath my jeans. I felt like a Russian doll, so many boxy, hollow versions of myself waiting to be revealed, and the smallest, hardest little nub right in the middle.

I had always been fascinated by my body. I started masturbating young. I explored the smooth expanses of my flesh, every pucker and hole, every sprouting hair or excretion of sebum. I'd examine the pores on my nose for hours in the bathroom mirror. It was weirdly calming. I once slipped a felt pen into my vagina to see if I could prod my cervix. I could not. I removed the pen, slick and ruined, staring at the length of it in total disbelief that there were depths in my own self I literally could not reach. I'd contemplate the big, brown mole on my arm, the tiny little cells that made it, each a slim oval with a porous dot in the middle, like the evil-eye trinkets you buy on the beach. My body felt so large and so small, so vast and so inscrutable.

And I suppose I'd always had a low-level hatred of all that flesh. It was never good enough, pretty enough, thin enough. But this was something different. It wasn't a case of wanting it to be better or more attractive or skinnier. I wanted not to have it at all. I'd lie on my back looking down at it. How my waist curved to my hips like an ampersand. The way my breasts slunk to the sides of my rib cage. I had a body that was not to be respected. That was a joke. I thought back to the times when I'd longed to be attractive, when I wanted slink and sex appeal more than I wanted anything, more than I wanted happiness and more than I wanted love. I wanted to be as narrow as a knife and hotly desired. I wanted eyes on me. I wanted men to want to fuck me. I could no longer imagine feeling that way.

It is the strangest sensation, to feel like a passenger in your own body. To look at your flesh as a too-starched suit, the overwhelming urge to strip it away from yourself. I'd imagine peeling it off, just unzipping it and stepping out, all skeleton and spirit. Hearing the slap of it on the ground, feeling the breeze on my bones.

I tried it just once. I thought of it as a considered decision. Crouched in our damp, drafty communal bathroom, I picked out the blade from an unused razor. It was a flimsy thing, really, though it did nick my thumb. A tiny bubble of blood plopped out. An accidental hello from my insides. The blade was clean, but I burned it with a lighter anyhow, turning it matte brown. My thigh seemed the most obvious place. My lap. It was where I went to work on things: a laptop or a newspaper. It was just right there.

I pulled down my jeans, sitting on the side of my bed with a fistful of balled-up tissue paper, ready. I held my skin taut with one hand and the blade with the other. I pressed it down and dragged it along, cutting four even lines. One on top of the other, left to right, no more than a few inches each. It hurt a bit. Little wriggles of pain beneath the satisfying, smooth motion of the blade opening up my skin. But mostly it felt like drawing on my leg with a pen. I pressed the tissue paper over and was surprised by how much blood I'd produced.

The blood was tomato red, not the lethargic brown goo I was used to seeing monthly. This was insistent, tenacious, and first in line, the way young things are. But mostly it made sense: all of this stored-up anxiety, zipping and coursing through my veins, released like weather on a low-pressure day. It felt as honest an articulation of myself as anything I'd ever done.

I fell asleep, crawling beneath my duvet. In the morning I woke fully clothed, my face dry and stiff, feeling no better or worse. My sheets were stained. I felt stupid. I wasn't going to do it again. I'd fashioned out a little space to be mad at, I thought, with only some pride. An area from which to feel a valid pain. And I suppose it did help.

On the last day, I walked around campus alone. The cold felt vivid and alive, the rain fell in a graceful smatter. Before, I could stand in the park and feel that beneath the dull absence of color, the cold dry breeze, there was life. Now my only feeling was mania and disgust and, behind those, intense waves of embarrassment. Michael pushing his hands up beneath my bra and wrenching at my nipple. The laborious way he'd lunged on top of me. The grimace of his face as he came. The dribble of semen across my stomach. The relentless carousel of those images.

I navigated myself around the university, looking at buildings I hadn't seen before, shortcuts I'd never needed to use. Walking from the art school to the student union, I found a small, fenced thoroughfare, narrow and paved, lined with hedgerows. In the distance I could see the towering blocks and golden cranes of the city as the sun crept out from behind the smoggy clouds and the rain almost completely stopped.

Without warning I started to cry, an aching, fundamental sob, animal gasps, spit and tears dripping from my lips. There was nowhere to sit, so I just kept wandering, tears running down my cheeks, dangling from my chin and seeping into my scarf, which rubbed and made my skin sore. *I am so terribly lonely*, I thought. *I am so sad.*

On Christmas Eve the trains were packed with weary commuters. I shuffled myself into the space beneath the baggage holders and crouched down. The idea of spending a significant amount of time back home filled me with a woozy trepidation. I was terrified of relaxing into it, of what would happen when it was taken away again. I closed my eyes, settling into the rhythmic thrum of the engine, the cozy claustrophobia of my position. I dozed off. When I woke, the open doors were blasting an icy gale, and I looked up to see my mum and aunt on the platform.

That night I crawled beneath my clean sheets and dragged Joan of Arc with me. She pawed at the pillow and settled in a heap. She had developed a bear-cub-like snore and would deliver wheezy little growls that became looser and louder the deeper she slept. I put my hand on her fur and felt her warm flesh, her stomach moving up and down, the humble thump of her heart. I lay with my face pressed against her; she smelled of yeast and dirt, of honey and soured milk. I barely slept all night, just concentrated on her easy presence, her tiny panting existence. I heard my mum go to the toilet three times. On the third time, she pushed open my bedroom door to check up on me. I snapped my eyes shut and pretended to be sleeping. She closed the door and went to bed.

Christmas morning I woke to the sounds of tinkering in the kitchen, the obnoxious blare of festive pop. My mum did the appetizers, and I did everything else. Hetty helped me in the kitchen, staring in appraisal as I sliced mushrooms using the julienne method I'd learned off YouTube. She couldn't cook at all herself, living mainly off party food: feta-and-spinach parcels and beer-battered shrimp. But she liked to watch me, regarding the proceedings with a cool admiration and a wonder that bordered on suspicion.

When we were stuffed full of Christmas dinner, we lifted Joan of Arc up to the table, and she guzzled everything she could reach from my mum's arms. Afterward we lounged around watching *Elf*, a meze of confectionery on the coffee table in front of us: a celebration box

of Maltesers, giant gooey dates on cocktail sticks, and chocolate caramel digestives. It was weird to feel contentment after such a long
while without it.

On New Year's Eve, I went out with my old school friend Jonathan and two large-haired girls from his course. Jonathan and his
friends went to Oxford and so were essentially in a different strato-
sphere, but they were polite about it. Their experiences seemed so
ritzy and unreal: formal mixers with ball gowns and imported cigars,
waking up next to athletic chemistry postgrads. Jonathan was learning Russian, had booked a trip to St. Petersburg. I felt so drab. So
lacking. But there was also something sort of bolstering about the
experience. These dauntless women who'd suddenly just appeared.
Everything in their lives so evidently possible.

Returning to university was better than I expected. I'd resolved to
switch courses so I wouldn't have to see Michael, deciding that
philosophy was as good a degree as any. I'd also resolved to be more
assertive and to wear a little more color. I was getting there. I asked
Mei-Ling if I could maybe tag along the next time her friends went
out to that pizza place she was obsessed with. One evening Adnan
was loitering around the kitchen, and I said I'd cook him dinner. We
ate pho and watched all of *Transformers*. Gradually I dragged myself
back from the margins of my own existence.

Spring drew on, and everyone started looking for somewhere
to live in second year. I replied to a couple of adverts from the library notice board, even went to look at a bedsit a half-hour train ride
from the campus, but generally had no idea what I might do. One
evening I was lying in bed, not understanding a word of *Tractatus
Logico-Philosophicus*, when my phone bleeped with a message from

June. Hey, you want to live with us next year?!! Someone dropped out:-) :-) I read the message a couple of times, trying to grasp the idea of living with my flatmates for another twelve months. I waited five minutes and then replied, Yeah, okay. Later I went to the kitchen to make a cup of tea and watched June and Mei-Ling microwaving some pasta, awkwardly negotiating the small space, and I felt quietly heartened. They, too, lacked options, or perhaps imagination, just the same as me.

The house they had found was in a suburb densely populated with students. I felt radiant with gratitude that they'd asked me to move in, and I offered to do all the rental admin: photocopying letters to evidence our exemption from council tax, taking pictures of cracks in the walls so we wouldn't get charged for the damage.

We had a meeting to determine who got which room. We wrote our names on a torn-up coursework form and dropped them into a mixing bowl. Adnan made a celebratory fist pump when he got the room that came with its own sink—also by far the dampest, dingiest room in the house. June looked over to Mei-Ling and mouthed, *Why?!* Samuel got the biggest bedroom, dancing along the back of the sofa, elated. June got the second-biggest, and Mei-Ling got the smallest. I offered to switch with her, but she refused. Nadeem had decided to live with some boys from his course. I imagined it would be a very loud house.

"Right!" Adnan announced. "I guess we're living together again. It's official."

We didn't have drinks to clink, but Samuel and June were eating cereal bars, which they pressed together with obvious satisfaction, and we all made generally affirmative sounds. I thought I should thank them for inviting me into the new house, for letting me hang around another year.

"I really appreciate it," I added. "And I promise I'll stay out of your way."

Samuel and June rolled their eyes and sighed theatrically, telling me not to be daft. But Mei-Ling looked annoyed.

"What?" she said. "What did you say that for?"

I froze, panicked, as it became apparent I had said the wrong thing.

"It's your house, too," she said. "You obviously don't have to stay out of our way. That's ridiculous."

She looked hurt, and I tried to form a smile that would look maximally reassuring, entirely nonconfrontational. I felt bad for having upset her but also strangely satisfied to find she cared.

As I fell asleep that night, I could almost imagine the five us living there. The image was faint, but I concentrated hard on it: making fun of crappy television shows, cooking and cleaning rotas, throwing parties. I told myself I would spend more time with them, would try to act as though they wanted to see me. I was even looking forward to it. But that was before I met Arnold.

Bigger on the Inside

By the end of the summer, we had four new members in Supper Club: Renni, Ashley, Monica, and Sash.

Renni was the first to find out about us, having seen one of the clubs in real life. She was working as the duty manager at this fancy bar in town, the Amore, which meant she was always the last to leave. Closing up one night after a double shift, giving the bar a final wipe-down, she noticed a well-dressed man slumped unconscious in the corner. She prodded him gingerly, and he came to, saying something about a hotel room and Vienna. She said she didn't know about that but she did know he had to leave. He stumbled to his feet, and before he left, he threw up, rather efficiently she couldn't help but notice, emptying the contents of his stomach just to the side of the main door and then going on his way. She retched while mopping it up, thinking about how nice it would be to feel clean more frequently. She thought about the bath she was going to have when she got in. That was something she used to do after a late shift: languish in a bath oily with lavender at four, sometimes five, in the morning. She walked past Supper Club as she made her way home.

We met her in the park. She was waiting on a bench, headphone wires trailing from her ears into her handbag, watching a bird hop across a pile of leaves. We walked laps around the park while she told us why she wanted to join Supper Club.

Renni remembered being happy until the age of sixteen. That was when her parents moved her to the UK. They'd been living in Lecce, a town on the south coast of Italy, where her parents had run a seafood restaurant built into the rocks. She worked in the kitchen, helping her mum and dad wash pots, then in front of house, showing tourists to their tables—and sometimes she would be treated contemptuously, but sometimes she would get good tips. She had friends, and at the weekend they would smoke weed and drink cheap wine on the beach. She had a boyfriend called Niccolo, and even though he'd pressured her into having sex sooner than she really wanted to, she liked him: she liked his smooth back and broad shoulders, the angles of his face. She liked how much he seemed to like her, how he would bury his face into her breasts and stomach, as if he were ravenous and she was a meal. But then her parents told her they were selling the restaurant and emigrating to the UK because of the recession. It broke her heart, and even though she and Niccolo said they would stay in touch, of course they did not.

She hated England. She hated the cold and the food and how instead of getting high and drunk on the beach she spent most nights in with her mum and dad, watching *X Factor* and eating crisps. She hated her parochial college, how she didn't have friends and even the teachers made a point of not understanding her accent. And she knew that something else was going on there, something not to do with her accent at all. "You don't know what it is like to be a black woman in this country," she said. "You've got no idea." She went to university, and it was better—not that much better, but at least she wasn't the only person of color within a ten-mile radius. She started dating a white woman called Liz, whom she liked a lot. They stayed together all through university, and when they both graduated (Renni in hospitality with finance and Liz in history of art), they moved into a flat together and got temp jobs that emptied their souls. Still, they were in love, and that counted for something. They'd cook elaborate meals out of store-brand food and eat them while watching their favorite films and television shows, cuddled on the couch. Renni wished the way she felt then, wrapped in a blanket with the woman she now recognized as the love of her life, could be the way she felt forever.

One morning they walked to the shop to buy toilet paper, jam, and a loaf of bread—and an ordinary-looking man walked past and said something under his breath. "What did you say?" Liz demanded, even though Renni begged her not to. "What did you just say to us?" And the ordinary-looking man turned around and said it again, and it was something not meant for Liz but intended for her, for Renni—and she hadn't needed to hear it up close. Liz shouted something back, but Renni couldn't remember what, and the man reached into his canvas carrier bag and removed a carton of milk, opening it and emptying it in their direction, then turned and walked on. They both stood dripping milk in the street, and Liz started crying, and Renni had to comfort her, had to hold her arm around her the whole way home. That evening Liz couldn't understand why Renni was being distant, lying on the couch with her eyes shut. There weren't the words to explain what was wrong. And so the fight became about something else instead, something easier: Liz raging over her girl-friend's avoidant nature, her passivity; Renni not speaking, not meeting her eye, confirming what Liz thought she knew. The following morning Renni moved out.

A few years later, she was living on her own and managing the Amore. Then one evening she walked past her local Italian trattoria, a restaurant that was almost always entirely empty, and saw a group of women inside, dancing wildly, wearing neon outfits and clutching handfuls of food. She thought about herself and Liz cuddled on the couch, and herself and Niccolo drinking wine and getting high, and herself on her own, moving through the world—how she'd spent years striving for comfort but had never thought much about joy. And that was what struck her while watching the Supper Club— joy—and it seemed like something to consider.

Since I had moved in with Stevie, I went home less and less. My mum had been talking about an off-season holiday with Hetty, booking a cottage in the Lake District or a few days in the south of France. I didn't dare tell them I'd just used what was left of my leave on a week in Berlin. Instead I took a Friday off work and went home to demonstrate that I did still want to see them. My mum picked me up from the station. "Well, you're certainly a sight to behold," she said, taking in my loose-fitting elasticated trousers, my visibly larger body. "I suppose I should be grateful you're here at all."

That night I cooked us both dinner. My mum was distant and preoccupied, busying herself with pointedly unnecessary chores. I rustled around the kitchen, focused on finding some alcohol as a priority. Discovering some hard, pale limes in the fruit bowl, I muddled them with vodka, ice, and sugar for a makeshift caipirinha. "Drink this," I said, handing it to my mum. "It's classy."

I took my time roasting a chicken with olives and fennel, thinly slicing potatoes for a gratin. By the time we sat down, my mum had loosened up, perhaps was even a little drunk, stacking far too many potato slices onto her fork and clumsily spearing strips of chicken. "So what's going on with you?" she asked, not unaggressively. "You seem different."

"What's that supposed to mean?"

"Well, love, you look different."

I put down my fork. "For Christ's sake, Mum. This is why I don't bloody come home."

"Don't be like that, Roberta. I'm just saying that, you know, it's good to keep moving. And it's wonderful that you're so into your food. We all like a treat now and then." She paused, casting around. "Why don't you go for a nice walk with Hetty tomorrow? Get some fresh air." She paused again. "Build up an appetite."

My aunt picked me up the following morning. We were going to the beach.

En route we pulled into a drive-through to get breakfast. She ordered us each two egg-and-sausage sandwiches, a large bag of hash browns, lattes, and juice. We parked and pushed back our seats, laying the food out across the dashboard, the car steaming up with cooking oil and coffee, the radio playing Billie Joel. Outside, it started to rain, but Hetty refused to roll up the window, rain spattering across the food. My aunt managed to imbue everything with a sense of wildness and the outdoors. She could be a strange woman.

The beach was a bleak affair. The sand whipped up in the breeze, spraying an assault like thousands of tiny spider bites. The wash was foaming and yellow. My aunt said she knew a particular stretch, nice and quiet, where she'd sometimes come to walk Joa, who was now old and feeble and did not want to walk at all. It was unmarked save for a single fish-and-chip vendor and a small, run-down pub. We were one of two cars in the car park—a gung ho family with a roof rack for their bikes and wearing Windbreakers blown flat got out ahead of us. As we made our way to the shore, we saw them eating cones of battered scampi, nodding at each other in hardy affirmation.

My aunt linked my arm in hers, and we walked headfirst into the wind. It seemed like the kind of place used only for field trips and education, as opposed to anything leisurely or fun. CENTIPEDES TO LOOK OUT FOR! a worn information board declared, illustrated with different types of squirming beasts, most of them graffitied to look like ejaculating penises. My aunt pointed at it and howled with laughter. We went right up to the tide and walked alongside it, our feet intermittently drenched. It was freezing.

"You haven't been in touch much," my aunt declared finally. "Like, at all."

"I've been busy," I said, kicking up the sand. "Work. Going out. You know."

"I'm sure."

The other family were far ahead of us, out on top of some dunes in the distance; the tall grass as blond and windswept as their hair. They walked in a long, straight line, holding hands like paper dolls: two boys, two girls.

"You see, love. I wanted to talk to you about something."

She glanced over to check I was definitely listening, and I nodded.

"Your mum's started seeing someone. A woman. Sheila."

I stopped still in the sand, my feet immediately engulfed in a frigid rush of water. My eyes started leaking from the cold. I felt all my goose pimples, every single one of them, sprouting like little friends, and then a deep heat in my belly like an MDMA high. I contemplated it a moment, then turned to my aunt and threw my arms around her.

"That's amazing," I said, pulling back to hold her at arm's length.

"Is it?" my aunt said.

I mentally audited my answer, playing it back, making sure I'd given her the right one. "Of course it is," I replied. "I mean, is she happy?"

"She's very happy. Though she's been going daft trying to tell you. I thought you were near crying then."

"It just took a second for it to sink in."

"There's something else I should mention," she said.

"Oh, yeah?"

"It's been going on awhile."

"Like, how long?"

"Just over a year."

I processed this information, mining my body for a response, deciding where to file it. Did I feel angry, betrayed, lied to? I wanted to summon something that wasn't there, or perhaps something that was not *yet* there. Like flipping an object over and finding both sides are the same.

"Right," I said.

"You okay?" my aunt asked.

"Sure."

My aunt strode on contemplatively. I followed behind, feeling a bit like a little girl whose legs couldn't keep up.

"Did I ever tell you about when your mum and I went on that trip to Croatia in our late twenties?" She didn't wait for me to answer before continuing. "It was before she got pregnant with you. She and your dad had just got married. We'd had lunch and spent the afternoon drinking, sitting in the sand watching the sunset. She told me she was worried about becoming boring. That your father didn't want to travel. That he'd sulked about her coming away with me. Then, suddenly, apropos of nothing, she starts stripping off. Takes off all her clothes and runs headlong into the Adriatic Sea, this mad, white, sprinting thing. Well, up until this. It was the only other time she had truly surprised me."

I looked out at the sea, the rough gray infinity of it, restless with living things. I thought about my mum, and my aunt, and Stevie. And I thought about my own life. I was still so afraid and yet so desirous of everything. Fear and freedom, occupying opposite ends of the spectrum, though inexorably tied. Freedom as abstract, fear essential to it, the necessary risk without which it was meaningless. The brain is as limitless as the sky. Our bodies won't last forever. The sun was falling lower, dropping into sight beneath the clouds, a coy egg yolk in the sky. It gave the beach a renewed quality, the sand a crystalline shimmer.

"I'm doing it," I said, unbuttoning my coat, pulling my sweater over my head.

"Me, too," my aunt said, like she couldn't quite believe her own words. We unpeeled our clothes and dumped them in a pile. We removed our bras, then our knickers, quickly yanking them down and simply stepping aside. The part of my brain ordinarily occupied by Supper Club took over, and I felt the two worlds collide—or perhaps bleed together. Running toward the sea, we squealed as water splashed our bodies, breasts cold and swinging, hair sopping and salted. My eyes stung, and I couldn't feel my limbs. I let the waves carry me, floating on my back, watching my body made glassed and foggy by the sea. My aunt swam a sturdy breaststroke around me. We must have been in only a couple of minutes, but it felt much longer. We finally got out and roamed around looking for items of clothing that had strayed from the pile. Our bodies were blue and puckered. We were shaking like leaves.

I leaned over, stepping into my pants and turning around to look for my bra, and froze when I saw the little boy from the other family suddenly in front of me. He promptly burst into tears and ran away at the sight of my naked breasts.

"Everyone's a critic," I said, and my aunt started laughing.

"I've missed you," she said, wringing out her hair.

We dried off in the pub, nursing two pints of Guinness, enjoying the soporific warmth of an open fire. I called my mum to tell her I'd heard the news and I that was very happy she was happy. We finished our round, and I bought another, tea for my aunt and a pint for me. I decided I was going to tell her about Supper Club.

When I'd finished talking, she stared into space for a long while. "It reminds me of a joke," she said. "The one about the wife and the mistress."

"How does it go?" I asked.

"Your wife and your mistress are both drowning. Who do you save? Your mistress. Because your wife will never understand. Or your wife. Because your mistress will always understand."

"I don't get it."

"Exactly," she replied. "Exactly."

I felt so sad that she didn't understand. My cool aunt Hetty, of all people. She'd once called us at midnight from San Antonio, announcing, "I think I just got engaged!" Another time she dropped off the radar for weeks, until eventually my mum rang to find out what was going on, and she replied, "Oh, yeah, I just got really into engines. Been dead busy learning about the different kinds of engines."

We finished our drinks and got up to leave. It was dark, and there was very little lighting on the walk to the car. My hair was still damp with seawater, the wind ever more insistent. I watched Hetty stride on in front of me, as she always did. Back in the car, I switched the radio on. *I want to go home*, I thought. *I just want to go home.* But I couldn't attribute this feeling to any place I knew of.

When we got back from the beach, we found my mum snuggled up on the sofa, sipping tea and watching the six o'clock news, with a person I had to assume was Sheila, and I thought, *Well, this is something I have to deal with now.* That evening Sheila made us a stir-fry, calling me into the kitchen to show me some bean curd, saying, "It's called mapo tofu, which means 'pockmarked woman,' because of the texture of its skin," and I thought, *This is not so bad.*

My mum suddenly having a girlfriend was not altogether strange. I'd grown up in a house populated almost exclusively by women, and so there was no change there; I could still go to the toilet with the door open. She'd dated before—men with unmemorable names like Richard or Dave, who could occasionally be found in the kitchen, plainly uncomfortable, asking whether I played any sports. The only difference apparent when she was going a date was a slight sheen of Vaseline across her lips, a faint trace of perfume. But there'd never been anyone serious. She'd always go to dinner parties and parents' evening alone. I used to wonder when she even saw them.

Sheila was Scottish, which for some reason surprised me more than the fact she was a woman. She worked as a community nutritionist, which meant I could talk to her about food, and she was soft-spoken and seemed as if she listened, really listened, to everything you said. I could see why my mum liked her. On Sunday we all had lunch before I left: Sheila, my mum, my aunt, and me. Joan of Arc scuttled into the living room as we sat drinking our coffee, dried flecks of blood dusted around her vagina, and my mum exclaimed she must be in season.

"My girl!" she said, lifting her up in her arms. "You've synced up with me."

"And me!" my aunt added.

"Me, too," Sheila said. They turned to me.

"Yup," I confirmed, and we toasted, clinking our glasses of cheap Buck's Fizz together to five simultaneously menstruating women— which seemed ridiculous, but beautiful also.

Roberta, hello.

How are you? Well, I should hope. The cats hope you are well also. Mildew is rolling around on his back and licking his paw in a contemplative manner that suggests he is thinking: I hope that daughter of yours is doing very well, Jim. I might be projecting.

I am nursing one heck of a hangover, having spent yesterday evening (and daytime) at my friend Jools's wedding. What a wedding. Have you seen what people do for weddings these days? No longer a quick do at the registrar's, then back to the house for some supper. These days there's bloody jazz quintets and canapés that do not resemble any kind of food I'd recognize, speeches that go on all flipping afternoon, bridesmaids doing dance routines that are, let me tell you, more than a little bit provocative. My word. Anyway, I was being all responsible and grown-up, having a glass of water after every glass of wine, as you're supposed to. Then Jerry shows up, trashed as a badger's whatsit, and demands—demands!—I do tequila shots with him. So I did—it can't have been more than maybe three tequila shots, and I was absolutely on my arse. Terribly embarrassing. I should be able to hold my liquor at my age (they call it "liquor" over here). So I woke up this morning with a cracking headache. The cats and I have just been sat on the couch all day, watching old episodes of *Seinfeld*. Do you watch it/like it? My favorite's Kramer. Elaine reminds me of your mum. We've been watching the series where George is engaged.

I've been trying to make more of an effort with the flat. Took myself down to IKEA the other evening. It was a roundly stressful affair, but I did get myself a nice new standing lamp (you can see it *here*) and a bookshelf, that I put up myself. Was dead proud of myself. I've attached a photo of it. Now I just need to fill it with some books, don't I? I'm sure you'd give me some great book recommendations. You always had your head in a book (or in the clouds—ahem). One of my pals that I have pizza with was telling me he's just joined a book club and he's the only bloke. He's really loving it. Says all the ladies make a right old fuss of him. Lucky bugger.

Did I ever tell you about the Frank Lloyd Wright exhibition? It was fantastic! Had loads of his original drawings and letters he'd written to friends. Spent a good few hours there and treated myself to loads of useless rubbish I can't afford from the gift shop. And a panini. Got you some stuff too, so if you ever do get back to me, you could give me your address and I could send it to you. It's nothing fancy, just a tea towel and some pencils. Or if you ever find yourself this way, I'd be very happy to come give them to you. Up to you, really.

Thinking this evening I might be forced to order a takeaway. Hard life. Just have to make my mind up between pizza or Chinese food. Have I told you the curry situation over here? It is DIRE. It's like they've never heard of chili. Spread the word! You can't get decent curry in Queens.

Anyway, I think I've told you all of the most exciting details from my life now. I'm sure you're simply seething with jealousy, thinking why is my old dad having all the excitement and not me? As ever, if you do fancy getting back in touch, please feel very welcome to. I'd love to know how you're doing. And your mum, what's she up to? Still running around after your mad aunt, I've no doubt.

Have a great weekend!

All best,

Jim (Dad)

X

Stevie came home confrontational. It often happened after she'd spent the evening with her studio friends. She would pace about the flat, picking up oranges from the bowl and asking if I'd bought them in Tesco, or pulling at the hem of my sweater and questioning whether looking nice was worth freezing for. She would clatter in the kitchen, throwing open all the cupboard doors and rattling around the washing-up, waiting for me to ask if there was something she was looking for. One time she came home and sat on the sofa, loudly unzipping her bag and removing a blister packet of Tylenol, evacuating two on the table before knocking them back with a bottle of water, all the while staring at me. During these moments I imagined all the hair on my body standing upward, like a cartoon cat made afraid. I'd temper my voice and make myself small and unobtrusive, offer her the remote or ask if she'd like some space, but this would only make her more angry. "My God!" she would yell before stomping up the stairs. Sometimes I would hear her playing music from her teens—Sleater-Kinney and Bikini Kill leaking ominously through the ceiling. Once I knocked on her door to find her lying facedown on her bed, listening to "Dying" by Hole on repeat. It was hard to know what she wanted. Like me, she could scream, *Leave me alone!* and *Where are you going?* in the same breath. My tactic was to wait forty-five minutes, then ask if she wanted a cup of tea. Sometimes I would set a timer on my phone. Often I would have to remind myself to breathe deeply, that it would all be over soon.

On this occasion she made for the fridge and removed a bottle of white wine. I'd been hoping to make crab-and-parsley linguine with it, but I didn't say anything, just watched her sniff at the nozzle and pour herself a glass. "You want one," she said, as statement not inquiry, and poured a glass for me, too. She placed it forcefully in front of me, sloshing some over the side, and I dabbed the wet bit of the table with my cardigan-covered elbow. I felt her eyes roll. "Sorry," I said, and she snapped, "Stop saying fucking sorry." We both drank, staring at the television, despite the fact it was not switched on.

"Look at this fucking room," she said after a while.

I looked at the room. Its beige walls. The pieces of furniture all facing each other like they were friends. It was a nice room. I felt it radiated kindness, that it wanted us both to be happy. It was perhaps my favorite room in the world.

"I like this room," I said. I curled my toes into the thick, round rug that sat beneath the central table, topped with books and nail varnish and gallery flyers and receipts.

"Have you ever thought about why we never smoke inside this room?"

It was true. We both smoked in our bedrooms, opening the window and hanging over the side. We smoked in the kitchen, huddled at the back door. Neither of us was above a cigarette while stewing in the bath. I wondered what made the living room a sacred space.

"I guess we just want to keep it . . . nice?" I offered.

"Nice!"

"Yeah, you know. Not cigarette-smelling. Clean. Tidy."

"Ugh, he's right. We live such parochial lives."

I looked at the felt blanket that covered my waist and legs. The tube of digestives to my side, sealed with the plastic twist tie. The cheap scented candle that made the room smell like lemonade. I still liked all of it. The easy sense of normality it represented. It felt safe, and I felt safe in it. More so than I felt in my own bedroom, even. A room that functioned only for us to sit in, together. It did feel sacred. It did.

"This fucking guy," Stevie said. "This fucking Tim."

I'd heard her mention his name previously. He was a lecturer of some sort, possibly in fine art. He'd done a show in Finland shortly after Stevie had met him, and for some reason this had really gotten to her. He did something with photographs and collage, and he wore a yellow ribbon on his wrist for obliquely alluded-to political motivations.

"He's got this real problem with Supper Club. Like, he said we think we're doing something really profound, but actually we're doing something which is at best basic and at worst just really fucking bourgeois and gross."

She put down her wine and threw forward her head, folding like garden furniture. I watched her hair fall toward the floor, the heavy mess of it. The back of her head was much flatter than I'd have anticipated. I thought about her head and all the ideas it contained. She once talked about how the larger a woman's handbag is, the more likely she is to be deranged. She also thought that short people were all into erotic asphyxiation. One morning she'd announced, with a vague and gray seriousness, that all video games were about rape. She had a theory about women being conditioned to become birds, fundamentally febrile and delicate, twitchy and on edge, with a ready sense of slight.

I always listened to her notions, though it was more the idea of them that I liked rather than their actual content. I liked to watch her follow one thought on to the next, surprising herself with where it might go. But the bird theory I got.

Sometimes I would sit in the park or get a coffee at the gallery café and just watch the women passing by, their flinty stares, their hunted way of moving around a room. I could feel the beats of their hearts. I could hear the dense, pink noise of their thoughts. And when I looked at birds, I felt it, too. Especially in migration: the bibbity-bobbity terror, the swooping movement, together but apart. I once read about how flocking and flock theory had been appropriated as computer code: a simulation program called Boids. A man called Craig Reynolds invented it in the eighties, an animation code that mimics the movements of a flock. He wanted to formalize it. To have it make sense.

"I'm going to bed," Stevie said. She stood up, and her face was flushed with blood and noticeably clammy. She climbed the stairs with restraint. She didn't play any music. I tidied the kitchen and the living room and made myself a cup of tea. I thought about Supper Club. There were ten of us now, which seemed unbelievable. Sometimes I would imagine the women we had collected like a large basket of apples: how proud I would feel parading it around. I didn't really expect anyone outside it to understand, what it meant to stretch every tendon of your body after being hunched over for so long.

The next morning Stevie was up before me, which made me feel anxious. I could hear her doing her frustrated clattering, and I dreaded going downstairs, but the thought of what I might make myself for breakfast overrode it. I found her in the middle of cooking, which was unusual, even slightly alarming.

"You're up!" she said, her eyes widening vertically somehow. "Sit down! Sit down!"

The kitchen smelled like bacon, and there was a stack of thick, misshapen pancakes on the side.

"I've already been out to get maple syrup," she said. "And I got the expensive stuff."

I sat at the little table, which had been properly set, with an elegant-looking bottle of maple syrup. Some minutes later she deposited the pancakes and the charred bacon in front of me, floating her hand across them apologetically.

"Eat up," she said, helping herself to a couple of pancakes and several strips of bacon. "So. I've had an idea."

I reached for some food.

"We break in."

"What?"

"We break into places. We don't fucking pay some dump of a dying-on-its-arse restaurant to use their stuff. We find other spaces, and we just fucking take them."

"Like what?" I asked. "How would we even do that?"

"We find spaces that are quiet and have facilities," she said, increasingly out of breath. "I've been researching it. You know most places don't even have working security cameras? I've been reading about it online. Most places don't even have decent alarms. So long as we find somewhere with a kitchen and where we can make a bit of noise, we'd be completely fine. Scot-bloody-free."

She abandoned her breakfast to run into the next room, coming back cradling her laptop.

"Like, this library. There's nothing near it. No way we'd be seen or heard. Or the gallery in town. Or, you know, restaurants. If they're out of the way. And they all shut on Mondays. There's, like—a million spaces we could use. We could use people's houses."

"Whose houses?"

"I haven't figured that out yet. But y'know. Rich people's, I guess. Rich assholes."

Stevie was making large gestures with her hands, like she was trying to spirograph something in the air. I wanted her to calm down. To eat her breakfast. To put her hands in her lap. I tried to reason with her.

"Forgive me for stating the obvious, but neither of us knows how to break into buildings."

"Well, of course I know that! I only just had the idea. But we can find out."

"Okay," I said. "Okay."

I cut off a rectangle of black-brown bacon and dipped it in a pool of syrup. Outside, it had started raining. Over Stevie's shoulder I watched water slither down the windowpane and thought about how I might spend my day. It rolled out in front of me, a pleasing nothing. Empty weekends had become something different, far removed from the blank edges of time before, time spent waiting for something to happen, for someone to present themselves to me. I felt a wave of warmth for Stevie, even though she was being absurd, and for the miracle of being part of something. And I suddenly had a thought.

"I know where we can do it," I said.

Babysitting

S ometimes after we'd had sex, Arnold liked to read in silence, for an hour, maybe two.

He wouldn't tell me when this was the case, but I'd intuit it from his rolling over, getting out of bed, removing a book from his satchel, putting on his glasses, starting to read, and refusing to speak or listen to me at all. Sometimes I would watch him, the fair hairs on his chest damp and erratic, the wild fluff near his ears. I had a theory that the volatility of his personality stemmed from the unpredictability of his hair growth.

"Look at this," he urged me once, pointing at the smooth underside of his arm, the skin mushroom-soft and hairless, save a single wiry strand, like something pubic.

"What do you know?" It was horrifying, grotesque. I ran my finger across it, then pinched and tore it out.

"The fuck!" he exclaimed. I shrugged my shoulders. Two weeks later it had grown back, and I never bothered pulling it out again.

When I was done watching him, or when he asked me to stop watching him, I'd leave the bedroom and walk naked through to the lounge. When we first started sleeping together, I'd feel his eyes follow me across the room and through the door, but after a couple of months he'd barely look up from his book, sometimes calling, "Shut the door behind you," while his eyes remained on the page.

I'd dress and wait for him to finish his reading and come keep me company. Two hours could feel like a long time. Eventually he'd come sit with me on the couch; sometimes we'd just hold each other, other times I'd give him a blow job, then I'd cook tea or order Chinese. "Children like to have a routine," I once said, cupping my hands beneath my chin.

"That's not funny," he replied without meeting my eye. It was something not to be said, only alluded to. The denouement of a sentence abandoned halfway. *When I was. You wouldn't remember. You'll understand when.* We didn't want to say it, to actualize it, though it was always there.

Strange things would date him: a maddening sincerity, an unusual turn of phrase. And in turn he would find me silly: naïve and uninformed. "Are the Falklands the ones with the sweaters?" I asked while watching *This Is England* on the couch. He didn't answer, just came through from the kitchen to top up my wine.

In the evenings we'd talk in bed, me on my stomach, him sat up straight. I'd be dreamy and whimsical, and he'd pretend not to be amused. I fiddled with his toes. "Which one is your favorite?"

"Favorite what?" he replied.

"Favorite toe."

He tried to smother a smile. I wondered what grown-up women were like.

Sometimes I'd step out of the shower and see him dressed for work, dropping my towel and pressing my still-wet and, crucially, young body against him.

"Hey," he'd protest. "That's not fair."

And like so much of our dynamic, it both was and was not.

We had met in the pub after class. I was trying to socialize out-side the flat more, mostly to have stories I might tell Mei-Ling when I got home. I was still desperately awkward and shy, my thoughts often slowed to a standstill while I navigated the inexpli-cable twists and corners of the social racecourse. But I had mystery on my side, which is not without its merits, and as the weather began to warm and I made a conscious effort not to seem quite so utterly unreachable, my coursemates started inviting me out for drinks.

By the time I arrived, they were usually already there. They were what I'd always imagined students should be: floppy, ill-washed, vi-tal though easily pleased. They sat spilling clumsily into one anoth-er's space, legs thrown over other legs, arms draped around one another's neck. It was like they had regressed to infancy, pressing themselves against other objects and bodies, determining which bit was them, which bit was other. The night I met Arnold, I got there to find one classmate knitting, another idly snapping stems off a whole raw broccoli, burrowed within her bag. Chewing, she offered pieces around.

It was good to be in a pub. The whistle of the jukebox and the chatter of drinkers. It smelled of chips and sickly-sweet beer. The conversation veered ludicrously, from processes in the home fermenta-tion of yogurt to Hegel, from characters in *Lost* to the eternal return. One of the boys told me what the definition of session beer is. One the girls evangelized a strong admiration for Nelly Furtado. What I

remember from the night is in unremarkable scraps: my utter con-
foundment at learning that one of my peers was a mother, the sweet
and creeping sense of communion. *Let's all sleep over!* I thought. *Let's
all just take a bath!* That end-of-the-night glow, like a glorious secret
shared among us, sitting in a pub at the very center of the world.

Eventually the group began its slow departure. Just one other girl
and I remained: I knew her from classes, she was called Suzanne, and
she was very drunk. Suzanne dragged herself from the opposite side
of the table to rest her arms heavily around me. Her head landed on
my shoulder, though we had never properly talked before. I could
smell the sour-sweetness of her whiskey breath, her mouth wet and
sticky on my skin. She started getting upset for reasons I couldn't
determine. I wanted to tell her it would be okay, but I didn't know
that it would. I draped my arm around her. "Let's get you home." I
tried to help her to her feet, and she staggered around, unable to lo-
cate a center of gravity, her legs liquid and useless beneath her. I
propped her up and walked her toward the bar. She was much heavier
than she looked. At the bar I rested her on a stool and asked for a
glass of water to sober her up. I tried to find out where she lived, but
she just kept repeating "Twelve fifty-three," like it was the most obvious answer in the world. Two men at the other side of the bar spotted
us. One of them said, "Suzanne? Suzanne Kielty?" before making his
way over, later joined by the other man.

The older of the two tapped Suzanne's hand while it rested on the
bar top. He said her name a few more times while she mumbled
incoherently.

"Oh, dear," he said to the younger man, and then to me. "She's
one of our students."

"Right," I replied.

The older man asked if I knew where she lived, and I said I did not. The younger man interrupted, saying as a matter of fact he did. "Clifton House," he said. "She mentioned it the other week."

Suzanne was near sliding off her chair, melting toward the floor.

"Listen," the younger one said, "I can give her a lift home."

"Arnold." The older one gestured toward me, watchfully. "You'd better take her as well."

The man called Arnold glanced indifferently in my direction. "Fine," he said. "Sure."

There are lots of different theories on how best to caramelize onions.

There is the Momofuku method, in which you use a twelve-inch cast-iron skillet and cook the onions on a very high heat. You have to warm the oil first, until it's bubbling but not smoking, then toss in the onions, six onions specifically, which, when chopped, should fill around eight standard American measuring cups. When thrown into the skillet, they'll pile quite high, usually reaching the rim of the skillet, but resist the urge to move them around or smooth them out, leaving them to cook undisturbed for two to three minutes. After this short period, season lightly with salt and flip them over; you'll be doing this for perhaps another hour. Though don't be entirely married to the clock, it's more a matter of color and consistency. For the first fifteen minutes, the onions at the bottom of the pan should be softening, taking on the beginnings of a nice, gravelly brown as they sweat out liquid. The onions at the top of the pan will look quite undercooked at this point, alarmingly so, but they're doing their job, their gentle weight pressing down the onions beneath them. Don't try to speed up the process by turning up the heat or, heaven forbid, smooshing them down with a spatula; just be patient and let them cook. Every four minutes or so, you should be turning the entire pile of onions over on itself, to help distribute both the heat and the caramelizing onion juice, oozing it out all through the pile. After a quarter of an hour, you should notice that the onion pile has reduced significantly in volume; the onions are looking softer, though still supple, and golden in color, ever so slightly translucent. You now need to turn down the heat, stirring and flipping the onions around every ten minutes, making sure that they don't burn or stick to the bottom of the pan. It's going to take a while, but it will be worth it. You want them to soften and sweeten, but you don't want them to dry out. After the full hour, season lightly with salt again; they should be brown, maybe a little crispy at the edges and mushy in the middle, with a rich, roasted flavor and a definite sweetness. Serve straight-away or, if you must, refrigerate in a large Tupperware container. Do not freeze.

The Julia Child method is a little more hands-off but just as time-intensive. Julia's method is used primarily to prepare the onions for French onion soup (which I've never made), but it works for a multitude of other dishes, too. The cutting of the onions is quite specific, cutting each onion from top to bottom and removing the skin. Once they are halved, slice the onions into small half-moons of even widths, then chop them in half again. Don't worry too much about quantities here, just throw in the whole lot. Again, it will seem like a lot of onions, but they will reduce quite significantly. Cook on a medium to high heat. Use butter, as most of Julia's recipes insist, a lot of butter and not oil, heating the pan and letting the butter foam up and release liquid; then, once they're settled, throw in the onions, tossing until completely coated in butter. Stir them a few times, adding more butter if required. You want them to be yellow and slippery at this point. Once they start to sweat, quickly cover with a lid and turn the heat down low, leaving for fifteen minutes before checking. The onions will have wilted down considerably; there should still be butter in the pan. Then season, stirring in a teaspoon of salt, a generous quantity of fresh cracked black pepper, and half a teaspoon of sugar. Leaving the lid off, turn the heat up to medium and leave to cook, occasionally stirring, until the onions are quite deeply browned. If the onions start to stick, turn the heat down. You want them to sizzle nicely but not scorch. Caramelization doesn't come from burning the onions but from even, persistent cooking.

If you're looking for a tang in your onions, then there is one more method, in which balsamic vinegar is used. It is a very specific and quite potent flavor and best served in small amounts, with, for example, soft cheeses or meats. Use three large onions, either white or red (red onions give off a slightly sweeter taste, but if you use red onions, you are a little limited in what you can eventually serve them with). Cube the onions and put them in a slow cooker with a tablespoon of oil, a tablespoon of castor sugar, and a pinch of salt and pepper. Stir, then on a very low temperature leave to cook all day, possibly all night, too. You may need to stir occasionally, but mostly leave them undisturbed. The onions should be soft and jammy, a deep dark brown, and not crispy at all. For the final half hour, remove the pan lid to evaporate some of the excess liquid. Finally, stir in two tablespoons of a thick, good balsamic vinegar (most balsamic vinegar is "thick" and "good") and serve.

When choosing your onions, there are a few different factors to consider, but generally you want something firm with a crisp and crackling outer skin that gives off a moderate scent. Too much or too little of a scent can mean it's not yet ripe or soon to spoil. In terms of size, something in the middle, for a combination of flavor and constitution. On cubing versus slicing, I always go with slicing.

Caramelizing onions takes at least forty-five minutes of cooking. Butter can slightly speed up the process but may also burn. It's a player's game. A lot of recipes will suggest that caramelizing onions can be done in ten or fifteen minutes; this is a lie. They may turn a light brown, but they will not be caramelized. There is another method in which you can chop the onions and throw them into the pan before adding the oil (virgin olive), which claims to take no more than twenty minutes, but I've never tried it, and I never will.

When Arnold asked me what I'd been doing with myself this term, I told him I'd been caramelizing onions.

His car smelled of cigarette smoke and air freshener. The interiors were cartoonishly glossed: chrome and vinyl, metallic and LED red. It seemed like a make-believe car, and I felt as if he in turn was not really driving, only pretending to. He switched on the stereo, pushing his hand down the side of his seat to retrieve a thick wedge of CDs.

"If you can find something you want to listen to here, feel free," he said.

I shuffled through them, choosing the only one I'd heard of: Dory Previn.

"So you're into cooking?" he asked.

I told him I was.

"But you're studying . . . ?"

"Philosophy," I said.

"Oh, good," he replied.

He fixed his stare on the middle distance, out onto the road, almost looking through it. I watched his hands grip the steering wheel. His large, square fingernails. I thought, *I am going to say something*.

"I find cooking sort of a radical act," I said.

He continued staring at the road. "Oh, yeah?" he replied, just mildly amused.

"Oh, yes. It's the transience. All that time for a fleeting pleasure. Nothing else is like that."

He seemed genuinely curious and turned his head toward me, and I noticed how large it was, how truly gargantuan. I looked down to his shoulders and chest, the crease of his chin, the peek of the soft skin beneath his wrists. He was, I concluded, very attractive.

I'd found people attractive before, obviously, though truthfully not that many. I'd had a mad crush on a boy from primary school, the son of one of my mum's friends. He was freckled and scrappy. I used to sit with my mum and her friend, watching him moving through the house with a searing intensity, brattish and filthy-kneed. They would ask if we wanted to go outside and play together, and I would protest "No!" and he would look panicked, and that was that really. Then when I was fifteen, there was a guy in the year above me. Greek, with olive skin and black hair that fell across his face in curtains. He was the sort of boy teenage girls vandalize their desks for, and on the one occasion he spoke to me, I thought I might throw up. Then, as I was nearing college, a boy from the local bookshop, possibly a university student, who I used to make pathetic small talk with until he asked me if I wanted to go to the pictures with him, and I was so horrified I refused to set foot on the premises ever again. And most recently Michael. Though I was still figuring out what that meant.

But my previous attractions were always in the abstract. Like watching *Ally McBeal* and wanting to become a lawyer. This was new. I was an adult now. And he was right there.

The more I looked at Arnold, the more absurdly attractive I found him. He had a certain sturdiness: blockish and stackable, like he might tessellate. And such a large head! His voice had the grit and bass of a combine harvester. Tufts of dark hair peeked out of his shirt collar. His face was gladiatorial in its bone structure and heft. But most of all, he seemed important and he seemed like he knew stuff. I felt I could ask him any question and he would have the answer: What happens in *Ulysses*? Where is Belarus? How do I bleed a radiator? I leaned against the car door, the wind dragging my hair through the open window. There is a thick sensuality to being driven somewhere at night—the hum of the traffic, the blur of the streetlights. I imagined reaching over and straddling him when we stopped at a pedestrian crossing. We could pull over, and I'd unbuckle his belt, slip my hand down his trousers. He'd ease off my top, put his face between my breasts. I crossed my legs. I felt something akin to a sneeze, a building of pressure, then something give, seep, and trickle. A nosebleed.

My second-ever nosebleed. I'd had only one before, when I was around fourteen, in French class. A slow, deliberate drip had landed on a note I was writing to a friend, a round red blob like the seal of an ancient scroll. I had looked up and felt the trickle from my nose and down to my septum, remaining completely still as if I could freeze it into not happening, but my teacher had already noticed. She dragged me off to the nurse's office, where there was a short but intense debate about how to deal with the situation. Do I pinch and lean forward, letting it flow out, or lift up my head and absorb it back into my body? I did neither, just held a tissue to my nose and wondered what made adults so hysterical. It was only blood. A few days later, I took enormous joy in prying the large clot out of my nostril and studying it in my hand, eventually flushing it away with a strange combination of loss and shame. And I hadn't had a nosebleed since. In Arnold's car I felt the same fullness in my nostrils and more. Dark splotches began dripping from my nose and running into my mouth before landing on my lap, my skirt made canvas to an increasingly chaotic Rorschach test. It seemed absurd, blood spilling liberally from my face with no apparent reason or cause. With nothing to stem the flow and my hands resembling those of a practicing surgeon, I pulled the sleeve of my top down and held it to my face, my palm damp and sticky. We were only a couple minutes from my flat, and my freeze instinct took over. I stared straight ahead with blood flowing down my nose, hoping to God he hadn't noticed.

"Right here?" Arnold asked, indicating and turning around.

There was a moment of disbelief, then a chime of horror, and finally, revulsion.

"What the fuck?" he yelped, registering the situation. I cupped my face to my hand, mortified and unable to explain my flatulent, leaking body. He looked pale and stricken, briefly removed both hands from the wheel—but panic quickly made way for action. He pulled over and leaned across me, pushing open the door.

"Out," he said. "You have to get out."

I stepped out of the car, a frightened and bloodied victim at the side of the road. I watched as he madly surveyed the interior. There was a smear on the dashboard and a thumbnail-sized splatter on the seat. It could have been worse. A late-night corner shop glared over the way and Arnold made his way to it, muttering, "Tissues!" Did I detect a gung-ho militarism in his tone? A shade of northern pluck? It is possible. But I couldn't escape the thought that aside from anything he just seemed angry. Angry at my inelegance. Angry at the blood on his car. I was chastened by this display, fully accepting that it was my fault. I had done something wrong.

He paced back across the road, producing several pocket-size packets of tissues and a tub of wet wipes. I pressed one of the tissues to my nose while he wiped down the car seat. He then held the slightly pinkened wipes away from his body like objects of unfathomable grotesquerie, while looking for a bin. It started to rain. "I'm going home," I said, and he didn't try to stop me.

The following morning he was outside my halls, waiting in his car with a bottle of wine and an offer to drive me to class. He wanted to say he was sorry. He had a weird thing about blood. He hoped I didn't hate him. We went out for breakfast, and then, for what felt like two weeks, we didn't stop fucking. He'd go to work, and I would lie in bed watching TV and reading. He'd get back, and we'd have sex, then order a takeaway. Then we'd have sex again and go to sleep. I went home when I found myself washing the same pair of underwear in his sink for the third time.

Back in my room, I felt a weird twitch and went to the bathroom to investigate. I pried the offending clot from my nostril and flicked it into the bin. Life could be one idiot circle, but things do change.

We'd been seeing each other for a few weeks, meeting at the margins of the day; after he'd been out to dinner with friends, he would pick me up on his way home, or I'd head over to his place before class. One morning as I lay in bed watching him get dressed and calculating whether I'd have time to steal one of his croissants, he announced he wanted to take me on a date. "I still don't know anything about you. Your hopes, your dreams, et cetera. We should do this properly."

And so we went out for dinner, meeting first in a pub near his flat, well away from the university. He wore a red checked shirt, desert boots, and a khaki jacket. I put up my hair and wore a dress. He seemed a little nervous, which was strange and sweet. He was still a teacher, but I wanted to look after him. We talked about my course, my flatmates, my family. We'd never really spoken about anything biographical before, nothing meaningful. Our discourse existed mostly on the physical plane. He rested his chin in his hand while I spoke, and it felt like the first time I'd been listened to all year.

We took a taxi to a vegetarian restaurant in the suburbs, and he held open the door to help me out. Inside, he prompted me to order the wine, and I chose the third, not the second, least expensive, and that seemed like a sophisticated move.

"What are your thoughts on vegetarians?" I asked.

"Oh, I couldn't eat a whole one," he replied, piercing a half-moon of beetroot with a peculiar violence. "Aren't you due a vegetarian phase?"

"Maybe," I replied. "I have to start my period first."

The food formed a strange and colorful topography on our plates: knuckles of giant gnocchi, slivers of green beans, black rice shaped into glassy, dark igloos. I speared a cube of avocado, relishing its slick and soapy mush.

"Can you believe the ground can produce that?" I asked, holding it up.

"All your gathered knowledge," he said, "of what is outside you will remain outside you to all eternity."

He bit into a spear of asparagus dipped in garlic butter.

"Gide," he said. "André Gide. *The Fruits of the Earth.*" He winked.

I thought, *Good heavens.* And then, *I am not the first person to sit opposite him at this table listening while he quotes poetry.*

He dropped me back at my accommodation, stopping the cab just a little bit down the road, not entirely out of sight. He kissed me on the cheek and leaned over to push open the door.

"Oh," I said, stepping out.

"Oh," he replied.

"It's just," I said. "Am I not coming back to yours?"

He smiled a bit too kindly, avuncular yet evasive.

"Another time."

"Sure. Another time," I echoed.

As the car pulled away, I smiled and waved, immediately regretting the self-conscious gesture. I knew I'd been shut out. I'd been given a glimpse inside a gold-leafed room, but I didn't really belong there and I wouldn't be invited back. I guess I was not surprised.

I reverted to my quiet, sad life. The year was nearly over, and soon classes would finish, leaving me with even less to do: a diary punctuated only by the occasional exam. I was never not smoking, standing outside the front door of my halls or leaning out the window of my room, hating the sunlight and the people drifting happily through it. I smoked right down to the stub, smoking in an urgent, desperate way. I'd smoke five cigarettes before I had my breakfast, enjoying the woozy buzz, the feeling of being a little fucked-up first thing in the morning. My skin was graying and dry, and I'd developed a hoarse, hacking cough. What was once an occasional yellow smudge on my right-hand index finger was now a permanent stain.

And my eating was all over the place. Cooking felt tragic somehow, a spinster cliché. Whenever I'd make anything of note, I'd plate it up, then slide it straight into the bin. Some spinach-and-artichoke chimichangas spring particularly to mind, and a pinto-bean soup, though I actually froze that, and returned to it later. Sometimes Adnan would wander into the kitchen, following his nose.

"What have you been cooking, eh?" he'd ask, eyes shining and greedy.

"Nothing," I'd reply, and he'd look hurt but mask it, smile and wander off.

June organized an end-of-term gathering, setting out crisps and mixers in the kitchen. I got dressed and spent a long time putting on makeup, then lay down on my bed. I heard people come in and the music get louder but couldn't bring myself to join them. It sounded less like a gathering, more an actual party. Mei-Ling tapped on my door sometime after eleven. "You okay?" she said softly from outside the door.

"I've got a headache," I said. "I'm just going to stay in here."

"Fine," she replied, palpably irritated. But then a few minutes later, she slipped some Tylenol underneath the door. I remained on my bed, staring at the ceiling.

Most of them left that weekend. Mei-Ling and Adnan knocked to say good-bye, June and Samuel yelled it from the corridor. Left alone, I felt the emptiness as louder than ever. I had always been an anxious person, knowing it without really acknowledging it. It was low-grade jitters, a jarring sense of unease, like a high-pitched electronic hum you could live with for years and never quite notice. I thought that being back at my mum's would help, as it had done over Christmas. But in the long summer days, with the heat and the dry air and very little else, it only got worse.

Anxiety felt shapeless and transparent and yet solid and whole. It felt like a shroud. Like a hive of static around me. It couldn't be described, and yet I fixated on its description. It was like walking into a room and forgetting what you went for. Going to say a word that is on the tip of your tongue. It was always there, always threatening a conclusion and yet withholding it: a clock's hand between seconds, almost ready to strike. It was the moment before the moment before the moment. It was a thick slab of uncertainty and a choke of indecision. An operating level of excruciating mindfulness that required constant assessment and reassessment. Reading the room. Monitoring who is in the room. Who has left the room. Gauging the effect that had on the general tone and atmosphere of the room. The interpersonal relationships that may or may not be inside the room. I surrendered myself up to it completely.

And I went back to cutting. It was both the same as and different from the first time I tried it. I still felt the shame afterward, and also the release. But unlike last time, I didn't feel the sickness, the terror at myself. It felt somehow obvious, less abject, less extreme. And it got easier. All through that strange, blank summer, it was my secret communion with my body, a way we could privately converse. I never understood people who do it on their forearms, their wrists. I'd always pick the most clandestine corners. The plump flesh tucked beneath my underarms where my breast met my back. The soft skin at the tops of my thighs. The very bottom of my stomach, just above my pubic bone. There could be something tender about it, something quite beautiful, and sometimes even loving. The cleaning and dressing of the wound. Waking up to red splotches of fresh blood on my bedsheets. A gothic love letter from my former self. I'd watch the skin heal and regenerate, the scar tissue a faint memory of the trauma before. I was exhilarated by my body's ability to mend and move on, even if I could not.

The Bottom of the Ocean

We planned to host a Supper Club at my old university building: the Department of Arts and Humanities. It was a large contemporary structure, tall glass panels and concrete columns with exposed steel trussing, fronted by amorphous blobs of grass. Though it was now more than ten years old, it still hinted at a level of modernity and vocation. But in spite of its imposing aesthetic, I knew it was relatively easy to break into. I had gotten into the building late one night with Arnold. One Friday evening he left his wallet, laptop, and grading in his office accidentally, so we drove back there, past midnight, and he showed me how to access the building. Through the service entrance, the alarm disarmed via a code written on a Post-it note, hidden on the underside of some shelving. The security cameras were dummies. The computer labs had their own security measures, which were essentially impenetrable, but you could get through to the atrium, the classrooms, and the café without setting anything off.

Stevie, Erin, Monica, and I had a trial run a few weeks ahead of the club. Lina had told us if we could get hold of a master key, we should be able to unlock the service door. She said the master keys at her hotel were all kept in the security cupboard, and I remembered visiting the security room at university when I'd lost my scarf. I found my old student card and sent Monica in with it. She was the youngest member of the club, looked the most like me, and I was too scared to go in myself. She feigned having lost a pair of gloves, and one of the security guards took her into the room where they kept the lost property. She made a big fuss, asking again and again if he'd look for the gloves, asking him questions about his day and what he got up to when it was quiet. She scanned the shelves for what Lina had told her to look out for, seeing what appeared to be several master keys kept behind a plastic casing. Imploring the guard to check once more through the lost and found, she wriggled open the lid and took one.

She lingered around the atrium for the rest of the afternoon, reading and sipping coffee from the canteen. When it started getting quiet, she wandered the upstairs offices and tried it on a few of the doors. It opened a supply closet, the reading room, and lecture theater five, so she figured it must be the one.

Monica was Erin's girlfriend. She had blond hair and a sweet detachment in the way she spoke, like a primary-school teacher or an animatronic doll. She and Erin had been together six months. They'd met at Mass. She'd started attending Mass after having an abortion, wanting to understand what it was these people objected to, wondering whether they'd gotten it right all along. Erin was there with her mum and dad. She used to go with them sometimes; she liked doing nice things for them.

Monica had the abortion after visiting her boyfriend's sister's house. She hadn't planned to get pregnant. The first missed period didn't spike too much concern: her periods were typically irregular, disappearing, then reappearing, usually at broadly inopportune times, while she was swimming or on a flight. The second missed period was a little more alarming; not menstruating for long stretches of time left her tense and uneasy, clumsy and in pain. On snapping at her boyfriend, Thoman, for turning off the TV too quickly, she apologized, explaining it was just the absence of her period and that as soon as it arrived, she'd feel much better. Thoman looked both stricken and eager, offering to go down to the chemist at that very moment, coming back with a pregnancy test, a bar of white chocolate, and a copy of the *Radio Times*.

She waited for the window to change, still sitting on the toilet, her knickers rolled around her ankles. A few seconds before it showed her she was pregnant, she knew in her gut that she was. She stayed in the bathroom a long while, feeling like Schrödinger's cat, trapped in the box, existing in two states. Feeling like maybe she didn't fully understand Schrödinger's cat. She emerged half an hour later, Thoman pacing the landing. "I didn't know they took that long," he said. "Oh, they do," she replied, and wondered what other things she could lie to him about. When she told him, he lifted her off her feet, and his smile was so wide it looked like his mouth might stretch out and dislocate from his face entirely, floating into the air like a balloon. She watched him that evening, how he'd made her a hot-water bottle though she'd insisted she was quite warm, how he primped and plumped the cushions around her, looking handsome and tough in his polo shirt and jeans. If one were to have a baby, it might as well be with a man like this.

But then she had visited his sister's house. His sister was called Lisa, and his brother-in-law was called Dirk; they were both solicitors, and they lived in a very big house in a very nice part of Birmingham. They spent the weekend there. His sister wanted to get to know the mother of her future niece or nephew. Dirk and Lisa had children of their own: two girls named Messalina and Anastasia. They did their food shopping in Harvey Nichols and had a wet room filled with herbal-smelling creams and gels. The whole house was decorated with uncomfortable but expensive-looking furniture: chairs like hollowed-out eggshells, a telephone table with paws. They went on holidays to the Bahamas and were thinking of buying a BMW or an Audi, they couldn't decide which—senselessly asking Monica for advice. Their children were grubby-fingered and loud, howling at perceived inequalities, such as Anastasia getting a slightly larger slice of cake or Messalina being allowed to watch half an hour more TV.

After they'd gone to bed, Monica noticed Dirk and Lisa drinking a lot more wine, gulping it down like medicine. She excused herself and went to the bathroom, which was covered in photographs of the girls. She studied each one: these toothy and flame-haired children, with large, demonic grins. *This is a house of horrors,* she thought, the phrase just popping into her brain. By the time she came back downstairs, she knew that whatever she wanted from her life, it had to be the opposite of this—this tastelessly decorated house and these badly behaved children. She booked the abortion the following Monday. By Friday she and Thoman had separated and she had moved out.

She quit her job as a cashier at the bank, too—instead she worked odd jobs gleaned from handyman apps: cleaning students' disgusting toilets and assembling flatpack furniture for people too lazy or old to do it themselves. She was even poorer than she used to be and living in a freezing-cold bedsit when she met Erin, and she was immediately impressed by this wonderful wild woman: a freegan and an artist. She fell in love quickly and moved into Erin's flat.

Still, she thought back to her time with Thoman, the comfortable ordinariness to it, how she knew exactly what she would be getting. She felt like their life together somehow still existed, hanging in the ether, a tangential narrative. She would be off her face, dancing at an illegal rave, and suddenly imagine what the other Monica might be doing: perhaps soothing her son or daughter after a bad dream before nestling into the soft cove of Thoman's stomach and chest. She would be up at the crack of dawn, protesting fracking or systematic racism or the banks and imagine the other Monica making pancakes or else propped up with pillows, watching cartoons, with her husband and children in bed. She still went to Mass from time to time; she felt it was the only way to bridge that rupture. But more than anything else, she wanted to do whatever Erin did. She wanted to absorb her. To drink her up like sweet, hot tea. And so she started coming to Supper Club. She took a little persuading when it came to breaking and entering—we left that to Erin.

Once Monica had retrieved the key, we did a test run. We drove back in Erin's car after midnight, again dressed in all-black clothes. The building was set apart from the rest of the campus, so it was quiet and undisturbed. We pulled up at the service entrance. Stevie worked the key into the lock, clicking open the door. As we stepped inside, the beep of the alarm began. Monica had located the alarm keypad and was poised in front of it. About three feet beneath her was the Post-it note—barely sticking to the wall, gray with dust. It was the same code. I'm pretty sure it was the same Post-it. Monica plucked it from the wall and began to type in the code. We balled our hands into fists and stared desperately at one another, willing it to work. It did.

We looked around, tentatively exhilarated. "So what do we do now?" Monica asked.

"We wait," Stevie replied.

We waited in the car for a couple of hours, seeing if security might come, if we had triggered anything without realizing it. I sat in the front with Stevie. Monica and Erin slept in the back, Erin's head resting in Monica's lap, Monica's face pressed up against the window. Stevie looked outside, craned her neck around to stare out the back window. "I can't imagine you here," she said. "I can't imagine what you'd be like at university. Do you think we'd have been friends?"

"I doubt it," I replied. "You'd probably have thought I was a drip."

"Sounds about right," Stevie joked. "Come on, I bet you were really cute. Turning up dead early to classes, doing all the extra reading . . ."

"Hardly."

"Go on, then. What was it like?"

"I don't know, Stevie. It was just normal. I can barely remember, it was such a long time ago."

I looked at my phone. It was close to three.

"Reckon we can go back now," I said.

"Yeah, I think we probably can."

The morning of the Supper Club, I went for a run. It was cold and crisp, but I ran so fast I felt hot, a plump heat pulsating at my forehead. I ran past rows of houses and school yards. Ran through the park and wove between the flower beds. Ran down the pavement that lined the big road. I didn't listen to any music that morning. I ran so I could listen to my thoughts. Running is a good way of modulating thinking; it makes you feel like you're doing something about it. Back at the house, I took a long shower, then ate some lunch. A lot of the women don't eat anything on the days we have Supper Club, but I always do. I no longer have the self-restraint. Or perhaps the inclination. I read in bed until it was time to get ready, and though my eyes moved over the pages, all I could think of was what we were about to do.

We'd decided on an ocean theme, on account of the building's looking like a wave—a blue curl rolling out of the sea. We'd come up with lots of ways to decorate the space in a short amount of time. We each made a bunch of these enormous papery things that looked like the kind of ribboned, translucent organisms you would find in the sea. Erin pinched some blue gels from the music studio where she worked part-time. She said we could slot them over the lights to create a watery feel. We bought reams of blue and green tissue paper and cloth, which we'd throw over the floor. There was no table in the main atrium, but we were determined to use it anyway because of the beautiful, triple-height glass ceiling—so we had decided to eat out of our laps. Stevie wanted to set up a projector that was connected to a live feed of the sea floor, streamed from somewhere in Canada. We were going to play whale sounds.

Emmeline prepared the booze, filling thermoses full of Sea Breeze: cranberry and grapefruit juices, vodka. Sash said that because it was a nautical theme and because it was at a university, we absolutely had to serve Fishbowls: rum punch garnished with lime.

We were having a seafood menu, but fish is not the sort of thing you want to eat out of a bin, so we had to buy a lot of it. It also had to be a later Supper Club than usual, to account for the security guards clocking out. Andrea dropped off everything we needed in the car, and the rest of us walked. Stevie, Emmeline, Renni, and Monica worked on setting up the decorations. Andrea and Lina helped me in the tiny cafeteria kitchen, figuring out how everything worked. Erin set up the sound, while Ashley and Sash kept watch.

The kitchen was mostly used for toasting paninis and heating up soup, but it did have an oven and a stove, so we could make do. Once most things were going, I came out to get dressed. We changed in one of the lecture theaters, draping our existing clothes on the backs of the chairs, running up and down the aisles to exchange glittery makeup or help backcomb hair. We wrapped ourselves in iridescent fabrics, fashioning extravagant togas and capes from the lengths of cobalt, malachite, viridian cloth. We emerged liked nightmarish sea sirens, material loosely fixed around our waists with lengths of rope, our feet bare.

We had fish fritters to start, juicy and thick, about the size of your hand. We began by cutting them into tiny chunks, administering peanut sauce with the tips of our knives, but soon we just held them between our paws like burgers and dunked. The room smelled of citrus and salt, filled with the wet smack of our mastication. I looked around the room, delighted to see so many women ferociously eating fish.

We followed with bouillabaisse. When first suggested, it generated a ripple of controversy. It is not the sort of dish that we would normally want to endorse: a nonfood, lacking the heft and substance we usually favor. Soup seemed the kind of joyless meal women feel they should serve, rather than doing so out of any sense of appetite or desire. In the end the bouillabaisse was served with the fish on the side (as is tradition) and with a little pouring jug of double cream (which is not). We switched on the whale sounds, and when we were done, we lay on the floor, watching the stars though the glass ceiling. We sipped our cocktails and talked about the sea, its terrible, bottomless beauty.

After an hour or so, I went to roast a round of tuna steaks. The kitchen was dense with spices and smells. I'd massaged the tuna with cumin and ground coriander, plus lots of chili, serving it with new potatoes and carrots. We mopped up the sauce from our plates with thickly cut bread. We tossed any bones onto the floor, throwing them over our shoulders as was now tradition. The fat and the tomatoes left a thin red tide line around our mouths, which we dabbed at with tissues.

After the tuna we had a smaller course of spaghetti puttanesca—served in sundae bowls we'd found in the kitchen. The pasta was a little overcooked, but the fiery anchovy sauce was delicious, finished with an extra drizzle of chili oil, its carmine flecks spitting and popping from the pan. We'd eaten all the bread, and so we cleaned the last of it with our fingers and hands, the heels of our wrists working the lips of the bowls.

For dessert we ate chocolate. We'd blown our budget, and Erin had found a full bin bag of plain and milk chocolate bars. We broke them all up and tossed them into the middle of the room, lying on our backs with our heads meeting in the middle, slipping fingers of chocolate down our throats like otters eating fish. We listened to music, and at some point Emmeline produced handfuls of psilocybin mushrooms. I ate a couple, ignoring their horrible dirt flavor. After about half an hour, I felt light and drawn out. I looked up at the star-speckled sky, imagining it as an ocean and the stars as silver fish. I imagined what it would be like to lie on the seabed: the certain softness of the sand and the whole ocean weighing down on top of you. I imagined it would feel terribly lonely. Stevie scooched up beside me, landing a hard kiss on my cheek. "We did it," she said.

I looked over at Emmeline and Lina, who were veiled in the light of the projector, standing up to trace shapes on the wall with their fingers. Monica was on all fours, splaying her hands out across the tiles. "They are *all* perfect squares," she said, her eyes moist with wonder. Ashley and Sash were slow dancing, their arms hung loosely around one another, and whispering half-remembered lyrics to Joni Mitchell's "Blue." I rolled onto my back and looked up at the sky once more. I thought, *I am never going to feel normal again. This is who I am now.* Stevie was lying on her side and giggling.

I got onto my feet and decided I would walk the entire periphery of the atrium. I began at the entrance and marched languidly around, circling the space with a grim reverence. I couldn't quite believe I was back here, that this place still existed. Even more that it existed in the same context, performed the same function. I pressed my hands to the wall. I often wondered about walls. About the things contained within them.

"Why are you squashing your face into that notice board?" Stevie asked, suddenly beside me. I peeled myself away from a flyer advertising bike repairs for women and dropped my head onto her shoulder.

"Hey," I said.

"Hello, little drunky," she replied. "You okay?"

I laced my fingers through hers and pulled her to the floor with me. "I'm going to create a safe space," I said, edging my face close to hers, drawing her long hair over my head, a claustrophobic tunnel. "Can I tell you a secret?"

She nodded, of course I could.

"I had a terrible time here." I said it with so much seriousness that I felt embarrassed, making a stupid sad face to temper it. Stevie's expression was a new one: sober and concerned.

"Really?" she said, untangling her hair and sitting up. She patted the floor next to her, gesturing for me to get up off the floor also. I felt dizzy being upright. The room came in and out of focus. I had the feeling of slipping inside and outside of myself, like a lazily inked cartoon. I closed my eyes and leaned into it, allowed myself to sway gently from side to side. I smiled, hoping to summon a bit of the easy happiness from before. I wanted to go back, to feel heavy and dreamy and not completely there.

"What is it?" Stevie asked again, her hand gripping my shoulder, rocking me with a gently insistent force. "Did something happen? Hey!"

"It's nothing," I said, allowing my head to fall back and my jaw to hang open, acting more drugged than I actually felt. "C'mon!"

I stood up and threw my head forward. I shuffled from side to side, watching my feet move slowly across the tiling. "I'm dancing!" I yelled, and then louder, "I'm dancing! I'm dancing!"

I began jumping up and down.

"I'm so happy!" I shouted. "I'm really just very happy!"

I called over to Ashley and Sash, who were no longer moving, just propped against each other, inexplicably still standing. They half shuffled toward us, wobbling and rolling their shoulders unconvincingly; and then Ashley said she didn't want to dance anymore. She balled her hand into a fist and mashed it into her mouth, eyes wide, then promptly vomited, trumpeting it all over me. I looked down and thought, *Of course.*

Stevie and Emmeline escorted me to the bathroom. Ashley followed behind, offering apologies interrupted by her efforts not to throw up again. I lifted both my arms in the air while Emmeline unraveled me from my costume. Stevie dabbed at me with a large wad of wet toilet paper. Somebody found my clothes, and I allowed myself to be helped into them. It felt like the end of the night. I was excused from tidying-up duties on account of I had been vomited on. I was told to sit in the corner.

I slumped beneath the notice board and watched them at work, the nightmare exercise of it. They laboriously pushed paper towels across the floor. Emptied cups of prosecco into black bin liners. I crossed my legs and thought about how I was both exactly the same person I used to be and exactly a completely different sort of person, too. Everything was happening in front of me while I sat at the side. I thought about lying down and placed my palm to the floor to feel how hard and cold it was. Beneath a table just slightly out of reach, I saw a fallen felt-tip pen. I stretched my arm to reach for it and colored in the tip of my left middle finger. Then I turned around and got very low on the floor. At the bottom of the skirting board, I drew the tiniest Supper Club sign I could.

I sat up to look at it. Stevie came and crouched beside me.

"Come on," she said. "We're going. We're done."

The next morning I spent hours in bed unable to move. I felt alternating waves of nausea and pain, underpinned by a thick sense of loneliness and isolation. Inside my bed it was warm, and outside my bed it was not warm, and I saw no point of leaving that warmth behind. I clenched my legs when I needed the toilet and only went when I was truly ready to burst. I forced myself to sleep more, though it made me feel sluggish and sick. I picked my laptop up from the floor and propped it against an alcove I had fashioned with the lumps of the duvet, watching predictable crime dramas, the kind that are set up and concluded in an hour. Renni asked if I fancied popping over to her place for a cup of tea. I ignored her message. Downstairs I heard Stevie moving around. Every now and then, she would call out, "Roberta! Wake up! I'm bored!"—eventually yelling from the bottom of the stairs that she was going over to Erin and Monica's, 'cause they "actually liked doing stuff and having fun." As the door slammed shut, I expected to feel something yet was also not surprised when I did not. I pulled the cover over my head but didn't have the inclination to cry.

I hadn't bothered drawing the curtains the previous night, so I could see a small section of the outside world from my bed. Birds tweeted intermittently from the branch that sliced my window in two, and I watched them, thinking, *Little bastards*. I watched the clouds move across the sky, and then I watched as it started to rain. I thought about the sensation of rain on my face, and it made me feel hungry. I hadn't eaten all day. I retrieved my laptop from its alcove and rested it just beneath my chin, logging on to a takeaway website and scanning my options. I eventually settled on Thai and ordered noodles with tofu and green beans, plus a portion of tom yum soup. I lay back in bed and stared at the ceiling as I waited for it to arrive.

An hour later there was a knock at the door, and I went downstairs still wearing all my clothes and makeup from the night before and possibly smelling lightly of vomit. If the deliveryman was horrified by my appearance, he didn't let on. I took the paper bag from him and asked if there was plastic cutlery included. He said there was, and I nodded and took it back upstairs and got into bed. I put on a film about popularity at an American high school, being careful not to spill the soup, then going at the noodles. When I was finished, I piled the tinfoil packets to the side of my bed, then lay back down to stare at them. I thought about Arnold, and I thought about the last guy I'd had sex with, the one who held his penis like a paintbrush, moving over me like he was redecorating a room. I thought about his horrible Scouse accent and the weird bald patch at the nape of his neck. I wondered whether I would ever have a boyfriend again. Whether I was too broken and wretched and wrong ever to deserve that. I went back for my laptop and googled "dating website," clicking on the first link that appeared.

I clicked through Facebook until I found three decent photographs of myself from the past year. One of them was taken at a work party. Two were from when I was out walking with my mum and aunt. Under "Interests" I wrote, "Cooking, reading, and the outdoors." When it prompted me to determine what sort of partner I was looking for, I wrote, "I don't know," then deleted that and wrote, "Clean?" For the section that asked me to elucidate my ideal date, I wrote, "Food." I scanned what I had written and thought, *I wouldn't date me.*

I pushed my laptop aside. Outside, it had gone completely dark, and I could see the reflection of myself in the window. My hair was matted and enormous. My bed was covered in junk. I was an absolute mess. It made me feel sort of proud. I stared at myself for a little longer, and then my laptop started to beep. I'd already received a message. Brady, a self-described "cheeky chappy," had sent me a message saying, "Hey." A few minutes later, I got a message from a blond man named Mikael saying he was over from Finland but only until Tuesday. "Let's cut the crap," he said. "Are you coming over?" A few minutes after that, a guy called Luke messaged me the peach emoji. Within an hour I had maybe ten men staring at me from my in-box. I scrolled through their pictures: selfies taken in the car, photos of them wearing suits while holding pints. I read their interests, their platitudes, their *Family Guy* quotes. I felt a weariness staring at the faces of all of these men I suddenly had access to. I watched them hoping for a flicker of something. I tried to imagine having sex with them, and when that didn't work, I tried to imagine them just holding me while I felt some semblance of comfort. It was pointless, and instead I read the news and contemplated the horrible state of the world before watching some old *SNL* clips on YouTube. Stevie still was not home, and my room was by this point completely dark save for the rectangular glow from my laptop. It made the beeping sound again, and I opened the message with a gloomy feeling all over my body. It was from a man named Adnan, and it said, OH MY GOD I CAN'T BELIEVE YOU'RE ON HERE! I clicked through the photos, thinking, *Is it?*—and it seemed that it was.

Adnan was working as a civil engineer for the council and listed his interests as "seeking adventures and meeting new people." His profile picture showed him standing in front of a grass field with his hands in his pockets. He still had a large, handsome face, though his hair was slightly thinning, and he seemed to have put on an even layer of weight, which I thought really suited him. He had two other photographs, one pulling a funny face in what seemed to be his office and another eating an ice cream outside the Eiffel Tower. Looking at his photographs gave me a nostalgic glow I didn't feel entitled to. It also made me feel strangely vulnerable, like he could see inside my room. I felt a not-unpleasant blush gliding up my neck and shoulders. Three undulating dots told me he was writing something else, and then several messages popped up in quick succession.

ADNAN: What have you been up to?

ADNAN: Your photos look really cool.

ADNAN: It is really great you are still cooking!

ADNAN: You used to cook the most amazing food! Mmmm.

Though I still held him in the same esteem as you would a cool person at school, I entertained the prospect of not replying to him. I looked at his messages and considered just shutting down my profile entirely, but even as I was thinking about it, potential responses began forming at the depths of my brain, a narrative kicking into gear. I imagined saying sparkling and witty things that would demonstrate what a laid-back and non-weird person I had become. I wondered if he kept in touch with any of the others. I wanted to know what he was like now.

ME: Hi! Hello.

ME: Thank you. Your photos sure look cool, too. And you're a civil engineer. That's great. Or, dare I say, civilized. Sorry.

ADNAN: Yeah, it's all right. Keeps me out of trouble anyway. What are you up to?

ADNAN: Ha!

ME: I work at a fashion website. It's mostly boring and awful, but sometimes I get free clothes.

ADNAN: You were always the stylish one in the flat!

ME: No way.

ME: That was Mei-Ling.

ME: I was the grumpy one that stayed in her room.

ADNAN: You were the cool girl! I always thought you were very cool. And that your cooking was AMAZING.

ADNAN: I remember that amazing dhal you used to make. And that banana bread.

ADNAN: And the regular bread!

ADNAN: Yeah, I was certain you'd be a famous chef now
for sure.

Having Adnan compliment me on my cooking made me so
pleased I thought my ears might start ringing. I ignored his saying he
thought I was cool. Forever the confident sixth-former, making the
weird girl feel at ease. Though I was flattered he wanted me to feel
at ease at all. I opened up another tab and looked him up on Facebook. He had lax security settings, and I could see most of his posts.
His last update was a video of a suspicious owl. His last check-in was
to his friends' wedding. It looked like up until a year ago he'd been
in a long-term relationship; there were photos of them on walks and
on holiday. She was very thin and very beautiful. I clicked on her
profile and saw she was a communications manager at a housing
firm. Her photos made me feel anxious and hot. There was one of
her at some sort of awards do, in a low-cut black dress. I looked it up
on my phone so I could zoom in on her face and then on her waist
and then on her face again. I tried to deduce the precise geometrics
that made her so beautiful and me so not. I stared at her face so much
it stopped resembling a face, like repeating a word until it becomes
emptied of meaning. When I looked back, he'd sent me a few more
messages.

ADNAN: I actually did a cookery class recently.

ADNAN: Well, a baking class.

ADNAN: I learned to make sourdough.

ADNAN: You can see it here. What do you think?

ADNAN: You still there?

ME: Yes!

ME: Sorry, got distracted.

We messaged back and forth for a while, leaving calculated gaps between replies. I'd have to force myself to read an article about something after he asked me an open question, relaying the words to myself without comprehending a single thing, all the while drafting a detached and amusing response. I started wishing I had an orange handy, so I could languidly peel it into soft, pulpy curls. I liked the idea of being a woman who talked to men on the Internet while eating oranges in bed.

The spaces between our messages got shorter and shorter. I told Adnan about the soap stars I'd interviewed and the inspirational phrases my boss kept on her desk. Adnan told me about his recent holiday to Paris, how he'd gone with his brother, then felt really weird, being in the city of romance, sharing a twin room. I told him about how I was regularly dumpster-diving and how smug it made me feel. He told me that when he'd informed his mum he had separated from his ex-girlfriend, she'd locked herself in her bedroom and cried loudly for a full two hours.

We kept talking. At some point I heard Stevie get back in. At any other time, I would have been oxygen-starved with anxiety at the thought of having upset her, eager to race downstairs and make things up, to go to bed knowing that we were still friends and I would not be left alone in this world. But talking to Adnan gave me a strange secret feeling, and I didn't want to let that go just yet.

At some point I looked at the time, and it was three o'clock in the morning. I had work the next day. I told Adnan to check his watch, and he sent me the emoji that looks like Edvard Munch's *The Scream*. I replied, I know!!! I wasn't sure how we would end our conversation.

It felt like a hurried intimacy that I wasn't certain could be recaptured in person. I considered asking if he'd like to hang out sometime but thought if I could leave it long enough, he might ask me. I was exquisitely tired, but I didn't want to go to sleep until I felt a sense of resolution. Some minutes later Adnan messaged asking if I wanted to meet him for coffee tomorrow. I counted to twenty, then replied, Yes.

"You worship at the altar of romance," Stevie once said to me. "You think regularly fucking someone gives you the elevation of faith."

And it's true. I would ascribe a certain profundity to entirely average heterosexual relationships. I had a tendency to stare at couples, trying to imagine what on earth it was they talked about. I would sit behind them clutching hands in the cinema, trying to picture them having sex, then degrouting the shower. I would follow them in supermarkets, imagining a rich ceremony of oven pizza, bagged salad, and television, imagining it must feel like meditation, almost transcendental. A normal relationship was something I was confident I would never have, and yet it felt entirely inevitable. *Surely it must happen eventually?* I used to think. *It's been a really long time.* Walking to meet Adnan for coffee, I felt weighted by that abnormality.

We'd arranged to meet in a place called the Botanist, which was furnished with plant pots and driftwood; it felt somehow unreal, as though the walls might crumble, revealing it to be a film set or an art installation. I'd finished work on time and had accounted for going to the bathroom to redo my makeup and fuss with my hair, so I needed to take the long route round, walking a good twenty minutes or so in the opposite direction so I could be elegantly late. When I arrived, I spotted Adnan already sitting down, looking reassuringly recognizable, in a pale pink shirt and blue jeans. I watched him for as long as I dared. He was adjusting his posture and intermittently checked his phone. He seemed a little bit nervous, which was weird. I arranged my face and walked over to the table. He hugged me hello.

I went to the counter and got myself a flat white, then sat back down to cup it with both hands, like I was terribly cold and this was all that was keeping me warm. After a while I started wondering whether I was doing this because I wanted to or if it was for him; then I began auditing all my other gestures: a lock of hair tucked behind my ear, my hands raised and fingers splayed outward to dramatize a point. Adnan's old easy confidence felt poised immediately behind his nerves, and every now and then he would forget himself and tell a story without realizing how funny it was, or all of the muscles in his face would relax and I would wonder how anyone could be so handsome.

He had not yet developed wrinkles, but there were little cracks and divots in his skin. One between his eyebrows. Another like an eyelash, half a parenthesis, cut delicately to the side of his jaw. I watched the vault of his frown, the scrunch of his nose and mouth, and I found myself worrying about the devil of time taking away his good looks. I imagined it must be much harder for very attractive people to age.

We talked more about our jobs and lives. We attempted some reminiscing about the old flat, our horrid student house. He told me he still saw Nadeem, who was now married with two kids, a son and a daughter. He said he ran into Samuel a couple of months ago on the train. That they sat together and talked for a while, and when they got to the station, they went for a drink. They've been exchanging messages since.

"Sam's going through a bad time," Adnan said. "He's had a few bad breakups and been struggling to get work."

I expressed sympathy, though when Adnan suggested we all get a drink together, I swiftly deflected.

I told him about my dad emailing me, about how I hadn't replied and didn't dare tell my mum because she got weird whenever I mentioned him. About how he was a total bastard to my mum, but from his emails he seemed sort of nice. Adnan took a deep breath, and his eyes moved to the side, and he was silent for a long while. He exhaled what seemed like all the air from his lungs, then began positing a series of solutions: that I talk to my mum, who might feel differently now she has a committed partner, that I ask my dad to no longer email me, that I talk to my aunt, that I see a counselor to get some impartial advice. I got the feeling that if I didn't stop him, he would continue spitballing indefinitely, that he would pass out on the floor doing so. I placed my hand over his and said, "Thank you, that's really good advice," and he beamed.

I finished my coffee and then drank another, just to feel occupied with action, with consumption. Once I'd finished my second, Adnan asked if I was hungry. I said I was, and we went to get a pizza.

At the pizza place, he held out my chair for me, and I sat down. "I had a terrible feeling then," he said. "I had a feeling I might pull the chair out from beneath you as a joke. Like, I actually thought that might be a funny thing to do."

He held his hands against his face. "Can you imagine?" he said.

"I'm glad you didn't," I said, and felt something unfurl in my chest, like a plant slowly growing, or something coming back to life. I wondered if he could see it, too, rippling beneath my skin like an alien.

We both ordered pizza margaritas: just tomato, cheese, and bread.

They were chewy and salty and delicious. I was going to tell him about Supper Club, but I couldn't quite get it out. I felt so embedded in the space of easy normality: the date, the conversation, the no-frills pizza. It was exhilarating to present as an entirely regular girl, who had a job and a flat, friends and a life. In the end I fudged it, making it sound more socially acceptable, just a group of women who take turns cooking.

"That's cool," he said with a firm absoluteness. "You're cool. I always thought you were cool."

After the pizza Adnan asked if I wanted anything for dessert, and I said I was full, because I was, not because I thought that might be what he wanted to hear. I watched him eat a giant chocolate sundae, without wanting to steal a bite, thinking, *Who orders a giant chocolate sundae on a date?*

We went for a drink at Renni's bar after, and Adnan handed me the cocktail list, giddily imploring me to order "the biggest drink on the menu!" I messaged Renni to tell her I was there, and she came out from the back to say hello to us. She had a professional composure that was physical; she held her arms to her waist, tempered her breathing in a way that made you feel relaxed. She extended her hand out to Adnan, who bypassed it for a hug, a meeting of worlds. When he popped to the toilet, Renni showered me with questions: Did I like him? Where did we meet? What were we going to do afterward? It occurred to me I'd never gossiped about boys before. I felt suddenly sad.

When Adnan returned, Renni excused herself. She messaged me a few minutes later: He's cute!!! Use protection. After our cocktails we went for a walk down by the canal. He held my hand, and I let him. I suggested we go back to his place to watch an episode of some program he'd been telling me about. I registered a small eye pop of surprise, which made way for precipitous affirmation.

At Adnan's flat I was informed he had damp: the assured noun of it. It hung in the air. It rested on my shoulders. The window frames were soft and rotting. The sheets were heavy with moisture. He poured us each a glass of water, and we made our way to the bedroom. It was a strange march; there wasn't a great deal of passion, more a sober sort of necessity. It was much better the next morning, when we had not yet accumulated a day's worth of hesitancy and self-doubt. But by that time I was quite cold, could feel the damp sinking into my bones, settling around my joints. After we finished, I lay in bed while Adnan slept, staring at those rotting window frames, watching the vapors from outside already worming their way in.

The Price of Admission

Spaghetti alla puttanesca is typically made with tomatoes, olives, anchovies, capers, and garlic. It means, literally, "spaghetti in the style of a prostitute." It is a sloppy dish, the tomatoes and oil making the spaghetti lubricated and slippery. It is the sort of sauce that demands you slurp the noodles *Goodfellas* style, staining your cheeks with flecks of orange and red. It is very salty and very tangy and altogether very strong; after a small plate, you feel like you've had a visceral and significant experience.

There are varying accounts as to when and how the dish originated—but the most likely explanation is that it became popular in the mid-twentieth century. The first documented mention of it is in Raffaele La Capria's 1961 novel, *Ferito a Morte*. According to the Italian Pasta Makers Union, spaghetti alla puttanesca was a very popular dish throughout the sixties, but its exact genesis is not quite known. Sandro Petti, a famous Napoli chef and co-owner of Ischian restaurant Rangio Fellone, claims to be its creator. Near closing time one evening, a group of customers sat at one of his tables and demanded to be served a meal. Running low on ingredients, Petti told them he didn't have enough to make anything, but they insisted. They were tired, and they were hungry, and they wanted pasta. *"Facci una puttanata qualsiasi!"* they cried. "Make any kind of garbage!" The late-night eater is not usually the most discerning. Petti raided the kitchen, finding four tomatoes, two olives, and a jar of capers, the base of the now-famous spaghetti dish; he included it on his menu the next day under the name spaghetti alla puttanesca. Others have their own origin myths. But the most common theory is that it was a quick, satisfying dish that the working girls of Naples could knock up with just a few key ingredients found at the back of the fridge— after a long and unforgiving night.

As with all dishes containing tomatoes, there are lots of variations in technique. Some use a combination of tinned and fresh tomatoes, while others opt for a squirt of puree. Some require specifically cherry or plum tomatoes, while others go for a smooth, premade passata. Many suggest that a teaspoon of sugar will "open up the flavor," though that has never really worked for me. I prefer fresh, chopped, and very ripe, cooked for a really long time. Tomatoes always take longer to cook than you think they will—I rarely go for anything less than an hour. This will make the sauce stronger, thicker, and less watery. Most recipes include onions, but I prefer to infuse the oil with onions, frying them until brown, then chucking them out. I like a little kick in most things, but especially in pasta, so I usually go for a generous dousing of chili flakes. I crush three or four cloves of garlic into the oil, then add any extras. The classic is olives, anchovies, and capers, though sometimes I add a handful of fresh spinach, which nicely soaks up any excess water—and the strange, metallic taste of cooked spinach adds an interesting extra dimension. The sauce is naturally quite salty, but I like to add a pinch of sea or Himalayan salt, too, which gives it a slightly more buttery taste, as opposed to the sharp, acrid salt of olives and anchovies. I once made this for a vegetarian friend, substituting braised tofu for anchovies. Usually a solid fish replacement, braised tofu is more like tuna than anchovy, so it was a mistake for puttanesca. It gave the dish an unpleasant solidity and heft. You want a fish that slips and melts into the pasta, not one that dominates it.

In terms of garnishing, I go for dried oregano or fresh basil (never fresh oregano or dried basil) and a modest sprinkle of cheese. Oh, and I always use spaghetti. Not fettuccine. Not penne. Not farfalle. Not rigatoni. Not even linguine. Always spaghetti. It's not the same unless you can slurp it down in gassy gulps, unless you slop it all over yourself.

Delia Smith calls it "tart's pasta." Italian-American restaurants call it "whore's pasta." But Nigella Lawson calls it "slut's spaghetti," and that's the one I prefer. Because there's nothing more terrifying than a woman who eats and fucks with abandon.

I'd spent most of the summer before term started indoors, so being outside made me feel exposed: pale and thin-skinned, burning beneath the glare. Hetty drove me to my new home, dingier and more decrepit than I had remembered from the viewings. I got there a day earlier than the others. I didn't want my aunt to see how awkward I was around them.

My room had a bright red carpet and peeling cream walls. I hung up an old sarong I'd found at home opposite my bed. I set out two candles on the little desk, then tidied away my clothes. After I'd put on fresh bedsheets, I realized this was the full extent of effort I was prepared to make with it. I went downstairs to inspect the kitchen. There was an oven and a microwave, some cloudy-looking pots and pans. It was not a kitchen I was particularly happy about, but it would do. I went to the shop and came back with ingredients for making a large and hearty vegetable lasagna. I left the lasagna in the kitchen, with a card saying "Help yourself!" When my flatmates arrived, I offered to help them carry things, asked about their summer. On the first night in the flat, we sat and watched *Love Actually* together, drinking vodka and Coke and eating the lasagna. But the following night, when I asked what they were doing, they all had plans: Mei-Ling was meeting her new boyfriend, Adnan was going out for pizza with friends, Samuel and June had been invited to a party. "It's, like, a really small party," June said. "Otherwise, you know, we'd totally say come along." I spent the evening smoking in my room.

Class started, and I slipped across the days as if they were an ice rink, reaching out for strangers to keep my balance. I signed up to a dating website, arranging to meet a thin, blond man named Tref, who taught English to Japanese business students. We went to the cinema to watch *The Wicker Man*, then smoked weed back at his flat while listening to Portishead. In the morning we ate cereal in bed, and I watched him splash milk down his chin. I couldn't sleep, ordered supplemental melatonin and Xanax off Craigslist, which arrived at the house in conspicuous little envelopes, always hand-addressed. Occasionally my flatmates would ask if I fancied getting a takeout with them, going for a pint at Wetherspoons, and I would think of new ways to say no.

Arnold was covering one of my ethics classes after the usual teacher fell ill. And although I was rattled, I'd stare at him, trying to force him to catch my eye. He never would. At home I googled him compulsively. I still didn't understand why I'd been dumped, whether I had actually been dumped—whether that was even the right word. In lieu of answers, I had only a blank canvas, and I threw everything at it—every color and shade of tormented emotion—and what I was left with was black, a black wall of my own inadequacy. There is something bottomless about inadequacy, like you will never quite reach the limits of your own insufficiency. There were the late nights staring at the ceiling, the duvet an unconquerable and oppressive bloat, time dry and unyielding. Then there was the drinking. Bottles of red wine squirreled away in my room. Vodka tonics premixed in tin cans, drunk like soda. The times when nothing but a whiskey would do, diluted with ice from the Spar on the corner. There was always a sense of pragmatism, a sense that this is just what I do.

When I eventually showed up at his flat, Arnold seemed alarmed, confused, and yes, even horrified, but also there was a hint of . . . was it relief? A certain, *Well, here you are.* He invited me inside and told me he was making curry—and I stepped over the threshold, already knowing I'd made a mistake.

That autumn I took up tai chi. It was something to do. I hadn't heard of it before, and it sounded like a phrase I might use to describe the wanton characteristics of a woman who wore bright coral lipstick, who had a string of lovers called Jimmy or Chad. Arnold suggested it; he'd seen flyers for it in the student union. Just the thought of it made me feel ridiculous, stupid, and out of place. I'd passed the class before, observing the seriousness with which the group posed. *What idiot religion is that?* I thought. If you were looking for meaning, could you find it in stretches?

"You should do it," Arnold said. "Your body shouldn't be an encumbrance. Also, you really need some friends."

I invested in the soft gray clothes that were apparently required; I ate nothing for a few hours before. The instructor was named Jessa, and she was older than I expected, with a thick Eastern European accent. She called us her "little cows," or at least I think she did.

Tai chi was a combination of breathing and movement, which sounded a lot like life. I enjoyed the fluidity of the motions (though my own practice was disjointed and clumsy) and also the strange locomotive narrative. *You pick up the bowl, lift it over your head, now shoot your arrow!* At the end of each session, we would lie flat on the floor, our eyes closed, gently breathing. This, Jessa told us, was corpse position, and it was my favorite.

"I could lie in corpse position forever!" I once told her.

"And one day you will," she replied.

After each session a group of girls from the class would go out for smoothies. They studied nutrition, social care, and community health, respectively. They used a wealth of different exercise regimes and pedometers, and they all had very thin arms. But it was nice to get out, to talk to people who were neither Arnold nor the sort-of-strangers I lived with. They were bubbly and sweet, giving me recipes for rice bowls and chocolate cake made out of beetroot or avocado. And still I knew I had not found my people. Evening after evening I'd find myself going back to Arnold's.

Arnold's apartment symbolized a very necessary respite: some grown-up home comforts between the crisp-packet tip of the seminar rooms and the towering stacks of unwashed plates in our much-neglected kitchen. It was so neat! I'd spend hours wrapped between the recently laundered sheets of his bed just to smell them. The gleam of the bathroom sink made me want to sing. His kitchen cupboards contained every type of spice. God, it was good.

Arnold made coffee with those individually packaged caramelized biscuits you get in nice cafés. He sent his ironing out, and even his towels would be delivered pressed and folded. And his flat had a slight ambient chill, like a hotel room in which you can't quite nail the AC. When he left me in the mornings, I'd pad around the flat wearing one of his work shirts, my legs cold and pimpled, trying to make sense of the TV. For breakfast I'd have flatbread and hummus and a cup of fennel tea, not because I enjoyed it, because I didn't really, but because it felt like such a treat: fennel tea and flatbread. Exotic.

I'd leave for classes feeling as if I were dipping in and out of two separate lives, definitely a little smug, like maybe I was above it all. I wrapped up in my wintry best and brandished a chai tea from the New Age vending machines like it was the torch of civilization. Around me my classmates were sallow and spotty, with three-day hangovers, often still drunk. I began to feel contemptuous toward a boy called Simon for always wearing a hoodie, always smelling of weed. I'd find my eyes narrowing on him, my face contorted into a twist of hostility. He'd catch me staring and smile dopily across. He probably thought I was into him.

Arnold was a cheek kisser. And there is something very specific about cheek kissers. My family used to cheek-kiss—me, my mum, and my aunt. Mwah! Darling! It was silly, and we were pretending. Our love was base and essential, not of the same world as cheek kissing. I was once constipated for a week, and my mum bought me laxatives. When eventually I was able to make a bowel movement, I ended up blocking the toilet. I told her, mortified.

"Sweetheart," she said, putting on some rubber gloves. "It sounds like you had a really good clear-out."

Cheek kissing meant never discussing bowel movements. It was lifting oneself above the shit and slop of humanity. Arnold was always catching me out with his cheek kisses, my mouth nipping clumsily at his ear.

Our regular meet-up was an espresso place near where he lived. The coffee was always burned and the pastries too shiny, but the seating was soft and the staff unusually friendly. I'd always order a latte. There was something about him that made me crave milk. He'd have an espresso, often two, the bitter dirt of it. Never with milk. Occasionally with one cube of brown sugar. He often seemed distracted—looking to see who else was in the room, watching people walk past the window. The coffee was a ruse, a pantomime of civility before we started drinking.

Something I learned quite quickly after the night I turned up at his flat, drunk and sobbing, wanting him to love me, was that I wasn't getting the Good Arnold. I'd had a chance with the Good Arnold. The one who would take you to a nice restaurant. The one who would ask about your parents. I had failed my audition somehow, and instead I'd landed the consolation prize: the Bad Arnold. The one who wanted to get indecently drunk. The one who wasn't afraid to ask for weird sex stuff. Though it was still Arnold, and I was happy, sort of. Happy I'd gotten my way. I suppose you could say I went into things with my eyes open.

Though Arnold was a great many things I hadn't accounted for: loud, unpredictable, entirely unreadable. Despite his seeming solidity, he was an erratic character. This usually meant making myself flat and accommodating, perennially tiptoeing around the edges of his existence. But occasionally he was in just the right mood and I didn't have to fold myself down. I could feel enormous, like he'd given me the platform to be so.

After coffee he'd ask what I wanted to do, offering me the illusion of a blank piece of paper. Of course it was not blank, it was densely populated with invisible ink. But I wasn't supposed to know that.

"Shall we get a drink somewhere?" I'd ask.

"If that's what the lady wants."

But it wasn't what the lady wanted. I wanted late-night suppers and trips to the theater. I wanted cocktail dresses and HBO box sets. I wanted Tuesday tacos and impromptu weekends. I wanted to be whisked off my feet. What I learned about desire is that it never goes, not really. But you can make it smaller, you can fold it up and tuck it neatly away. I felt like I was carrying a solid-gold pillbox of my wants and needs somewhere in my chest, just behind my rib cage. I kept lifting the lid to slip things inside. It was getting more and more full, but there was still room. There was always room for more.

There was a particular kind of pub Arnold liked to go to, nothing too young, too expensive, or too contrived. He liked going to places he described as "real"; he was averse to "bullshit." Places occupied primarily by men, with pun-driven drink names and a house band. The sorts of places that had their own dog. It was a gross pretension, obviously, but in those pubs I'd get a sense that there was something broken in him, though I didn't have the maturity or experience to figure out what.

All Arnold wanted from me was to be game, and so I pretended to be a free spirit. I was game for spending the whole night drinking and talking to strangers. I was game for doing shots in the early afternoon. Once I was even game for administering a hand job in the men's bathroom of a horrible pub called the Lighthouse. As nasal country or chart pop drifted from the cheap speakers, I would catch sight of myself, sitting between a couple of middle-aged women or buying a round for a foreign exchange student visiting just for the night, and think, *Who am I?* The rigidity with which I moved, the tightening of my vocal cords as I tried to seem relaxed, would always betray me in the end. I'd catch him registering my discomfort with a certain shame, like I'd let him down.

"It wouldn't disservice you," he said as we walked home one night, "to lighten up."

We detoured down the canals, the streetlights on the water making bright white sea snakes in the black.

"Here," he said, finding a small gap in the railing at the side, ducking through it. "Do you trust me?" I did, and he clutched my forearms while I clutched his, my feet pressed on the angle of the drop, my body suspended over the muddy brown water below. We stared into each other's eyes, mine wide-open, a plush, empty room, his muscled and evasive, though nonetheless fixed on mine: the long corridor of eye contact. A siren sounded, which must have startled or distracted him, and I felt his grip relax as my arms drifted out of his and I fell backward, landing in the canal.

I must have been beneath the surface for only a few seconds, but it felt like much longer. I remember opening my eyes in the black, gritty water, thinking, *I am safe down here.* It took some inner corralling to reject that thought. As I struggled to the surface, retching at the rotten-sewage stench, I watched him standing hopelessly over me, scarcely able to maintain his balance. I fought my way out, scraping the length of my forearm, which would later become infected. Slumped at his feet, a soaking and sodden mess, I asked him to hail us a cab.

"We can't let you in a taxi," he said. "Not in that state."

It was always me who was the problem.

And so we walked home. He wrapped his coat around me, a fact he would remind me of the following day, and once back at his flat I fled into the shower while he fixed me a coffee and two slices of toast. I switched the temperature of the shower up and up until it burned, my skin bright red and hurting, and when I couldn't stand it, I switched it up some more.

December came around, and we had the usual weeks off for Christmas. I'd been hoping I might spend some time with Arnold—perhaps we might go away, even. I broached the subject one evening. I was eating dinner on the large leather sofa, watching television, while he sat tapping at his laptop on a separate armchair.

"You know our classes finish next week," I said, consciously tempering my voice. "I don't have to be back at my mum's for ages. You maybe want to do something?"

"I don't think so," he said, not looking up from his screen. "I'll be staying with some friends in Norfolk."

It only occurred later that he might have invited me, that that was not beyond the realm of possibility.

And so I went home for Christmas early. I did tai chi in the mornings, pushing aside the curtains so the low sunlight flooded the front room. I moved through its weak heat like I was swimming, allowing myself a brief lull amid the shudder and quake of my nerves. I found if I did it first thing, I could quiet the clatter of my brain for a few minutes.

The days carried on: large, empty rooms in which the color scheme was awful and I was the only occupant. Rooms that were too poorly lit for me even to daydream. The walls were papered with my absence of imagination. Not clear or transparent, just beyond perception. And not on account of their complexity but because of their total inability to engage or generate interest. Just like: whatever.

Boredom is the hollow space that comes before anxiety. It is a void that needs to be filled. And anything you have flattened and confined—any tiny, manageable bad thoughts, not to speak of the larger, less yielding traumas—in this space they bloat, becoming big-bellied, and surrounding them are a thousand feeding horseflies, buzzing and nipping and whipping up the radio static that drives a person mad. I rang Arnold every night, feeling the cold horror as my calls went to voice mail.

The anxiety was making me irritable. I found my mum alternately comforting, necessary, and insufferable. Even Joan of Arc's incessant yapping, her lunatic joy when I walked through the front door, had become intolerable, a joke at my expense. As anxiety made way for depression, I started staying in bed until the late afternoon. I'd stopped calling Arnold, instead sending him messages, emails; text felt less transient, something he couldn't ignore. In the morning I would wake up and immediately check my phone, willing so desperately for his name to be there that I would occasionally imagine that it was, joyfully clicking on an email to find rows of summer sandals or the latest deals on trains where his words should be.

One morning my aunt hammered on my bedroom door. I called for her to come in and watched her silhouette against the tense light of the landing, her dark and sturdy body.

"Right," she said. "You, me, and your mum. We're going for a walk."

To Hetty the outdoors offered near-medicinal properties. She didn't wade into cold water but walked into it, like, *Come on, then*. I imagined a cold trudge uphill, a soggy trip to the woods. I could not bear the thought of moisture on my skin. I wanted to remain dry and brittle, warm and still—like something synthetic.

She marched into my room, throwing a still-damp towel onto my bed.

"Shower," she said. "We're leaving in twenty."

We took Joa with us, and she pulled on her lead, raring to be a few inches in front of wherever she was. My aunt led us, followed by my mum, and me at the back, where they couldn't see my face. We hiked up a steep incline, and when we were nearing the top, the wind started hurting my ears. I looked out onto plains of grass and little pockets of housing and life. The thing about the countryside is there's no pretending. It is cracked ground and howling wind. It is animals for the slaughter and enough water to drown in. I thought, *I am exhausted*. It was a fresh kind of exhaustion, one I had never experienced before. It was beyond tiredness. Surpassing overworked or fatigued. It was an all-encompassing collapse. I craved only darkness, the bliss and nonexistence of sleep.

I dragged my bag over my shoulder and walked forward. My aunt didn't ask me any questions about why I was nervous and down. Neither did my mum. But I noticed how watchful they were. How later, at dinner, they eyed my untouched plate. The resignation in their faces as I pushed it away.

I came back to university on New Year's Day, as I had told Arnold I would. I'd spent the previous night watching television with my mum, entertaining the notion that if I'd been invited out, I would have politely refused.

My mum offered to drive me all the way back. I enthusiastically protested—emphasizing the long drive, the unnecessariness of it, somewhat panicking that she might insist. Eventually she conceded, driving me instead to the station. It was dark and raining. On the train I imagined myself on a roller coaster, falling into a black abyss, having paid for the pleasure. I texted Arnold saying I was on my way, then put my phone back in my bag, not looking at it again until I'd arrived. On the platform I found I had received a reply from him: I'm here.

I went down to the agreed pickup zone nearly giddy with joy. I spotted him waiting in his car, the one I had once bled all over. Throwing open the door, I exclaimed, "I didn't think you were coming!"

"Why did you think that?" he said, irritable and curt. "I said I'd meet you, and I'm here."

A rnold had started hosting dinner parties.

He'd entertain friends, other lecturers, almost always male. I'd survey the crowd, the naked ambition of academia—later the drugs—and feel I'd slipped into some parallel life, something I was not supposed to see. The room was heavy with jazz, smoke, and ego. I'd wear a slip dress to show off my shoulders. I was impossibly, enviably thin. I'd steal glances at myself in the mirror near the door, wondering if any of his friends wanted to fuck me. Thinness had made bravado possible.

Arnold was a social creature. He thrived on conversation and company, feeding off it like a vampire. I'd watch him pour drinks and play records, thinking once again that he was quite exceptionally good-looking, though knowing it was very much the appeal of someone who had gotten attractive in his thirties—suddenly, unexpectedly, a tentative handsomeness like a transient superpower. He wanted to fight all the bad guys in the shortest amount of time but he hadn't quite learned the rules.

I couldn't determine my own attractiveness; it ricocheted up and down like the trace on a heart monitor. In a room in which everyone was at least ten years older than me, I was young, and that contained some currency. Tai chi had given me small muscles in my back, thighs, and arms, but my hair was thin and kinky, an encumbrance that I'd recently had the urge to shave off entirely. I'd stare at my face so much that I became unable to recognize it as a face at all, more a collection of unwieldy trinkets pressed into my skull. I'd compare photos of myself with press shots of celebrities or classmates on the Internet. *What makes that one a good face?* I would wonder. *What makes a bad one?* They were like weddings. All the same but different.

But Arnold's parties had made me consider something else about myself, something I'd never begun previously to venture. Perhaps I was smart?

For a nineteen-year-old I had read a lot of books. I cared about stuff: science and art and the environment and buildings. I liked French films and graphic novels and Elliott Smith. I watched the news. I had opinions. I liked listening to people. Being smart in this context was inherently wound up with being likable—whereas previously being likable had always seemed mostly dependent on being superficial. I spent a lot of time thinking about what it meant to be likable. Did being likable mean being agreeable? Did being likable mean being charming? Was it about sense of humor? Or just good looks? Did the criteria change as you get older?

As a child I'd felt an easy acceptance among my peers. That stopped around fourteen, when puberty kicked in, metabolism jacked out, and suddenly everyone was wearing a bra. It was around that time I started feeling out of place. I woke up with breasts, bulbous and asymmetrical things with large, flat nipples. My thighs suddenly rubbed, and my stomach touched the bottom of my desk. "You've got to hold it in," Becky told me in history, patting her own. "Mine's always in." Then came boys, and I honestly did not know what to do about that at all. But sometime around college, everything sort of settled. The swamp of hormones and the scorch of embryonic sexuality leveled out, and while we still felt each other up and cried in the toilets at discos, we were mostly able to sit in the common room and speak more or less normally. But university had seemingly undone that. In the world of freshers' weeks and three-day hangovers, I had always been too much of a stick-in-the-mud to be liked. Until now.

Arnold's friends, mostly academics or public-sector workers, asked about my thoughts on gender politics, on the EU, on wine, trading mine with their own like they were worth the same thing. Though they referred to me as "the youth," their faces soft and open when they spoke to me, they made me feel like I mattered. And in these settings Arnold was very affectionate with me, crooking his arm around my shoulder, kissing me tenderly on the head. He would ask whether I needed anything, if I was tired. I'd feel special and spoiled and high on the whole episode. Later, on the more tangible high of tramadol, Adderall, Xanax, I'd sit on the settee and enjoy the blissed-out half sounds of music and talking.

One time I was tripped out on something or other, slumped across the antique apothecary table (one of Arnold's most beloved possessions), and one of my tutors sat next to me, asking if I required a glass of water. I told him I was fine and felt his hot palm on my knee. "I can see why Arnold likes you," he said, pushing it further along. "But what I cannot tell is—why you like Arnold?"

Arnold likes me! I thought, pushing away his hand as it edged further toward my underwear, clumsily getting to my feet and making my way across the room toward Arnold. I hooked an arm around his neck. "You like me," I said, pressing his nose with my index finger. "You like me!" He squeezed my bottom, whispering in my ear that perhaps I should go to bed. I kissed his cheek and did as I was told. As I crossed the room, I noticed Suzanne, the girl from the pub the night I'd met Arnold. She was limp and drooped, lounging across the lap of one of his friends. We made eye contact, recognizing our own. I felt heartened by her presence and diminished by it at the same time. After that we spoke a couple of times in class but never mentioned the encounter.

I was half glad and half disappointed I'd chosen philosophy. I was glad because it gave me something to talk about with Arnold but disappointed because I don't think it really interested me. Technically yes, I was interested in stuff and ideas, and philosophy seemed a repository for people who were interested in stuff and ideas. But I didn't know any stuff and I didn't have any ideas, and as witness to literally hours of clumsy proselytizing on the logic of Wittgenstein, the existentialism of Sartre, I realized that it quickly felt useless and absurd and almost comical. In the library especially, I felt myself literally surrounded by the physical heft of all the stuff I didn't know. But it was strangely comforting, too. How could I be expected to know all this? How could anyone?

I'd always felt comfortable in the library. I liked the particular sense of stasis in the cool, dry air, the tumble-dryer scent of clean clothes and the abstracted triangles and antiquated fonts on the covers of sociology texts from the eighties. I invented a pastime in which I'd identify random facts from esoteric texts to memorize and drop casually into conversation with Arnold, occasionally rewarded by a raised eyebrow, his surprise that I knew such a thing, that I knew anything at all. So although I didn't use it strictly as intended, the library was an antidote to the boredom of my university experience. It was a safe space, the cool relief of a sip of wine after a stressful day. And I suppose it's when our guard is down, inevitably, that we are caught out.

One afternoon I was fetching a cup of water from the cooler in the corridor when I sensed the shadow of someone too close behind me. I knew it was Michael before I'd even turned around. Time slowed, and I felt the urge to put my hands to my face, to make sure everything was still where it should be. I briefly panicked about where I'd left my phone—was it on the desk I was working at, had it fallen out of my pocket in the bathroom? Why didn't I have anything to hold on to? I turned around because I had to.

"Hey," he said, no more and no less—and moved past me to get himself a drink.

That evening I invited myself round to Arnold's. He vocalized his displeasure, but, entirely unlike me, I insisted. It was pouring rain and, as I carefully applied my makeup and selected an outfit I thought might make him be nice to me, I looked out the window and felt foolish for not just staying indoors.

I tried calling a cab, but there were none available. I put on the nearest thing I had to a raincoat and went outside, furious at every droplet of rain, enraged at the trickery of the puddles, all much deeper than they appeared. I was determined, and I felt stupid for it.

I turned up at his place late and dripping wet. He told me there were fresh towels in the bathroom, then went back to his laptop. I had started having a recurring dream in which I jumped up and down on his laptop until it was smashed into shards, which I then threw out the window. I went to his bathroom, dried my hair and body, then redid my eyeliner.

Presenting my hastily reconstructed self, I felt desperate. Desperate for his attention. Desperate for his kindness. Desperate for him to love and save me. I lay on the sofa and stretched out like a cat. I made a racket in the kitchen. I removed a book from my bag and sat at the opposite side of the room from him, pretending not to notice he was even there, not reading a word.

As it approached midnight, he got up from his desk and told me it was time for bed. We had sex and then he went to sleep.

Force, Mass, Acceleration

Soufflé is an egg-based dish originating in France. The word "soufflé" comes from the French word *souffler*, which means to puff, or to breathe.

A soufflé is a good dish to serve at a dinner party or for a date—if you get it right, it can be quite impressive. Getting it right is a matter of hot air. Beat enough air into the mix and the thing will rise; as the air heats up, it will expand, swelling the blend and occupying more space. But it is important to remember that the air is only partly responsible for the soufflé's expansion—you are also depending on the evaporation of water from the walls of the bubbles, steaming inward within the bubbles themselves.

You can make either a sweet soufflé, mixed with a crème pâtissière or a fruit puree, or a savory soufflé, with a béchamel sauce. This will serve as the base of the dish, adding flavor and strengthening the shape. For a basic Gruyère soufflé, begin by preheating the oven. Place a baking sheet inside. Wash your hands.

Coat the insides of two ramekins with butter and Parmesan. This will improve the flavor and help it rise. You might also use bread crumbs or grated cheddar instead of the Parmesan. Choose wisely. Next make your béchamel sauce; heat gently, season generously. Toss egg yolks into the béchamel, separately whipping the whites into stiff, glossy peaks. Beat a large spoonful of whites into the sauce before folding in the rest using a gentle figure-eight motion. Work quickly and decisively. It is too late for second-guessing.

Fill your ramekins three-quarters to the rim and run your finger around the edge of each dish to create a narrow gap between mixture and porcelain. This will help the mixture to rise cleanly away from its container. Some suggest prechilling at this stage, but that has never worked for me: it makes the soufflé too heavy.

Place the dishes on the baking sheet in the oven and leave until golden brown and, hopefully, risen. Try not to open the oven door until they are done. Serve immediately.

Seasoning is very much up to you. You can sprinkle your soufflé with tarragon and chives, then dot with Tabasco sauce, or grate over a dusting of fresh nutmeg or some final shavings of Parmesan. I prefer to eat it unseasoned, concentrating on the texture. It should be delicate but large, light and yet rich. It should look big on your plate. It is supposed to be voluminous. It has a reputation for going wrong.

I used to come back cool. "It was all right," I'd tell Adnan, taking a pointedly cruel swipe at his choice of shirt or taste in music. But the truth was, I was already smelling him. First thing in the morning, or while he slept, I would lean over to inhale his skin. When he cooked for me, I would creep up behind him and bury my face in his back, breathing deeply.

"Are you sniffing me again?" he would ask. "You're so weird." Hooking his arm around my neck and holding me close.

But it wasn't always easy to be close to his body. Sometimes when we were having sex, I would feel overwhelmed, not by pleasure but by anger, the certain white spear of it. We would be entangled, Adnan inside me, maybe halfway there, and it would come over me suddenly, hot rage jet-planing from my eyes, from my crotch, from the palms of my hands. I would slap him away without warning; once I even bit him on the mouth. The first time it happened, he was afraid, he was actually very upset, something I hadn't even considered. He pulled the duvet up to his neck, and I could feel the choked prickle of tears behind his eyes, the strain of his vocal cords as he asked, quite reasonably, "What the fuck was that?"

In that moment I was still angry, but I concentrated on letting it go, consciously feeling it run off me, like drip-drying after a shower. He trembled beneath the floral print of my bedding, his pale brown gooseflesh. My body hummed like a tapped tuning fork, my heart as busy and thrashing as the sea. As I felt the energy drain from the tips of my fingers, I suddenly ached. My muscles stiffened up, my bones throbbed. Anger leaves me like this. Leaves me with this flat, dull pain. I felt his body go pliant, moving into a crescent moon, as he often did, instinctively making space for me. I was the cat that crawled there, that belonged in the curvature he had created.

We lay like spoons for hours before I told him. He stiffened, then loosened, then just held me a little tighter. He always held me tighter after that. And sometimes, as we slept, he would place one of his palms over my eyes. Just the gentle flat of his hand pressed against my face. His arm wrapped around my head. Once when we were drunk, he told me he'd like to pop my head off my body, as he'd done with one of his sister's Barbies. That he would like to cradle it, to set it in his lap. "I could look after your head," he said. "I could look after your little head like that."

We were on the bus when I told Stevie I was moving out. She was staring out the window, talking idly about the light. "I'm getting somewhere with Adnan," I repeated. "I'm really sorry." She continued staring out the window. Tree branches brushed the top deck of the bus. They made me feel uneasy.

"I heard you the first time," she said, removing her phone from her bag, suddenly engrossed in an article about hookup culture. The windows were fogged with condensation. I had an urge to draw something in the steam, but my mind was a blank, so I just wrote my name in large capital letters: R O B E R T A. I examined the sheen of water that coated my fingertip and noticed my hand was lightly shaking.

I had been feeling sick with guilt for the full month Adnan and I spent discussing moving in together. Sometimes I could manipulate that guilt into indignation, recasting myself as the victim. I would imagine some small slight on Stevie's part, dwelling on a time she'd treated me callously or not invited me to something she knew I might have liked to attend. I'd have heated arguments with her in my mind until my heart was beating hard in my chest. I would catch myself walking down the street, mentally lecturing Stevie on the times she'd undermined me or willfully misunderstood what I was saying to her, my lips just perceptibly moving, mouthing the words. But I never managed to convince myself for long: I knew that she'd been betrayed and that the betrayer was me.

When we reached our stop, Stevie leaned past me to ding the bell. As we walked down the road to the cinema, she broke the silence, demanding, "Why did you tell me on the bus? What, were you scared I'd make a scene?"

She was walking half a step in front of me, and when I sped up to meet her, she simply moved faster. By the time we arrived at the cinema, we were both breathless. As we bought our tickets, she was irritable. I couldn't find my debit card, buried somewhere at the bottom of my tote bag, and she sighed and produced hers, saying, "I'll just get it"—like this was something that happened all the time. When I said I needed the toilet before we went in, she rolled her eyes and told me to hurry, despite the fact we'd purposely arrived very early to watch the trailers. As we looked for seats, she said, "I suppose you want to sit right near the front, then?" and began demonstrably massaging her neck.

As the film rolled, I tried to determine her mood by gazing sideways at her posture in the dark. Sometimes her shoulders were hiked right up to her ears, and I'd think, *Oh, fuck.* Other times she slid into her seat, and I'd wonder whether she'd forgiven me. We were watching a horror film, and I spasmed violently in my seat at every jump. As we left, I felt hyperalert but exhilarated by nerves. I asked if she wanted to get a drink, and she assented indifferently. After staring at her phone for ten minutes, bending her straw into an inelegant concertina, she snapped.

"You know that being in a couple is the ultimate in individualism, right? It's you two against the world, and fuck everyone else."

"I don't have to move in with him," I offered, and she made a face like I was the most ridiculous person in the world, finishing her drink and leaving without me.

I'd heard that Sash was looking for somewhere to live after her landlord decided he was selling the flat she'd been renting. Sash and Stevie got on fine, though not brilliantly. I would have preferred Erin or even Emmeline to have suddenly required somewhere to live. Stevie and Erin had an easy intimacy, while Stevie and Emmeline had struck up quite a friendship, in spite of the fact that Stevie had repeatedly had sex with her then boyfriend. But someone was better than no one. I emailed Sash telling her my room would soon be free, and she replied saying she'd like to come and see it. I ran downstairs to tell Stevie. She was blasé. "Sure," she said. "If that makes it easier for you."

I reasoned there was at least symmetry: we'd first met Sash a little while after she had moved out of a flat she shared with her best friend, Emma. That had been months ago, and she was still really hurt, not enjoying living alone. We met her in a quiet Mexican restaurant she'd suggested. We hugged her on arrival and asked if she minded our recording the conversation. Stevie flipped over her phone and tapped the red circle to begin.

Sash had been a skinny boy, and he found something pacifying about being able to crawl into small spaces. He liked the feeling of being hemmed in. He dragged his single bed's frame to the far corner of his bedroom and moved his wardrobe, desk, and chest of drawers around it, accessing it by a small crack next to the wall. On Saturday afternoons he would climb into the top chamber of his mother's airing cupboard, reading comic books with a torch, enjoying the sweet aerial smell of the freshly laundered towels. In school he would retreat to the library at lunchtime and slip between the spaces under the shelves, lying there facedown, his nose pressed against the carpet. When they discovered that hiding place, he found another, a little corner of the cleaning closet that was cramped and uncomfortable but warm. When they discovered *that* space, he begged to be home-schooled, and his mother agreed to quit her job and teach him history and geography, mathematics and French, even though she could barely remember any of it herself.

Being homeschooled had its ups (no broken noses) and downs (no friends). In the evenings he'd log on to his father's old Dell and talk about *Buffy the Vampire Slayer* and *Dawson's Creek* and *Roswell* and *Charmed*. He'd spend hours online, feeling an energy running from his brain through to his fingertips, a bright white light like the glare that travels backward and forward inside a photocopier. He would exchange theories on forthcoming episodes and postulate on certain characters' motivations. He started writing speculative fiction that slotted between seasons and found people who really loved what he wrote. Some sent him their own writing, hoping he could offer them some critical feedback. He would say very nice things about their writing even though it was mostly absolutely dreadful.

At the weekend he would stay awake until the sun came up, blinking sleepily at his screen. One late night spent discussing the recently proposed romantic coupling of Willow and Tara, somebody started talking about queer politics, and he looked up what that meant, and then somebody else used the word "transgender," and he looked up what that meant, too. Reading the Wikipedia entry, he felt that same energy, that bright white light, except this time he felt it all over his body and beyond his body, lighting up the entire room. He started visiting forums and chat rooms that used phrases like "body dysmorphia" and "gender incongruence." These words stirred something in him, and he realized that he did not want to be a boy.

He wanted to be a girl. And then he realized that he was in fact already a girl.

Sash spent three years in possession of this information, imagining it a brilliant and solid pearl that she had to keep clenched tight inside. At night she would imagine her life as a girl, willing her body to change into that of a girl's, of its own accord.

She met Emma online. They would hang out at comic-book stores and drink milk shakes and eat American candy. One Saturday the actress Amber Benson came to sign some of her comic books, and they met her and had their photographs taken with her. They started talking to some other kids at the store, who invited them to the park later. The park was hazy and cold and loud and thrilling. People were passing around bottles of vodka, and everyone had similar interests. Somebody complimented Sash on her hoodie, and she was struck with the knowledge it was perhaps the first compliment she had ever received that had not come from her mother.

She drank a lot of vodka that night, and when Emma asked her if she wanted to go for a walk, she said sure she did, even though she was so drunk she could not properly see her own feet. They sat on a bench together, and for the first time in her life she said aloud that she was really a girl and that when she got out of this godforsaken town, she would live her life as a woman and everybody would just have to deal with that. She said she'd never told anyone and she was only telling Emma because she could see she was a person good all the way through, with an open and receptive heart. Emma wrapped her arms around Sash and squeezed, telling her she was so glad Sash had told her and that there was nothing to be afraid of. Sash felt a great unburdening, like there was nothing in the world heavy enough to tether her to the ground, like she could lift away in the slightest breeze. She looked at Emma's strong and fierce face, the freckles and scar tissue that puckered it. She thought it was the very best face she'd ever seen. And then suddenly this face was leaning in toward her own, and her lips were on Sash's, and they were moving in a way that she knew meant they were kissing. She stayed incredibly still and hoped it would be over soon, and when Emma finally peeled her face away, Sash could see she was crying, and it was Sash's turn to comfort her.

They never spoke about the kiss again, not when Emma was holding her hand as she told her mother, not when Emma escorted her to the pharmacy to receive her prescription, not even now that Emma was engaged to be married, and Sash felt a deep void of terror.

Emma said that nothing would change, and perhaps it wouldn't. But when Sash met Andrea at group counseling and Andrea told her about a collective where all women were welcome and everyone had fun and learned about taking up space, she thought, *Well, I do need some new friends.*

Sash moved in the same day I moved out. It was a strange day. I had terrible period pains, and midway through carrying boxes of books and clothes I had to stop to lie down on the sofa and press a hot-water bottle to my stomach. I lay staring at my abdomen, the hot-water bottle perched on top of it, feeling my insides twist and pulsate, melting and easing just slightly with the heat. It lasted two hours, and for two hours I lay in the house that was no longer my home but still contained all my stuff. I apologized to Stevie. "I'm so sorry. Soon I'll be out of your hair."

She looked blankly at me. "What?"

When I was feeling better, I helped Sash arrange her things in my old room. Adnan drove my belongings over to our new flat, a place in the center of town with enormous square windows and exposed floorboards. I was lingering, finding excuses still to be there. At some point Stevie left, calling up the stairs that she was going out for a bit, slamming the door behind her. When Adnan came back, we waited at our old table, the table with just enough space for two, and I told him we couldn't leave until she'd gotten back. Later we sat on the sofa, and Adnan might have fallen asleep. The light went milky and gray, then dark. We left without having said good-bye.

I was bigger by then than when I first started dating Adnan. Sometimes when I held his hand, I felt so much stronger than him, and it made me feel good, radicalizing the natural order like that. But sometimes I yearned to be tiny, to feel delicate and light, a person requiring protection.

I would catch myself observing Adnan with a degree of remove. I was watching for signs, monitoring how his hands touched my body, how he regarded me as I walked into a room. I would watch him as he watched me eat, imagining a tiny shift, an expansion, his irises swelling to fit me inside.

Our flat felt much bigger than it was. The first night we moved in, I cooked a huge dish of imperial rice while Adnan mixed cocktails. We sat around eating from paper plates, getting tipsy, and cursing how much we'd spent on agency fees. Cardboard boxes and black bin liners littered the floor. We had to weave in between them to make our way to the bedroom or to the kitchen. It was a pre-apartment, an apartment in flux, poised to become a home. I thought, *How are two people supposed to share a space like this?* We ended up throwing an awful lot out, negotiating exchanges. *Well, I threw out all my Alice Munro books, so you can get rid of your* South Park *figurines.* Taking stuff to Oxfam, I thought about how much time Stevie and

I used to spend trawling through charity shops, giddy to find a nice sweater, an old leather handbag. How happy someone's unwanted or forgotten stuff could make us.

Our nights together felt expansive, long and dry, the sort of inert cuddling that couples acclimate to. We always had food in the fridge. It was a fridge from which you could mostly compile a plate of leftovers. Adnan had a thing about waste. At the end of every meal, he would huntedly scour the table, grasping for literal crusts, smearing them with the last of the pasta sauce. I'd throw away hardened heels of bread or the softening stalk of a long-gone head of cauliflower. He would bite his lip and list ways we could have used it.

I did the ironing and Adnan did the washing-up. It was choreography. He would also fix things around the house. Sometimes I, too, would fix things around the house, flexing my muscles, planting my legs like an explorer: *Which way's the beach? I am very strong!* But whenever I'd fix things, he'd need to fix them properly, so that they'd actually work later on.

For a while it occurred to me that maybe I would like a baby. That something was missing, an absent space about my calves where something should be clinging to my knees. Sometimes I'd be standing at a bus stop or waiting for the kettle to boil, and I would ruffle my fingers through an imagined mess of brown curls. I'd find myself pulling faces at babies—on the train or in the changing rooms at Topshop. I'd widen my eyes and purse my mouth. The babies would stare and sometimes laugh, in their palsied baby way. "Babies like me," I once said to Stevie as I acted the buffoon before a captive infant strapped into a buggy while his mother drank a flat white.

"Babies like anyone with a symmetrical face," she replied. "They're stupid."

I would still email Stevie about Supper Club. We would still see each other at work. We would even go out for dinner or to the pictures. But I'd noticed that when I walked past her in the corridors and she was with other people, my eyes would drop to the floor and I'd walk sheepishly past her like a prisoner. I would hope she hadn't told the people she was with about what I'd done. Once I was eating a salad and reading a gardening magazine in the staff room. I must not have noticed her in there, or perhaps she came in after me, but when I looked up, she'd been staring at me, and in that second before she glanced away, I registered an unmistakable emotion on her face, and it was contempt.

I rarely bothered speaking to Adnan about this. He would tell me stories of fallouts with friends, and I would have to maintain a semblance of composure, check the muscles in my face for tells or spasms. *It's not the same,* I would think. He was so unshakably blasé—I didn't know whether to find it comforting or deeply annoying.

I'd started spending more time with Renni. I'd pop into the Amore on the walk home from work, and she'd make me a mint tea, set her laptop on the bar, and complain that it made her elbows sticky. But she would stay there with me for a little while, working while I sipped my drink. I liked to think Renni and I were the sensible members of Supper Club. The ones who had it together a bit. I suspected she liked to think that, too. In my head this coincided closely with my imagined arguments with Stevie. I mean, of course she didn't get it. She was not an actual adult like me. She didn't have responsibilities. She was risking very little.

I liked to talk to Renni about work because Stevie never would allow it. She'd dismiss my frustrations about how a meeting went or a new system for logging calls as "meaningless." When I relayed anecdotes about how I had to pick up somebody else's slack or that someone had done a task in a senseless and unthinking way, she would say I had told her the story only because I liked how it made me feel, and that was pathetic. But when I told Renni these stories, she would share in my outrage and it would occur to me that we both liked asserting ourselves in this way, as thinkers and doers, and perhaps there was nothing wrong with that.

A couple of times, we went out for dinner and talked about the terrible men we'd encountered. She'd tell me how some customer had gotten so drunk he urinated into one of the indoor plant pots. I'd tell her about one of the managers calling me "doll." After I'd felt that an adequate amount of time had elapsed, I would table the subject of Stevie. I would ask Renni what she suspected Stevie's problem might be. "I am *so* not getting into that," she'd reply, and I'd feel bad for having made the atmosphere change.

One afternoon at work, I was emailing Adnan about our toilet. There'd been a problem with the plumbing since we moved in: every time it flushed, it would ring out this unholy sound for a good half hour afterward. I wanted to joke that it was howling to be fed, but the joke was too unpleasant, too scatological, to prompt anything beyond discomfort. I was desperate to ring the landlord, to have him pay to get it fixed, but Adnan was insistent he would work out how to do it himself from YouTube. He was always working out how to do things from YouTube. He knew how to do yoga for menstrual cramps, how to toilet train a cat. He kept emailing links to new YouTube videos and plumbing equipment he'd found listed on eBay. Then he said his brother was coming round to help. I was sick at the thought of it. He wanted me to be out of the flat when they attempted the repair and kept sending me speculative dates and times. Eventually he rang me, listing weekday names in no logical order ("Friday? Tuesday? Monday? Friday?"). I told him that whenever was convenient, I'd just get out of the flat. At the end of our call, I held my head in my hands and released all the air from my lungs. Kate asked me what was the matter. I told her my boyfriend was driving me mad, a sentence I felt privileged in the saying. I was a member of the club of women who had boyfriends who were getting on their nerves. "Oh, babe," she said, recognizing my elevation. "Let's grab a coffee."

I got back to the office to find an email from Stevie. The subject line said "WHAT." The email said, "So now you're hanging out with KATIE?!" I moved it to my Deleted folder and stared at my wallpaper: a dog in a sou'wester, looking confused. I realized I felt, as I had always felt, as I had felt my entire life and probably would feel forevermore, lonely. There were gaping spaces that I still didn't know how to fill. I opened up a new email and typed in her address. I wrote, "I miss you," and stared at my screen for a long while, thinking about how it was always me doing the chasing and the emotional work, how sad that made me feel. I stared at the words on my screen a bit longer, then deleted them letter by letter. I wrote instead, "I suppose we need to start organizing the next Supper Club." I clicked SEND.

It was Monica's idea. She had been temping and working seasonal shifts the entire time we'd known her. She had worked the reception desk at a clinical-research company, instructing floppy-haired students on where to get their experimental flu jabs, asking them if they wouldn't mind not kicking the vending machine. She had processed data for global banks, making eight pounds an hour for the privilege. She had sold tickets on the phone to *Les Misérables* and *Cats*, taking timed toilet breaks and being docked pay for bouts of IBS. And for a spell she worked the Clarins desk at Selfridges, rubbing lotion into strangers' hands and making recommendations on how best to apply liquid eyeliner.

She would come home from Selfridges exhausted from having been on her feet all day and would very often completely lose her voice from talking. Erin resented the job. "It is *everything* that is *wrong* with the world," she once told me, fired up about something or other. "But she's weird about money. She's weird about not having it."

Monica made friends with one of the girls at the MAC counter, and they'd visit the Selfridges prosecco bar after shifts: one glass each of prosecco and a shared bowl of truffle fries costing about the same as what they'd pay at the nearby pub, once their staff discount had been applied. Sometimes Monica's friend's new boyfriend would join them; he was the night control-room operator for the store. One evening she came home and told Erin what he'd told her: that the cameras inside the department store were all dummies, that the only area actually surveyed was outside the front and the back, that the security guards finished their shifts at eleven, and that it would be easy to break in, really easy, anyone could do it, so long as they used the entrance to the lower-basement car park, which had a lousy lock. Erin relayed this to Stevie, and it was decided: the next Supper Club would be held at Selfridges, on the bottom floor—the best floor, really, the floor where they kept the alcohol and makeup.

Stevie asked me to meet her for a drink to discuss the plan. She'd suggested this weird little continental-themed pub she liked to go to sometimes. It was the sort of place that made me feel uncomfortable, awkward and out of place. I couldn't situate myself in it, couldn't arrange my body correctly.

When I arrived, Stevie was already there. I scrabbled my phone from my pocket, panicking that I'd arrived late. "It's okay," she said, holding her hand up ceremonially in front of me. "I was early." She pushed one of the two glasses of red wine before her toward me. "Here," she said. "You need to loosen up."

I set out my ideas for the menu. I'd been thinking about the sort of food that was ordinarily served in Selfridges, the glut of canapés and nibbles left over from the winter party season, their fussy redundancy. I wanted to do gigantic and kind of crass versions of those dainties. So a goat-cheese-and-beetroot cup became an enormous cheddar-and-onion pie. Chorizo-and-prosciutto wraps became immense German bratwursts rolled up in thick, salty bacon. I set out some sheets of paper containing my ideas, and Stevie arranged them in front of herself. She paused momentarily. She pushed them back toward me.

"We're not cooking this time," she said. "We're just going to eat what's in there. There's tons. I had a look on their website. Huge hampers of cheeses and chutneys. Loads of chocolates and fancy cakes. Alcohol. Plus lots of weird stuff, too, like edible insects and astronaut ice cream. It's perfect."

I placed the pieces of paper on top of one another, folded the sheets in half and half again.

"Well," I said. "I guess that's that."

"Don't be like that," she replied.

"I'm not being like anything," I said.

"Sure," she said. "Whatever. So do you want to know the plan or not?"

"Of course I do."

"We'll get there for twelve. We're not going to bring anything. We're not going to decorate anything. We're just going to show up."

"Okay."

"Then we eat and drink what's in there. And we dance. And do the usual Supper Club stuff."

I made a shape with my mouth, the beginnings of an objection.

"Listen," she interrupted me before I even spoke. "All this planning—

menus, themes—it's not necessary. You make such a big deal out of *everything*. And it's not like you have time to organize them these days anyway. We've not done a single one since you met Adnan." She paused guiltily—as if she'd said more than she meant to. "We're just going to do this one relaxed. Can you cope with that?"

I nodded, and Stevie twisted her face into an expression of skepticism, then picked her phone up and appeared to reply to a message.

"Right," she said. "I've got to go."

She finished the last of her wine, wound her scarf around her neck, and put on her coat.

"Who are you meeting?" I asked.

"No one you know," she said. And then she nodded at me. And then she left.

Adnan and I had started going out for breakfast on Sundays. We began by choosing a new place every week but quickly lapsed into returning to the one place we knew we could get a table. I had poached eggs and halloumi. Adnan had maple syrup and pancakes. We each allowed the other one bite of our food.

Adnan had a tendency to cut his food up before starting to eat, spearing each piece on his fork. He sliced his pancakes into thick little triangles, dipped them in far more maple syrup than they actually needed, and chewed while staring out the window. He wasn't being indifferent, rather seemed cozy in the knowledge that I was right across the table. I reached my hand over to squeeze his. He grinned at me, food bulging at his cheeks.

"Hey, so what restaurant are you using for your dinner party?" he asked.

I felt something spiral in my stomach: the flex of a doubt.

"Um, we're not actually doing it at a restaurant this time. We don't always use restaurants."

Adnan continued chewing, gazing out the window.

"So where are you doing it?" he asked, swallowing.

"At Selfridges."

"Like, in the café? Can you do that there?"

"Uh, more like . . . we might be sort of sneaking in."

Adnan stabbed another triangle, dipping it in what remained of the syrup, pushing it around his plate and puzzling it out.

"What do you mean?" he said eventually. "'Sneaking in'? What does that even mean?"

I tried to deduce whether Adnan was feeling curiosity or suspicion, whether it was something I could brush off or giggle through. I decided I might as well tell him.

"Well, Monica works there," I ventured. "So, like . . . it's fine. We know how to get in. There are definitely no cameras. We're definitely not going to get caught."

I had to touch his hand to elicit a response, and he let me for just a second before pulling back, a sea creature snapping back inside its shell.

"I don't get it," he said. "I thought this was just like a cookery club with your girlfriends? For dinner parties. Like when we had Sophie and Dan round for paella."

"I guess it is kind of like a cookery club," I replied. "But it's not just about the actual food. It's sort of about how we assert ourselves in a space. In different spaces. It's about taking up more space."

"And how do you do that?"

I gestured toward my food. "Well," I said. "We eat. We eat as much as we want to. We get bigger. We take up space with our bodies, I suppose."

"Oh," he said. "I didn't know. I didn't know that was part of it."

Adnan thumbed the edge of his plate, the pancakes seemingly turned unappetizing.

"But I still don't get why you're breaking in." He glanced up sheepishly. "What does that have to do with being fat?"

I let the word ring in the air for a while, then pushed it out of my head. I thought about how he'd said "cookery club," the sweet naïveté of the phrase. But *fat* kept pulsating below. *Fat. Fat.* I let myself breathe.

"Okay, so it's all connected," I conceded. "Like I said before about the dumpster-diving? It's about existing in spaces we're told we shouldn't exist in or how we behave in spaces that expect us to behave a certain way, to be a certain thing—and what if we don't want to be that thing? What if we don't want to behave in that way? And then what if actually everywhere is one of those restrictive spaces? What if the whole world is designed to inhibit you and just to exist in it is to break some deep taboo? So what if you give up making yourself smaller all the time, like *all the time*, and you make yourself bigger instead? And what if, to make space for yourself to *be* bigger, you have to take it?"

I felt breathless, triumphant. I readied myself to gauge his response. I thought about how even in that moment I was bundled up, compromised and defensive. I uncrossed my legs and stretched my arms out across the table. Adnan put down his knife and fork and tugged hard at the flesh between his eyes. I wondered how far he might stretch it, whether he might pull it a foot out of his face like a teenager blowing bubble gum.

"What?" I urged. "What is it?"

He went to touch my hand, the one he had flinched away from before.

"I think we should just think about this," he said. "I think we should just think about whether this is a good idea or not. But for now—I think we should just finish our breakfast."

The morning of the Supper Club, Stevie texted me. Monica's out. I replied. What?

> STEVIE: Yes, she's out. Because Erin hadn't exactly told her the plan yet, and when she did, she went totally mental. Moved some of her stuff out, too.

> ROBERTA: Oh God. Is Erin okay?

> STEVIE: Yeah. I mean no. She's obviously really, really sad, but this is definitely for the best.

> ROBERTA: Really?

> STEVIE: Totally.

> STEVIE: You don't think so?

> STEVIE: It is so obviously for the best.

> ROBERTA: Okay.

> STEVIE: She was totally using Erin. Like, Erin was her chance for a wild life, but she will INEVITABLY go back to that Thomas guy, I've no doubt.

> STEVIE: Sash is certain they're still in touch all the time.

STEVIE: Monica and Thomas.

STEVIE: I'm actually glad she's not in Supper Club anymore. I don't think she gets it.

STEVIE: Like at all.

STEVIE: Anyway, meet me at the car park at twelve.

STEVIE: And remember not to bring anything.

STEVIE: And wear whatever you like.

That evening I spent a long time throwing clothes around the living room, putting something on, then tearing it off again. "Are you sure you're not nervous because you're, you know, going out to commit a crime?" Adnan said, watching me toss T-shirts aside and rummage through the wardrobe. "Because you know that what you're doing is fundamentally wrong?"

He had taken to assuming this chilly imperviousness when he was upset with me. Watching the steady gaze of his eyes, the careful composition of his mouth, I got the feeling he was working incredibly hard to maintain control of the various quadrants of his face. When he was in a bad mood, he would often have to retire to bed by nine o'clock, worn-out from demonstrating his animosity. Now he stood with his arms folded, addressing me from the doorway, refusing to step inside the room. "I can't believe you're going through with this," he announced, both to me and to himself and also, I suspected, to some omnipresent arbiter, addressing the splinters of wood in the doorframe, the specks of dust hanging in the air. "I can't believe it."

I met Renni ahead of everyone else. We walked to the car park together, talking about what we were going to do, all nerves and thrill, like planning a midnight feast. We arrived a little late, a calculation so we wouldn't have to be the first ones. "Who's missing?" I asked, hugging Stevie, an instinctive gesture that surprised us both.

"Just Erin and Ashley," she told me. "Ashley's had some sort of emergency, but Erin will be here. She'll be here."

I hugged everyone else hello, then stood beside Stevie. I thought about what we must look like to passersby, so thoroughly unassuming in our large bodies, our sensible winter coats. So entirely nondisruptive.

We saw Erin coming from the distance, swaying extravagantly from side to side.

"Uh-oh," said Stevie.

"Uh-oh," I replied.

"I'm here, bitches!" she bellowed, underscoring her point by raising her arms into the air. "Let's fucking do this!"

She walked straight past us and led us down through the underground car park. Once inside, we had to use the lights on our phones.

"This is the door," she said, splaying her arms out and pressing her whole body against it. "Now, this is the damned door."

"Sure is," Sash replied, patting her lightly on the back, peeling her away, and making a face of concern to the rest of the group. "But how do we get past it?"

Erin wriggled free and positioned herself in front of it. "We shove it open, of course."

She flung herself at it. It didn't shift. She tried again.

"Hey!" Sash exclaimed, grabbing her arm. "You're going to hurt yourself."

Stevie stepped in and began banging it with her side.

"It's going," she kept saying, rubbing the length of her arm. "It's going to go."

"I know it's dark," Renni said. "But people can still hear us, you know?"

"I'll go and keep a lookout," Lina offered, and Renni went with her. Stevie was still hurling herself at the door. After a couple more attempts, she asked if somebody else would have a go. Sash tried pushing but didn't really try very hard. Emmeline made an even more halfhearted attempt.

Stevie stood slightly to the side of us and began staring at her phone. Lit by just the screen, she looked ghoulish—blanched and lopsided. I felt the jump of anxiety I often did when I sensed that something wasn't making her happy. A propulsive need to step in.

"Let me have a go," I asked, and Sash and Emmeline eagerly stepped aside.

I pressed my hands up against the door. It was thick but not heavy, plated with some sort of corrugated metal. I pushed my whole body against it. I wondered why pushing my whole body against something was not enough to break it. It seemed a terrible injustice. At the same time, I felt something underneath the indignation— something that felt a lot like relief.

Behind me Stevie said, "Okay, come on," and I turned to find her calmly brandishing a crowbar. The mere presence of it seemed to change the temperature of the entire space. This large piece of metal, its vicious hook, so antithetical to the soft buoyancy of Supper Club.

"I might have brought one of these," she said, twizzling it non-chalantly in front of her, like a veteran showgirl. "Just in case."

I watched in outraged silence as she swirled the crowbar, waiting for everyone else's reaction, hoping it would be the same as mine. Nobody spoke or moved. Only Erin seemed unsurprised, too drunk to pay much attention. Or perhaps, it occurred to me with an uneasy dropping feeling, she'd been forewarned. Stevie strode forward, businesslike, and angled the bar against the doorframe. Pressing down, she popped off a foot-long strip of wood with ease. Turning back to grin at us, she carried on, working her way around the frame methodically, kicking each piece aside as it landed on the ground. I watched her, thinking, *She had that thing in her bag the whole time.*

Her movements were fluid, confident. Once she'd removed the bottom of the frame, she slipped the hook of the bar inside the now-exposed crack on the lock side of the door, pushing against it. We watched a little space open up, the door straining and quivering but holding shut. "Pass me that," she said, gesturing at the pile of wood on the floor. I did as I was told, baffled, picking up the nearest piece and watching as she inserted it into the gap, unhooking the crowbar and leaving the wooden chock wedged in a now-slightly-wider gap. She hooked in the bar again, higher into the crack of space. The dull shine of the metal lock peeped out. She moved the piece of wood even higher, following the path the crowbar made. We were enthralled, mesmerized by this strange dexterity. When the lock eventually broke and the door sprang open, we shouted and clapped. Stevie stepped aside, slick with sweat, and watched us walk in. I hung back from the others, wanting to ask her where she'd learned all that, but she just smirked and trotted away from me.

Once inside, we had to navigate the service corridors, all beige and waxy with signs imploring good customer service and hygiene.

"I mean," Stevie said, "this would be much easier if we had Monica to help us out."

Erin walked ahead, the veer of her chin toward her shoulder telling us she'd heard but was declining to comment.

At the end of the main corridor was a pair of double doors. We understood that this would be the entrance to the shop floor, but we diligently tried all the others, just in case. Most were locked. Once we'd exhausted all the options, we gathered in front of the doors. Erin pressed her hands against them, one on each door. "Okay," she said. "I'm doing it." She squeezed shut her eyes and pushed. We emitted the second collective yelp of the night as the doors swung open.

We emerged into the cosmetics section, the hard marble of the floor lined with white columns and strip lighting, all switched off. There was some debate over what to do about the lights, concerns that the main lights would be visible to the security cameras on the floor above. In the end we could not find where to switch them on anyway and were facing the prospect of groping around in the dark all night when Emmeline found a control panel for the individual display lights tucked under the Dior counter. Suddenly we were bathed in the honey glow of Charlize Theron's smile, a gold watch hanging from her wrist, her nails a gleaming crimson. Searching around the other counters, we found more buttons: film-star dressing-room lightbulbs surrounding mirrors, LED panels illuminating tubes of lipstick. It felt both grotesque and exhilarating. The darkness pooled around the fluorescent displays, beacons guiding you to a better self. All the different ways you could color in a face. I dunked my index finger into a pot of pale blue gel, rubbing it against my thumb, holding it up to my face to sniff. Once it had dried, my fingertip felt like velvet. I thought about how if you had enough money your whole body could feel like velvet.

"Okay!" Stevie shouted. "Food first. Let's set stuff out here. Find what you can."

She gestured to the space between the Clinique eye shadows and the Tom Ford perfumes. I looped an arm through Renni's, ready to forage, but Stevie chased after us. "Aren't you forgetting something?"

she asked, producing a handful of peppercorn-size MDMA bombs. "Here, have one now."

"Fuck it," Renni said, taking three and knocking them back at once. Stevie turned to me, palm unfurled, imploring me.

"Sure," I said. "Fine."

The food we managed to gather was considerably more limited than we'd been led to believe. An excess of individually wrapped panettone and reindeer-shaped chocolate—the dregs of Christmas. Baskets of savory biscuits and variations of chutney. Kitsch American stuff like packets of Froot Loops and jars of marshmallow spread. Large decanters of flavored oils but nothing to dip into them. There weren't even any cheeses or cured meats. But the alcohol was good: bottles of champagne and prosecco, Żubrówka in sculpted glass jars. We sat on the hard floor. Stevie had brought blankets and paper plates, plastic cups and cutlery. It felt like a picnic at the end of the world. I made a plate of Gruyère cheese twists and port-and-fig chutney. I slathered salted caramel dip over savory oatcakes. I had a slice of hazelnut panettone. I finished with some shortbread and sea-salt truffles. I felt sick but not really full. But as I sipped from a miniature bottle of whiskey, I started to feel myself coming up. Sash suggested we each pick a different makeup counter and present back our looks. I got the Illamasqua stand.

I began by covering my face with iridescent powder, then applied liquid eyeliner, too wasted to do anything beyond just ham-fistedly color in my entire eyelid. I completed the look with some forest-green lipstick, at first carefully lining my mouth, then just smearing it around my lips and chin. I made my way back to the group. "Beautiful," Sash called over as I placed my hands in a childlike V underneath my face. Emmeline was playing pop music on her phone, just loud enough to dance to, so long as you really concentrated. We started singing along, drowning out the music, relaxing into the night. Stevie returned, having colored all her teeth red. Andrea had painted her face like a cat's, with whiskers and a black blob of a nose, and Lina had drawn a luminous turquoise strip across both eyes and the bridge of her nose. They climbed on top of the Bobbi Brown counter, kicking a display of bronzers, then flipping over neat rows of lipsticks and liners, jerking their legs in an inelegant can-can, raining makeup across the floor. We wolf-whistled in appreciation and sang even louder.

Erin was the last to come back, her whole face a burnt orange, some sort of matte cream bronzer. She was a lot drunker than the rest of us, dancing in a boneless and syncopated way, knocking things over and flailing around. "I don't like this," she said, tugging at the plain gray dress she had on. "I want to wear something else." She broke away from the circle and made for the static escalators, doing a kind of showgirl dance, hanging her legs over the sides. When she was about halfway up, I remembered how Monica had said the ground floor was the only one that was alarmed. And I imagined myself on a tiny stool at the very center of my head, trying to communicate my thoughts to Erin, to anyone, like shouting beyond the walls of a ballroom. But it was too late—the alarm was ringing, and Erin was crying, and everyone around me was hysterical. I stood on the spot, stunned, an ant set in molasses.

"We have to get out!" Stevie shouted. She grabbed both my shoulders, shaking them. "We have to get out *now!*"

And so we did.

I didn't wake up until late in the afternoon, and it took me a moment to remember why I felt so sick. Sticky chunks of chutney and crushed biscuits mashed into the floor. Makeup smeared all across the counters. I had a feeling Andrea had thrown up somewhere, but I couldn't remember where. I had a feeling I might have thrown up, too. I thought about whoever's job it would be to clean it all up. I thought about the squeal of the alarm, us scrambling to find our way back through the tangle of corridors, the cameras we'd been assured were just for show. Why had we listened to some security guy who Monica kind of knew? I lay staring at the ceiling but wanting to be beneath the bed, wanting to feel small and trapped and unaccountable, not large and conspicuous, too big to ask for any favors. When my phone rang, I let it. I wasn't sure where Adnan was, but he wasn't in the flat.

I stayed in bed for the rest of the day. I'd sleep for an hour or so, then wake and lie staring at the ceiling. Sometimes I would frantically scroll through my phone, anxiety compounded by my hangover, avoiding all my news apps. I messaged Adnan a couple of times asking where he was, staring at the tiny tick hanging from each communication, the small and faint lettering that said READ.

When he eventually arrived home, I was drifting in and out of consciousness, woken by the rattle of his keys in the door. As he walked into the bedroom, I instinctively snapped my eyes shut, pretending to be asleep. He must have stood watching me for a few minutes before I heard him shuffle out, switch on the TV. About an hour later, I made my way to the living room. He was watching *Match of the Day*, despite the fact that he did not like football.

"I'm ill," I said.

"You're hungover," he said. "And God knows what else."

He flicked over the channel, suddenly self-conscious.

"I'm serious," I said. "I really am ill. And it's not a hangover. I think I've got that thing that's been going around the office."

Adnan trained his eyes on the TV.

"Where have you been?" I asked.

"Been to my brother's," he replied, not looking at me.

"How is he?" I asked. "How's Emma?"

"Apparently Dad's not very well," he said. "Had flu for ages or something."

I stood staring at him, having run out of lines of interrogation, ways to pretend that things were normal. I had not yet met his brother. I had not met his sister-in-law. I had not met his parents. In a sense I had so little access to his life. I thought about starting a fight, spinning around the lazy Susan, exclaiming, "*There!*"

As I turned to go back to bed, he called after me. "Robs," he said, his inflection too neutral for me to determine whether or not he'd forgiven me. "If you're hungry, there's leftovers in the fridge."

Roberta, hello.

How are you? The cats say hello. It's been a quiet week for me. I've had a bit of a nasty cold and have been tucked up in bed for days. It's a nightmare, because I'm far too sick to leave the house, and I've been running out of near everything. I've had to send just the most pitiful texts to friends and colleagues, asking if they wouldn't mind dropping off throat lozenges and toilet paper and other such glamorous effects. One great thing about New York is that you can have bloody anything delivered to your door. Like, literally to your door. You can order one burrito or a bunch of woodscrews, and somebody will bring it to you.

I've been treating myself to a different film on Netflix every night. I rewatched *Fargo* yesterday, which is obviously brilliant, and the night before I watched this film someone at work recommended called *The Neon Demon*, which was completely dreadful and awful, and when I eventually get back to work, I'm going to walk up to this person and say, "What is wrong with you?"

I've also been watching this BBC thing with Idris Elba called *Luther*, which is really excellent and scary. Does make me think of you, though. You know, these days you have to be so careful. I hope you get taxis everywhere (licensed). I hope you don't take unnecessary risks. And I hope you don't drink too much. My friend Eric was telling me his daughter went to her first party the other night, and this kid is like fifteen, and when he picked her up, she was stumbling everywhere and then was sick all over the back of his Honda. He says he's going to have a talk with her, because God knows what might have happened to her if he hadn't been there to pick the poor thing up. I dread to think, I really do.

Oh, I forgot to tell you! I ordered a cross-trainer. I ordered it off Amazon, and it arrived about two weeks ago. It's meant to simulate hiking, but it is absolutely exhausting. I did five minutes on it when it first arrived, and I thought my lungs might explode. But I'm building up, bit by bit. It's also got this little ledge at the front which is the perfect size for my Kindle, so I've been reading loads of John le Carré books while going at it, pretending I'm a tough spy. Sad, eh?

Anyway, why am I rambling on and on about the various mundanities of my life when there is BIG and EXCELLENT news?! The news is, I am popping back to the UK! I'll be in Bristol the tail end of next week and then over visiting relatives near you early the week after. My proposition to you is: Would you like to meet up for dinner? Absolutely on me. And I'll take you somewhere especially fancy. Don't feel you have to, of course. But that would be really wonderful if you did! Is that expensive Chinese restaurant still in business? The one that was on the telly? Maybe we could go there.

I must say all this excitement has rendered me a bit tired, and according to the notification currently flashing on my phone it's time for another Lemsip. Hurrah! Also, I should probably do something about the gigantic pile of washing-up that's looking at me from the kitchen. Such is life.

I do hope you're very well. Would be lovely to hear back.

All good things,

Jim (Dad)

X

I took Monday to Wednesday off work. On the first day, Adnan saw me still in bed at eight fifteen and asked whether I was planning to demonstrate interest in maintaining my employment today. When I told him I was taking the day off and that I'd already texted Margaret, he just said, "Right," leaving without kissing me good-bye despite the fact I'd arranged the bedsheets to make me look needy and wan.

I lay in until midday, still swamped with anxiety. I thought about texting Stevie to let her know I wouldn't be at work, but the thought seemed terribly presumptuous—why would I assume that she cared? I scrolled through her Twitter, seeing what she was reading: she'd liked a photo from a Guns N' Roses–themed hen do of a person I'd never heard her mention and a review of an immersive play called *In Want of a Shirt*. I put off reading through the news for as long as possible. When I eventually did, I found our break-in covered just twice: in the local paper and on the regional BBC news site. What was worse were the comments beneath it. A user called OrangeTango wrote, "What would possess a person to do this?" Another named Did I Miss Something wrote, "These idiots should be locked up for good." I'd click through to the profile of every username, seeing what else they had commented on, trying to get a feel for their moral compass. I dismissed one commenter for leaving thirty comments complaining about the language from the workers opposite his office but was later dismayed to find his measured response to a piece about the housing crisis. It was hard to determine who was right.

Adnan kept working late, not sending me the usual Facebook updates about his day, not punctuating his texts with the garland of kisses and emojis I'd become accustomed to. He'd send me one text every three hours: How are you feeling? I wondered whether he'd copied and pasted it or if he kept writing it out from scratch. In the evenings he'd get in after seven and make a point of cooking dinner, sighing and asking, "Who left the colander *here*?" to no one, not even to himself.

Midweek he asked me outright what had gone on. I told him we'd only stayed there an hour, then thought better of it. Said we'd gone back to Renni's to watch a film. When he asked why I was such a mess the next day, I said we'd ordered some pizza and the anchovies must have gone bad, that everyone else was sick afterward, too. He looked like he'd entered a strange liminal space, weighing up my reply, deciding whether he could bring himself to believe it. Finally he sighed and cupped his hand around my ear. "Sensible," he concluded.

When I returned to work on Thursday, I held back from emailing Stevie. She hadn't been in touch with me since Saturday, and I would

206 · *Lara Williams*

not make myself even more needy and pathetic by reaching out to her first. Margaret trilled about the office, her hair recently dyed canary yellow, a Post-it note attached to the underside of her shoe. I watched her, feeling the familiar combination of tenderness and irritation.

At home that night, Adnan was still distant, going to bed early, claiming exhaustion but then sitting awake for hours, propped up on pillows, staring at his phone. The next morning while he showered, I slid his phone from the table, opening his email, Twitter, Facebook, and Instagram for clues. When I found none, I opened his web browser to check what he'd been reading. I flicked my thumb against the screen: several pages of ASOS items, a video where a cat hides beneath a sombrero then peeks out, an article about how to remove ads from Hotmail (he used Hotmail), and buried between them the BBC report about the damage we'd done.

I left work early that afternoon, went to the supermarket, and came home with two plastic bags stuffed with food and drink. I marinated a leg of lamb in yogurt and ginger, then set about making a lemon tart. While the tart cooled in the fridge, I roasted carrots tossed in Dijon mustard and sautéed baby leeks with pancetta. I texted Adnan to find out what time he'd be home, anxiously checking on the lamb. I set everything out on the table, lit candles, and opened a bottle of red wine. At the last minute, I panicked that the gesture was not enough and threw rocket, goat cheese, and a chopped peach into a salad bowl, drizzling with olive oil.

I rushed to meet him at the door, insisted on pressing my hands to his eyes, as he sometimes did to me. I shuffled him toward the living room, revealing my feast, then swiveled around to see his reaction: a rubbery contortion of gratitude. He placed one of his large hands on my head. "This all looks delicious," he said. "What's this in aid of?"

"It's for you," I said. But of course it was not.

S tevie texted me absurdly early on Monday morning. It was the first I'd heard from her since the Selfridges disaster. Her message said RING ME NOW. Over the phone she said she had something to show me, an article. I replied that she was always wanting me to read articles and that was what work was for. Now was for sleeping in bed. She told me that I would probably want to see this one immediately, then abruptly hung up. A few seconds later, a link appeared in my messages.

The article's headline read SECRET FEASTS PUT GIRLS TO THE FRONT. My stomach turned.

It's four o'clock in the morning, and I am high on MDMA, having eaten a metric ton of soufflé.

I read the first line several times. I read the next few sentences. It was a first-person account of one of the Supper Clubs. I read it again, confused, then scrolled back to the byline. A woman called Rowena Clifton, with a little photo next to her name. It was Ashley.

I tried contacting Ashley via the email she'd given us, and she replied immediately.

Hello, Roberta,

You are no doubt disappointed, but I thought it important to tell your story, and the story of Supper Club, in the most authentic terms possible. I believe I have effectively concealed your identities, the locations of the clubs, and any distinguishing personal features.

You should also know that I have been contacted by a representative from the police force about the clubs, the break-ins. Please be assured I have protected your identities and will continue to do so. These things don't often end well, as you might imagine, and I'd advise you to be more careful in the future.

I believe I have exercised sound journalistic judgment, and I do not regret my actions. I wish you the very best luck with the Supper Club. Thank you for welcoming me into it.

Yours,

Rowena

I forwarded it straight to Stevie. She replied a full day later, a message just saying And?

In the following weeks, I left studied gaps between contacting Stevie, but still she kept retreating from me. I'd ask her if she fancied popping out for lunch. I'd invite her for a drink after work. Occasionally she'd message back to decline—more often she simply ignored me. Eventually I started making up excuses, saying I thought I'd left a book somewhere in the house, asking if I could come round and look for it. I felt the same panic I felt ten years ago, with Arnold. A flailing, not quite understanding why I'd been cast out, why I'd been abandoned—and urgently wanting to fix it. I'd send her meeting invites with cutesy titles—"*Extended cigarette break on opposite side of the road*," "*YO! Sushi Blue Monday + I Need To Tell You About My New Shoes*"—and she'd click NOT ATTENDING. Then, a few weeks after Rowena's article, I got an email from her via the Supper Club account, a proposed date and a request for venue suggestions for the next party. I scanned the message feeling breathless, looking wildly around the office for witnesses. That evening I went to Stevie and Sash's uninvited, just showing up.

Sash answered the door, and I told her I was in the area, meeting someone for a drink. She regarded me with a combination of pity and resignation, like she'd been expecting me.

"I'll just get her," she said, not inviting me inside.

Stevie arrived with her hair piled on top of her head, wearing a dressing gown I didn't recognize, cradling a large glass of white wine. I knew from the moment I tried to speak that I would have to work very hard not to cry.

"What are you doing here?" she said.

"I told Sash," I replied. "I was meeting a friend."

"What friend?"

"Someone from this class I'm taking."

"A class?"

"Yeah."

We faced each other, not talking for a moment. Stevie slumped onto her right hip, hand pressed against the doorframe, me a little colder, a little lower down. After a while she said, "I don't know what you want from me."

I removed my hands from my pockets, instinctively displaying my upturned palms. I wasn't sure what I was trying to say. That I was posing her no threat. That I was trying to divine something from the air. That I was forever presenting her with some invisible, weighted void: *Here, can you not see this? This thing right here!*

"Actually," I said, "I came for another reason, too."

"Yeah?"

"I came to say I think doing another Supper Club this soon is maybe not a good idea. We don't want to be irresponsible. I mean, I think it would be irresponsible. I don't feel comfortable with it."

As I spoke, I watched her face twist, and I had an urge to ramp things up, to say something that would hurt.

"I know you have literally nothing at risk," I continued. "Just because you have absolutely nothing else going on in your life, why put the rest of us in a dangerous situation?"

"A dangerous situation?" she replied, eyebrows stretched in incredulity. She looked like she was going to turn around, to just leave me waiting there with the door still open, then seemed to change her mind.

"Let me tell you something," she said. "You have changed. You used to be an interesting person. You used to have a rich, full life. You used to have opinions and things you actually cared about. Now all you talk about is Adnan. What Adnan is doing at work. Whether you'll meet Adnan's brother. Adnan hasn't replied to one of your texts and it's been half an hour."

She trapped the stem of her glass underneath her arm, used her hands to tighten the cord of her dressing gown, wine slopping down her front. She shut her eyes to take a breath, to telegraph that she was summoning strength.

"And you are all weird and meek around him. It's like you're constantly second-guessing him, trying so desperately to be the thing he wants from you. It's actually sincerely depressing to see. It's actually pathetic."

"Stevie." I could feel my eyelids strain closer toward each other, the way they did if I was confronted by the assertive girls at school. The same tension at my throat. My words came out sounding very small. "I just think you're being really unfair."

"You think *I'm* being unfair?" Stevie replied, her voice growing looser and louder. "You know what's unfair? Being a single woman in your late twenties, that's what's unfair. Everyone treats me like I'm fundamentally broken because I don't want this thing I'm supposed to want. I'm precluded from so many experiences. And it didn't matter because I had you, but you just abandoned me. I was just your stand-in for someone else. You think you're entitled to determine the exact nature of our relationship with your new, coupled-up entitlement. It's fucking embarrassing for you, and it's smug and it's fucking rude."

Stevie held my gaze for a second, then suddenly became very interested in the contents of her wineglass, swirling the liquid around, watching it crawl down the side. I carried on standing there, still committed to the belief that if I just presented myself, undefended, willing, eventually we would work it out.

"You know what?" she said. "You think we can't do Supper Club without you? We can. So you enjoy your break. You enjoy your Netflix and your takeaways and your sofa."

She looked me up and down.

"Now, go home," she said. "Go home to your boyfriend."

I walked home fast, replaying the conversation all the way, thinking of everything I should have said to her. Adnan was already in bed by the time I got home. I passed the open bedroom door, and he called me over, pulling back the duvet on his side so I could perch, half in and half out. I tucked my head beneath his chin. He asked me why I was crying.

"We've fallen out," I said. "Me and Stevie." Adnan pressed his hand against my hair and ear, rubbed his chin against my head.

"Poor thing," he said, and I thought, *I am. I am a poor thing.*

My phone vibrated from my coat pocket, and I felt Adnan tense. I thought it might be Stevie, apologizing or even continuing the fight—that would be better than nothing. I slid off the bed and padded across the room to check. It was another email from the Supper Club account. It said that Supper Club was on hiatus, that Stevie would be in touch. It said that she might not be in touch, actually. It said to see what happens.

"So Supper Club's over," I called from the hall, with more bravado than I felt.

"It is?" Adnan's voice was performatively casual. I scrunched up my face at his gesture of indifference, at having to be near him at all.

I brushed my teeth for longer than I needed to, then washed my face, studying all my pores. When I got into bed, Adnan dragged me over, and I felt grateful for some affection, nuzzling into his neck.

"You still have me," he said, raking his fingers through my hair. "You'll always have me."

I pictured Stevie's face. The hair piled on top of her head. The dry skin around her mouth. Her pink forehead and the beginnings of a spot. I thought about how, dancing in Selfridges, I'd suddenly remembered Adnan: evenings on the sofa with him, indifferently searching for something to watch on the television, both too tired and inert to make conversation. In that moment I had thought, *Christ, I'm glad I'm not there now.* And I thought about how, when I was with Adnan, flicking through Netflix with my feet cradled in his lap, his face soft and southward with exhaustion, I would reel back to a memory of Supper Club, see myself climbing on a table or doing a line of coke before screaming in hysterics with Stevie, and think, *Christ, I'm glad I'm not there.* The two scenarios were like silver balls, either end of a Newton's cradle, endlessly spurring each other on.

"I have you," I said to Adnan. Then, picturing Stevie's face again, I thought, *And you have no one.*

Eternal Return

A dnan had a new girlfriend. He wanted us to have a house meal so everyone could get to know her.

His girlfriend was called Freja, and she was so Swedish and so impossibly beautiful, with a blunt, asymmetrical haircut and long, slender limbs, that it was a joy just to look at her.

She was studying animal behavior and was in the UK for a year overseas, which I suspected gave her an elusive quality. I'd catch Adnan looking at her in a taut, hunted way, like he was starving and she was a meal about to be snatched from him. I wondered whether I could do such a thing. Fall into something so innately transient. Whether that ephemeral quality would allow you to relax into things completely or whether knowing that it wouldn't last would be a sustained and reckless grappling, a slow torture. I imagined I'd fall into the latter camp, and I imagined so did Adnan.

He asked us all to bring or make a dish, something from our heritage or background. Freja was bringing cinnamon pastries, and

Adnan bought Imarti from a local South Indian sweet shop. I thought about making something German, strudel or potato noodles, but settled on picking up some Eccles cakes from the shop. June baked muffins. Samuel got a Swiss roll. Mei-Ling was hungover and had forgotten.

And so we had a dinner of desserts. We thought about ordering takeaway or popping out for hummus to allow us at least the illusion of sustenance, but the whole thing seemed so unbelievably naïve and charming that we just went with it.

I'd settled into a comfortable thrum around my housemates; I was no longer worked up about my inability to connect with them on a deeper level, not laboring after the nearsighted antidote to isolation I saw in them. We'd lived in a state of tolerant and mutual disinterest for about year and a half—and that was working fine. I went about my life, and they went about theirs; only occasionally did we intersect. A few weeks earlier, a drunk student, stumbling home from a heavy night, had barged into our living room and promptly thrown up all over the floor. What began as a witch-hunt for whoever left the front door open became a collective admonition and insistence he clean up after himself. There was a certain bonding exhilaration as we all stood over him, calling him disgusting and flinging open the windows, watching him scrub the floor, hailing a cab and bundling him into it. We bitched and griped companionably for hours after that incident, well into the early morning. But we hadn't spent time together beyond it.

We'd all seen and met Freja countless times. She stayed over almost every night and could be found walking nimbly through the hallway in uniformly cute and coordinated tank tops and sleeping shorts, in search of the toilet or kitchen. But Adnan had insisted on a very formal introduction, ushering her into the kitchen while we sat around the table waiting to receive our guest.

We helped ourselves to cakes and biscuits piled onto our ramshackle bric-a-brac of dishes and bowls. The sight of so many treats produced the sick buzz of sugar coursing through my veins before I'd even had a bite: the gloopy sheen of the imarti, the buttery yellow of the pastries, the sticky sludge of frosting oozing from the Swiss roll. The sugar brought on an intense dry thirst, like a salt hangover, and we drank liberally from bottles of cheap wine, chitchatting with the ditzy fervor of a cocaine high. It was basically a children's birthday party, all of us jazzed on e-numbers, ham-fisted with overstimulation.

I'd invited Arnold knowing he wouldn't come, he couldn't come, getting annoyed and falling out with him anyway.

"You don't even like your housemates," he'd defended himself.

"That's not the point!" I retorted. "I don't like anyone except you."

Arnold was a strange secret. In the seven months we'd been together, he had never met anyone I lived with; I hadn't told my family about him; in lectures and passing in the corridor at university, we were studiously professional. He felt so present and so absent in my life, invisible yet essential, occupying all my thoughts like a deity.

"Roberta's a mystery," Adnan announced while slurping back the remnants of a glass of Blossom Hill. "Nobody knows the whole story."

"Yeah," added June. "Where do you sleep when you're not here?"

"She's got herself a little boyfriend. Or girlfriend," Adnan added quickly, turning to Freja for approval. I smiled knowingly. At least I believed I did. On most days that was half the battle.

When we couldn't bear the sight of cake anymore, we squashed into the living room. June and Samuel had fixed paper decorations to the walls, tattered streams of yellow and red, but the smell of the stranger's vomit had never really come out, so none of us especially wanted to hang around in there. It was a bright, sunny day, the first of its kind that year. The suggestion we sit in the park down the road was put forth, and suddenly we were piling treats and bottles of wine into supermarket carrier bags and heading outside.

Kicking off my shoes and lying in the grass, I felt the heavy weightlessness of alcohol supporting my body, the sun hot on my face. We languished against one another's body, limbs arranged casually around each other. The park was full of others similarly entangled—mostly students, with their make-do tribes and easy, laconic chatter. I couldn't remember the last time I'd socialized with my housemates outside our house. They could be doing any other thing, I thought. They could text their friends and be somewhere else. But they weren't.

As the light faded and the temperature cooled, we wrapped cardigans around our shoulders and gathered our knees beneath our chins. The conversation had mostly dwindled, and we were dead drunk, happy just to be there, happy to be anywhere. Adnan sat upright with Freja's head in his lap, clutching her hair in his fist like a ponytail. Mei-Ling absentmindedly checked her phone. Samuel had lost the power of speech. We clung to the feeling, knowing it was draining away, until Adnan eventually stretched and stood.

"I think we're going to take off," he said, helping Freja up. "Thanks for such a lovely day."

I watched them walk away, holding hands loosely, pausing as Adnan removed his jacket and helped Freja into it.

"I'm gonna go meet this guy." Mei-Ling gestured at her phone, pulling herself up. She looked sun-dappled and gorgeous, her hair a tangle of shiny black, her sweet summer dress made haphazard by the evening. She wrapped her thin arms around us before drifting away toward the park gates. Just Samuel, June, and I remained.

"Let's go meet Trish and Savannah," June said to Samuel, retrieving her phone from the embroidered canvas bag at her side. "You, too, Roberta."

"It's okay," I replied. "I'm just gonna stay here for a bit."

They exchanged a look I might well have imagined and departed.

Bathing in the gray wash of the early-evening light, the grass dampening beneath me, I lay there watching the different groups break off and go home, or out, leaving me staring up at the darkening sky alone. I imagined what it would be like to have somewhere to go, someone waiting to meet me. I felt suddenly sad and, strangely, a little aroused. I considered touching myself right there in the park. There was nobody else around. No one could see me. I liked the idea of coming in the fresh air, sending spirals of energy into the universe. But my thoughts turned to Michael, as they often did when I was thinking about sex, and I was suddenly extraordinarily aware of my vulnerability: lying on my back in an empty park, all alone and horny. I hoisted myself up, and instead of heading home, I went to Arnold's.

As I stood outside his front door in the luxuriantly carpeted corridors, my face felt tight and salty from sweat and sunshine, my eyes squinting as they adjusted to the artificial light. I could hear the sound of classical music playing behind the door, below it the murmur of voices. I tapped on the door and waited, feeling a swell of anxiety. I already regretted dropping in on him. As footsteps approached the door, I thought about turning to run and hide, but it was too late; it was open, and he'd already seen me, and I couldn't unsee the look of horror in his eyes.

"What are you doing here?" he asked, the sallow light a poor illumination, the space behind him a portal to my mistake. Oh God. Why had I done it?

"Can I come in?" I asked.

"It's not a great time," he said. He'd been drinking. "Why the fuck didn't you call first?"

"I ran out of battery," I replied. "I wanted to see you."

His aversion to my being there, his obvious indifference to my desire to be invited in, made me feel like I was going to cry. My throat tightened, and I knew if I said anything, I would sound pathetic. Instead I simply stood in front of him waiting to be allowed inside, as I had done many times before.

From within the flat came the boom of a voice I didn't recognize.

"Arnold! What's going on out there?"

"I think it's best you go home," Arnold said, removing a twenty-pound note from his pocket and pushing it into my hand. Shoving me back toward the corridor. "Get a taxi."

The owner of the unfamiliar voice suddenly manifested from behind him, a man several years older and a couple of inches taller than Arnold, though with the same bone structure, the same pale brown eyes.

"Oh," he said, noticing me. "I'll leave you to it."

"No. No, Chris," Arnold replied. "This is Roberta. One of my students."

Abruptly he ushered me inside, removing a jacket from the coatrack, wrapping it paternally around my shoulders.

"I had a few of them over after class a few weeks ago, you see.

And it seems she's got herself into something of a state and found her way here. Isn't that right, Roberta?"

"Right," I confirmed. My face parallel with the floor.

"I'm just going to call her a cab."

He fixed me with a blank stare I couldn't interpret, and suddenly I realized how wholly out of my depth I was.

As I advanced through the apartment, I saw two slim, attractive women in long, tapered dresses, hair tucked elegantly behind their ears, drinking wine and nibbling olives at the breakfast bar.

"And who's this?" one of them asked, her voice soft with sympathy.

"I'm Arnold's student," I said. "I'm sorry for disturbing you. I had a bad night."

"I try to reach out to some of my more troubled students," Arnold added, speaking as if I were not in the room. "Pastoral support and all that."

"Pastoral support," the other man, Chris, repeated, pointedly raising an eyebrow.

"I'm Arnold's brother," he said. "Christopher." He offered his hand, which I tentatively shook. "This is my wife, Alicia."

I shook her hand.

"And her friend, Durga."

"We've just got back from the theater, you see, and we were going to crack open a bottle of wine. Why don't you join us?"

Arnold glared furiously at his brother. Durga patted the seat next to her.

"Sit down, darling," she said.

I did.

"What have you been up to tonight?"

Arnold preempted my reply. "I'm sure Roberta won't mind me

saying so, but she's had quite a few problems making friends." I nodded, and my throat tightened again.

For the rest of the evening, I barely spoke. Christopher rested his hand on the meat of his wife's thigh. Durga and Arnold exchanged heavy-lidded glances that I presumed must mean something. They discussed the organizational politics and minutiae of their respective jobs, considered the best places to visit in Portugal.

Christopher asked if I wouldn't mind fetching some more olives from the fridge, and I dutifully obliged, trotting them back over to him and placing them on the table as he reached around his arm and squeezed my bottom, in full view of the room. When I caught Arnold's eye, he quickly looked away like he was terribly embarrassed that I even existed. After a couple of bottles had gone, Christopher, Alicia, and Durga called for a taxi and then left. As the door shut behind them, Arnold walked past me and poured himself a large glass of whiskey. I followed him, hovering in the doorframe.

"Hey," I said, because I wanted to say something, to hear my own voice out loud. Arnold knocked back some, exposing his teeth to demonstrate the manly punch of his chosen drink.

"Why aren't you saying anything to me?" I asked, his silence intolerable. He wouldn't meet my eye, just resting his hand on the kitchen counter and staring at it, like the world and its miseries were his alone to bear.

"You are a disgrace," he said after a while. "A fucking disgrace."

He moved to the living room without meeting my eye, sat, and switched on the television, something I had never before seen him do.

I followed meekly and sat next to him.

"I'm sorry," I said. "I just wanted to—"

"You just wanted to what? You think you can just show up here whenever you want?"

"I don't—"

"And yet you always find a way, don't you? You always find a way to be here."

He flicked through the channels, knocking back more of his whiskey, swirling the liquid quickly around the glass.

"And you stay! You just expect to be able to stay."

I didn't know what to say, and so I stared straight ahead, watching the channels change, a succession of advertorials featuring white women in kitchens, police and courtroom dramas with hammy fonts and poor film stock, late-night panel shows about the issues. Finally he settled on one, a pay-per-view cam girl with long, flat hair and impossibly shiny lips. He leaned back into the sofa and straightened out his legs, taking deep and deliberate gulps from his drink. His eyes were fixed on the screen. The woman was a couple of years older than me, in red pants and a tank top that said BABY. Periodically she'd flip up her top, revealing her pert, perfect breasts, or push down her knickers to show her thin sprinkling of pubic hair. At one point she dragged her left breast out of her bra and fed her nipple into her mouth, flicking it with her tongue. Eventually she produced a sex toy and lay back, her legs high and wide like a gymnast's, humping the pink phallus, screaming like she either was or was not having fun.

I noticed Arnold's hand, balled into a fist at his side. He'd nearly finished his whiskey. A tear rolled down my cheek, but I was too scared to catch it, feeling it slide down my neck and land on the skin beneath my T-shirt. And I understood, for the first time, there could be an anger that was different from fists and yelling, that was beyond those things entirely.

Winter Sunshine

My favorite thing about making Thai red curry is adding the sugar. There's something about the grit and sparkle, the texture of it as you push it around the bowl.

Begin by frying up ginger, garlic and chilies, then blitz the lemongrass, which will make the kitchen smell very clean. Put it all into a mortar and smash together with shrimp paste and fish sauce. You don't actually add sugar until the very end, once you've worked all the ingredients together. You don't want the crunch of it to get lost. You only ever need a pinch.

Fry the paste again until it goes a deep red-brown. Fry it until it makes your eyes burn. Then toss in any vegetables or meat—my preference is duck with green peppers. Once the meat is browned, you can begin spooning in the coconut milk, watching the silky white emulsion of it turn orange. Reduce the heat and leave it to simmer for around twenty minutes. You might use this time to reply to messages on your phone or, better, to scan Netflix for something to watch. You really don't want to have dinner ready and the evening's viewing still not determined. After twenty minutes it should be ready to serve.

Thai red curry always catches me by surprise. I always expect it to turn out much thicker than it does, for it to have more form, more substance. I will often stir it and turn up the heat, willing it to thicken, awaiting some transformation. But it is not a thick curry. It is thin and watery, and there is nothing wrong with that. It should be served in a bowl and eaten like a soup.

M y mum asked if Adnan and I would come up for the weekend. Sheila had recently moved in, so now my family home was also hers, and with it came the clutter and ephemera of her life, which sort of made sense and sort of didn't. She had a collection of tiny teacups and saucers, hand-crocheted blankets and throws. The porch now bore a dream catcher, a webbed circle with a dangle of feathers. She had a thing for schnauzers, and so little pottery approximations of the things could be found across the surfaces, stitched onto pillows and the pockets of aprons. The bathroom smelled of mint and patchouli oil. The cupboards had foods I was unfamiliar with, which was the most dislocating detail by far. Who the hell was buying cheddar oatcakes? Who ate pumpernickel bread? Who would even want to?

My mum had always been characterized by a quiet spirit and re-solve. Coming home, I found that this had changed a little. She had softened. She'd leave the washing-up for Sheila, ask her what was wrong with the Wi-Fi, looking sweetly on as Sheila reset it. And while I was pleased she'd found somebody she loved, someone who loved her back, I felt an infinitesimal curl of, I suppose, disgust. She mollified her voice when talking to Sheila. She fussed girlishly with her hair at the mere mention of Sheila's name. She teared up at the news. She was talking about early retirement and moving to France. She had become lazy and weak—just like me.

Mum had made a fuss about having a special dinner, the occasion of which I presumed was Adnan. I said I would cook, making a lamb-and-thyme stew, pan-fried herbed potatoes, stuffed cabbage. I could hear Adnan talking to my mum, Sheila, and Hetty in the living room, holding his own and making them giggle. He kept loudly appraising the smell of the stew, saying, "Am I a lucky guy or am I a lucky guy?"

After we had eaten, I fetched the heavy-bottomed crystal glasses from the kitchen and poured us all a measure of whiskey. It was a ritual of ours, a private tradition, and tradition was something I was always happy invoking. But my mum sprang to her feet, saying she actually had a little something else cooling in the fridge. She came back with a bottle of champagne and five glass flutes. I started feeling embarrassed; she was about to do something humiliating, like toast to my having a boyfriend, such an occasion was it for her daughter to bring home a man.

"A little announcement," she said, and I noticed Sheila looking flushed. She lifted her glass.

"As you know," she said, "Sheila and I have been together for a little while now. Well, we're very happy, and we want to do something to mark that happiness."

I stopped breathing.

"We're getting married!" she said, and turned to kiss Sheila.

Nobody said anything until my aunt got onto her feet. She shuffled over to clink glasses, merrily said "Congratulations!" and kissed them both on the cheek. Adnan followed suit, warmly embracing them, saying they were a lovely couple who had made him feel totally welcome and at ease. I remained seated and stunned, squeezing my fist beneath the table so all my fingernails dug into the doughy flesh of my hand. I thought about biting my tongue so hard that it bled, imagining the coppery taste of blood, its base relief. *Here I am. I can still bleed.*

I'd been to only a handful of weddings in my life, always marveling at their total abstraction, like finding out your friends own a yacht or are furries. I wondered what sort of people even had weddings—and how they planned and paid for them. It was like my mum was revealing herself as part reptile. I noticed Adnan looking at me from across the room and felt duly chastened, getting up to say the normal things that were expected of me. I thought about what Stevie had said about couples and individualism, how she felt squeezed out of that community.

That evening, getting ready for bed, I whispered my main points to Adnan. They hadn't been together long enough. They were making a stupid mistake. I felt angry at them but I didn't know why. He listened silently and rubbed my back and looked concerned. Eventually I ran out of things to say.

Staring down at my socked feet resting on the faded carpet, I thought about Sheila and her long, draped clothes, the pendants that swayed at her navel. I sort of hated her. But it was something else, too. Of course I was capable of feeling authentic joy on behalf of other people—I was happy for my mum and had been since the beginning of her relationship—but the feeling was in flux, undulating. It couldn't be summoned on demand. I would squeeze toothpaste from its tube or grate cheese into a mixing bowl and think suddenly of my mum and Sheila with a warmth of sincere pleasure. I felt the same about my own happiness: it wasn't something I could perform.

I slipped out of the bedroom to fetch a glass of water and found

Sheila and my mum lingering in the hallway, holding hands and fidgeting. I was struck with an urge to do or say something cruel.

"Oh, yeah," I said. "I've been meaning to say. I've been emailing Dad."

I was hoping to sound flippant, but it came out acidic and warped. My mum went pale. Sheila wasn't sure what was happening, offering my mum catchall looks of comfort anyway.

"He got in touch a while ago," I said. "We've been emailing back and forth. He's cool. He lives in New York now."

"Right," she said. "I didn't know that. I didn't know you'd been doing that."

"Why would you? It's really nice, you know. To have the opportunity to actually, like, get to know my dad. It's sort of ridiculous I've not had it before. I guess it was never an option for me. For some reason."

She looked more troubled than I'd anticipated, but somehow I didn't care. "Can we talk about this more?" she said. "Can we talk about it properly in the morning?"

"If you want," I said, shrugging past them and down the stairs.

The next morning I asked Adnan if we could leave immediately. I just wanted to be home. I wanted to lie on my own bed, with its specific shape and lumps. I wanted to be tucked between my own sheets, which were soft and pliant from having not been recently washed, not the unyielding sheets I was currently trapped under, stiff with starch and smelling aggressively of detergent.

I got up as he snoozed, started packing my bag, then packing his—prodding him awake to ask what he was planning on wearing today. He rolled onto his back and made a show of rubbing his eyes.

I picked up his blue sweater and a pair of clean boxers. "These?" I asked. "Can I pack everything else away?"

He made a low moan, one that began in his nose and reverberated around his throat. It was a significant articulation of displeasure for him.

"What?" I said, snapping, spoiling for a fight. "What have I done now?"

"Fuck's sake, Roberta," he said, moving through the syllables as if each one contained a specific clue to my own absurdity. He clambered out of bed, and I momentarily thought about how good his body looked, that I could not believe he was in a relationship with me. He pulled the blue sweater over his head. I thought about asking him whether he was going to have a shower. He usually had a shower. Why wasn't he having a shower?

"Why are we rushing?" Adnan asked, watching me peer beneath the bed, sweep my arm underneath it to make sure nothing was lost there, something I had never previously done. "Why are you being so weird?"

"How am I being weird? Don't call me weird. You know I hate being called weird."

"You're acting all manic, and I don't know why."

I felt a sudden pain in both my wrists. I wanted to flip from fighting to care. *My hands hurt! Adnan! Give me a break!*

"I just want to get out of here, okay? I feel suffocated. I can't breathe. I want to go home."

"Why do you feel *suffocated*? Why are you being so dramatic?"

"I'm being dramatic? Oh, I'm the one being dramatic, am I? *I've* not just bloody announced I'm marrying this person I've known for about thirty seconds. *I'm* not acting like somebody's long-lost bloody son."

I watched Adnan's face flicker, a defensive gesture. There were no casual cruelties with him, and I knew I'd been reckless. He picked up the case I had packed for him, then put it back down, surveying the room, searching for a purpose.

"Have you ever thought about us getting married?" he asked finally. "Have you thought that might be something I'd like one day? Because you being horrified at the thought of it really upsets me. Can't you see that? Do you ever actually think about *my* feelings? Do you even want me here?"

I watched how he presented himself to me, the way he turned out his wrists so I could see them, his feet placed so close together that pushing him over would be easy. I *had* given marriage a lot of thought, as it happened. Sitting on the sofa watching television. Eating breakfast out of the flat. Lying in bed and talking in the dark. I felt the word "marriage" pulsate like the chug of a train beneath us. I was almost thirty. All his friends were married. It was the right time. But the concept of marriage seemed an impossible one, like picturing a color you'd never previously seen. And yet I knew I wanted things from him. I wanted how we were never to end. There had to be a price for that.

He moved around the room in his sweatshirt and boxers. Bent over to unplug his phone charger. Plumped the pillows and arranged the duvet. I stood to the side of the bed staring at him with a quiet feeling of terror. This large adult man in the bedroom of my childhood, this perfect stranger who wanted me to consider spending the rest of my life with him, to make him a deal.

"I mean, would it really be so terrible? Christ knows you like a fucking party. Clearly just not one where I'm invited."

"I'm sorry," I said, sitting down on the bed. I started to cry, and though I wasn't crying intentionally to get out of the argument, I knew it would help.

Across the room I noticed Adnan soften. He moved toward me. He sat down beside me and a few seconds later pulled his arm around me.

"Hey," he said. "I didn't mean to yell. It's just that I love you, and I'm serious about this."

I felt hurt by this thought, but I wasn't sure why. I also did not dare unilaterally state anything that might compromise our future. And yet the prospect of that future felt blurry and opaque. I wanted to perch on this tightrope forever.

I put my hand on top of his. "I love you," I said. And then, "And there's no one else I want to be with."

Done, I thought. *I've done it. It will be over now. It will be a conversation from the past.*

We heard the scrabble of dog feet and then yapping at the door. Ordinarily Joan of Arc would sleep on my bed, but Adnan was ever so slightly allergic. Life seemed like a series of some people coupling up and others being shut out as a direct result.

Adnan suggested we take her for a walk. In the park we let her off her lead, and she did her best to race ahead. She was slow and unsteady, tired with age and wobbly with cataracts. Adnan and I sat on the bench. When I made a gesture of being cold, he put his arm around me. In a thick coat, he felt even meatier. I wondered if his body was my favorite object in the whole world.

Walking back to the house, Joa trotted alongside us as Adnan clutched my hand tight. We were wrapped up in our winter finest, looking cozy and cute in our woolen hats and scarves. I thought about what I'd said, about not wanting to be with anyone else, and realized I hadn't even considered being with anyone else, that it hadn't occurred to me at all. I wondered if that meant I loved him very much or not enough.

We got in, and my mum was watching television while Sheila

washed up in the kitchen. "Come look!" my mum was shouting through to her soon-to-be wife. "It's that dog advert you like. The one with the paws." I rolled my eyes at Adnan. He shook his head, indulging me. We went through.

"Good walk?" my mum asked, wrapped up and eating biscuits on the sofa.

"A lovely walk," I said. "We're ready for some breakfast."

My mum got to her feet and began apologizing for having not made us anything.

"We've just had some poached eggs, I'm afraid," she said, her voice higher-pitched than usual. "I'm sorry. We should have thought you might like some."

She started fussing around the kitchen, looking for a pan and switching on the kettle.

"It's okay, we'll just have cereal," I said. I poured us both a bowl. We sat side by side eating Weetabix. *We're like brother and sister,* I thought. *We're like two little kids.* I put down my spoon and pushed forward my upturned wrists to him. "I've really hurt my wrists," I said. "They're really sore."

"Oh, no!" he said, gathering them into his hands, kissing them all the way around and then rubbing them with his fingers. "You poor little thing."

Sometimes I would be drying the dishes or hoovering the carpet or watching television while plucking bobbles of wool from Adnan's sweatshirt, and I would feel certain I was about to scream. I would have to concentrate very hard on not screaming, like it was a sneeze or a yawn, something beyond my control, almost impossible to avert.

And I flip-flopped between anger and an indefinable guilt about

Stevie. Why could she not just be happy for me? She had spent so much time telling me I never went for the things I wanted, that I couldn't even name my own desires. I'd find myself arguing with her in my head more and more often. Walking to the shop or sitting at my desk, I'd feel the dull crescendo of a migraine, having spent hours with my face bunched up, mentally defending my position. I wondered whether it was normal to be chopping potatoes and have to set down the knife and lie on the bed just to catch my breath because I was so wound up by the mere thought of my friend.

Some mornings I would watch Adnan sleeping and want desperately for him to wake up so I could share the insights and analysis I had generated the night before, staring at the ceiling, unable to sleep. I'd make him a coffee just to wake him, just so he would listen to me. But I knew he was not listening, was bored and frustrated, wondering why we were still having this conversation. He would tell me to stay in bed while he made breakfast, leaving me alone with my grievances multiplying and nowhere to put them. When he returned, I would have to play up my gratitude, and he would watch me dunk toast into a boiled egg and tell me that, see, all I needed was a little looking after. I wanted to weaponize his kind gestures. *Adnan made me the most delicious breakfast in bed this morning*, I imagined telling Stevie. *We had the most wonderful day at the gallery.*

At the weekends Adnan invited his friends over. He enjoyed acting the host, taking all their coats and getting them a drink. He would turn up the heating or open a window. "Too hot or too cold?" he would ask, lingering in the doorway, expecting a response. "Too hot or too cold?" One evening we were eating noodles on the sofa, hosting a film night, and someone spilled apple juice across the carpet. It left behind a stain that we did not try to remove.

We booked a trip to Skiathos. I bought beachwear and a large hat. Adnan spent hours trying on sunglasses, but none of them suited the shape of his head. He researched podcasts and loaded them up on my phone. He made a playlist for the flight. He made a playlist for lying by the beach. He made a playlist for getting ready before we went out at night.

At the airport we had our first giant fight. I cried in Boots after he'd yelled at me in Carluccio's. I didn't realize fights could have such longevity, such . . . fight. It was like a game of whack-a-mole. Just when we thought it had been bopped on the head, it shot back up, as shameless and insistent as ever. It was horrifying, but there was also something exhilarating about it. Testing our boundaries. Finding out what we could come back from. We sulked for days.

On the island we sat by the pool. We read in the sun. We walked up a hill. We visited an old church. We went out for pizza. Adnan asked me to photograph him swimming in the sea. One night the hotel ran out of halal meat, and so for dinner he was offered margarine and bread. I went to ask the waiter if they could arrange something else. If they had any fish they could give him or a vegetarian option. He told me it was a set menu and there was nothing he could do. I went back to Adnan. "What are you doing?" he asked.

"I'm just doing my best," I snapped.

On the flight home, I flipped through a magazine while Adnan listened to music. We ordered rum and Cokes and toasted to our holiday. I wanted to buy a duty-free perfume, but Adnan told me not to bother. He said I smelled good enough. Not good enough to eat— just good enough. For the last half hour, I fell asleep, dribbling a round patch of saliva onto his shirt.

As we queued for a taxi, I shivered in my beach shorts and camisole. Adnan gave me his jacket. "I actually prefer the cold," he said.

"I never did like the heat." When we got home, we ordered Chinese food and ate it in bed.

The boiler broke. Then the curtain rail broke. Then the toilet broke again. The windows always smelled of bleach. One morning while making breakfast, I drank the last of the previous night's wine.

Often I felt as if I were positioned outside my own body. Sometimes I would be on the roof. Other times I perched on the telephone wires outside. Sometimes I was much farther away—out in a forest or up in the clouds. Some evenings Adnan watched me as I was cooking in the kitchen, and I noticed a panicked look in his eyes.

We fought about the boiler. Adnan kept fixing it, only for it to break again. I kept asking if we could just get a plumber in or ask the landlord—but he refused. "I can do it," he said. "I can fix it." We would fight about it, then go to bed in terrible moods. Sometimes he would pull me toward him in the middle of the night, forgetful in sleep. Sometimes I would creep my arm around him, wanting the comfort of his back. One night I stared at Adnan's shoulders, watched the curve of his spine heaving up and down. I heard a little gasp. He was crying.

"What's wrong?" I asked. I rubbed his back beneath his T-shirt. His T-shirt looked blue in the dark, though I knew it was red. I wondered how something could look like one thing, then all of a sudden, look like something completely different.

It was unusual for Emmeline to invite herself over—not because we didn't hang out sometimes but because she was not ordinarily so assuming. She was very softly-spoken; during the first Supper Clubs, Stevie would have her scream at the top of her lungs. She would have her sing along to songs as loudly as she could. "Use your *voice*," Stevie would implore. "I can't *hear* you!"

I laid out several plates for summer rolls. I'd spiralized carrots into long, thin ribbons. I'd chopped avocados and dressed them with lime juice. I'd made a chickpea-and-peanut curry and a big pan of rice. When Emmeline arrived, I offered her a glass of wine, which she declined, and it occurred to me that I didn't have to drink either. Instead I made a pot of mint tea, giving her the cup that looked like a glitter ball while I had the one that said KEEP CALM & WATCH STAR TREK. It was Adnan's favorite cup.

I showed her how to dip the rice papers into hot water and fold them up into rolls. I sensed that there was something she wasn't saying, but instead of making the requisite silence for her to tell me, I began chattering nonsense, nervously filling the expectant space with words. Eventually I just said, "So Facebook tells me you're back with André?"

Emmeline's mouth was stuffed with rice and curry, and she made a small slurping sound as she struggled to chew and get it down. I apologized, told her to take her time, at which she pointed to her mouth and animatedly chomped, demonstrating her compliance. Once she had swallowed, I watched as she mined stray bits of chickpea and fragments of rice from her teeth, sweetly dabbing her lips with a napkin.

"Yes," she said with the somber tone of confession. "We got back together about two months ago. We ran into each other at the cinema. We were both there watching some J. J. Abrams thing on our own. Pathetic, really. We saw each other just before the trailer started, so we sat together and ended up going for a drink after."

She lifted and then dropped her shoulders like *It must have been fate.* When we'd interviewed Emmeline, she told us she'd been raised to understand two fundamental truths: that light mayonnaise was an abomination and that the universe was trying to speak to you.

Emmeline's mother worked for a rental agency, and her job mostly involved showing sullen and ingrate students around rotting houses, trying to convince them that with a lick of paint and a flush of the toilet these places weren't quite as hideous as they seemed. Her father was a manager at Marks & Spencer and was always coming home with expired yet edible food, with really good cardigans and socks. But one time instead of coming home with an aubergine Parmesan or a discontinued thick-knit wrap, he came home with a woman he'd met at the pub, sitting her down at the dinner table and introducing her to his wife and two children before taking her up to his bedroom. That was the first time the universe had tried to speak to Emmeline, and it was saying, *Your dad is trash.*

Despite this hiccup, her mother stayed with him, and though for a while he made a show of attending Alcoholics Anonymous and Sex and Love Addicts Anonymous, he soon went back to his drinking, to his philandering. One night her mother knocked on Emmeline's door and threw herself on her daughter's bed, wailing, "What do I do, darling, what am I supposed to do?" The next morning at breakfast, her mum plainly told her she must have had a bad dream, because she was looking very tired. And that it wasn't nice to tell people about your bad dreams, but if you wanted to tell them about a nice dream, then they would likely be all ears. That was the second time the universe had tried to speak to Emmeline, and it was saying, *Your mother is crackers, she is weak and sad and damaged beyond repair.*

Emmeline moved out when she was seventeen, living with a friend's family over the Thai restaurant they owned and ran. She'd work in the kitchen at the weekends and in the evenings. During the week she would go to the art galleries around town, catching every exhibition she could, sometimes visiting the same exhibitions several times, sometimes just sitting in one of the rooms and closing her eyes. One afternoon she was returning to an exhibition about artists influenced by Chagall and one of the gallery staff asked her which course she was on. "Which course?" she replied, and the staff member said, "Yes—history of art, fine art, interactive arts—which one?" That was the third time the universe had tried to communicate with her, and it was saying, *You should study art, dummy.*

She enrolled on a history of art BA. She wanted to carry on studying for as long as she could—so after her BA she did an MA, and after that she got funding to do a PhD. It was during the PhD that she met André, who was doing a PhD by practice, at the same school. One evening she went to one of his performances and as part of it he removed his shirt. That was the fourth time the universe had tried to communicate with her, and it was saying, *You really want to have sex with this man.*

André and Emmeline had been together for two years, including six months in Berlin, when he first introduced her to Stevie, this beautiful, extroverted, charming woman he swore he had no feelings for. Emmeline started getting suspicious of the amount of time they were spending together, suspicious of the fact he never invited Emmeline along to any of their meet-ups. Eventually she demanded they hang out as a group, and so they went over to her place for dinner. It was fine, and Stevie was very nice to her, but this didn't quell her suspicions, and so one evening she looked through all the texts and emails in his phone, establishing that, yes, he did have feelings for Stevie, had acted on these feelings, and they'd been sleeping together for months. That was the fifth time the universe had tried to communicate with her, and it was saying, *Your boyfriend is trash, just like your trash dad.*

She had split up with André and was concentrating on her PhD when she heard about the plan to start a secret society of women, run by the woman who had literally given her irritable bowel syndrome. She had agreed to meet Stevie and hear her out, mostly to have the pleasure of telling her to fuck off in person, and had been surprised to realize, firstly, that she liked Stevie a lot and, secondly, that she didn't hold the affair against her. She attended one Supper Club, then another, then found herself a member. Over a year later, she ran into her ex-boyfriend, André, at the cinema, while they were both alone, both about to watch the same film. That was the sixth time the universe had tried to communicate with her, and it was saying, *You should get back together with this man who treated you poorly but who says he is sorry and who you have been in love with all along—also, this time maybe it will be different?*

I asked her how it was going. She told me it was going very well. He was willing to do more of the stuff she liked and was spending a lot less time in the studio.

"I just love him," she said with some resignation. "I just do."

I swirled a summer roll through the sweet chili sauce. I got the feeling she wanted me to collude with her on this point, to tell her, *Yes, I understand, I'm the same, too.* I decided to change the subject. I asked her about her work.

"Actually," she said. "That's what I wanted to talk to you about."

"Oh, yeah?"

"So I'm part of this new research cluster, and we're doing lots of work around the visual arts and philosophy. Anyway, there's a small group of us who are hosting a conference together. We went out for dinner the other night, and I got speaking to this guy, and it turns out he knows you."

"Oh. Right?"

"Well, he used to know you. He was asking lots of questions about you, how you're getting on and everything. He said he'd thought about getting in touch with you, but he's worried you might not want to hear from him."

"Well, who is he?" I said, straining for an answer. "Who is he?"

"He's called Arnold. Arnold Falvo. Apparently you dated?"

The Rice Bowl was famous for once having been on TV. They were part of a makeover show where they fired their chef, a hulking guy with tattoos covering his lower arms and probably his upper arms, too, but only the lower section was visible in his chef's uniform. They invited him to sit down at one of the tables beside the window and told him he would have to find a job somewhere else. His menu had become bland and uninspired, and they needed to modernize and bring in someone fresh. He stared outside for a long while, and in the background you could make out a tiny dog staring back at him, and it seemed terribly sad—this gigantic man and this terrier gazing at each other through the glass. Then he stood up to leave, shaking his old manager's hand, saying he was grateful for her candor, and they played sad music as he walked out the door. The camera followed him all the way to his car, and I wondered how he felt having to maneuver out of a tight parking spot, whether he was worried he might stall, how they probably wanted him to seem ineffectual and pathetic. Now the restaurant is very busy and popular, and they have their own line of expensive sauces. I booked a table for late afternoon on a Sunday. I was meeting my dad.

They gave me the table by the window, the one the old chef was fired in. I arrived first and ordered a gin and tonic, then immediately worried that my dad would think me gauche or unseemly, his grown daughter drinking alone in the middle of the day. I changed my order to a sparkling water with a slice of lemon, though I do not like pieces of lemon in my drink. I can't stand the stringy bits of pulp and the half flavor.

I'd spent a long time curating my outfit. It's hard to know what to wear to a fancy restaurant. I'd opted for a pleated skirt and a button-down blouse, a pair of patent Mary Janes. I was considering heels but remembered my mum telling a story in which she wore platforms on one of their first dates and he had commented that in those boots she was taller than him, and she had understood not to wear them again. I looked down at the shoes I'd chosen instead, how childish they seemed: the strap making two broken ovals, like the droopy eyes of a cartoon. I thought about how my dad might respond to seeing me, whether he would be disappointed to find I was not thin or even thinnish. I wondered whether I might embarrass him by ordering too much or the wrong things from the menu. I started shifting in my seat and thought about draping my coat across my waist to disguise the indent of my skirt into my belly. I could tell him it was keeping me warm. When the waiter came back, I told him I would have that gin and tonic after all.

I checked the time on my phone. It was fifteen minutes past when we were supposed to meet. I felt a wriggle of nerves, or perhaps anticipation, imagining that he was probably having a hard time finding the place, that he had not been back here in a while. I looked around the room, pressing my elbows against the hard surface of the table, and wondered about the circumstances under which other people were meeting. Everyone in the room seemed as uncomfortable as I was, shifting their weight in the solid wooden chairs, trying to arrange their arms on the too-high tables. There was so much hardness everywhere, so many sharp angles, different ways to fall and break a bone or get jabbed in the hip by a table's edge.

I checked my phone again. Only three minutes had elapsed. I felt stupid for having not brought a book. Now, when my dad arrived, he would feel bad, finding me awkward and restless, with nothing to occupy my hands. Or else he would find me staring at my phone like some slack-jawed teenager. It occurred to me that I should look up an interesting article, so perhaps we would have something extra to talk about. I scanned Twitter for things he might be interested in, but they all seemed so banal: *Is this TV show feminist? How women are erased from work.* Instead I visited some of the news sites I no longer had time to browse in the office, finding an article about evolving drug policies in Norway. I read the first paragraph a number of times but couldn't get it to stick.

I had a sudden pang of panic that I'd gotten the date wrong, checking the last email he'd sent me, which I had screen-grabbed onto my phone. The twenty-fifth. I checked my calendar. As the waiter walked by again, I asked him if today was definitely the twenty-fifth. He said he would check, went away, then came back over and said that it was. I reluctantly replied to the last email my dad had sent me—"Still on today?"—adding a kiss. I removed the kiss. I added it again in case I seemed annoyed. I ordered another drink and decided I would not check my email until ten minutes had passed. When he hadn't replied after that, I decided to give it another ten. The waiter asked whether I was ready to order food yet. I said I still had not made up my mind, and he did me the kindness of pretending that really was the case. "No problem," he said. "I recommend the moo shu pork."

I got out my phone again and watched it with a feeling of wildness and urgency, this stupid metallic slab that I poured so much of myself into. I thought about ringing my mum, but she didn't know I was planning to meet him. I thought about ringing Stevie, but she hated me now. I thought about ringing Adnan, but I couldn't bear the thought of it, couldn't bear him offering to come meet me, telling me everything would turn out fine. I thought about the email I'd written to my dad, how I initially confessed I was having a tricky time with my boyfriend but deleted that and instead wrote, "I live with my boyfriend, who is just lovely!" How that no doubt came across insipid and braggy, insensitive because he lived alone. I opened up my email to reread it, to decode the clues. I spotted a new message from Emmeline.

> Hey, girl, thanks for dinner. Here's Arnold's email address, in case you want to get in touch (he insisted I pass it on!). See you soon
>
> x

I stared at it for a long time, annexing off the part of my mind that told me to delete it, that told me not to look at it again. I opened up a new message.

> Hi, Arnold. It's Roberta. Long time no see.

I paid for my drinks and went home.

I kept imagining the look of Arnold's name in my in-box, bracing myself for that moment. I checked my phone constantly. Adnan reprimanded me about how much time I was spending gazing at it. He said he'd started having a dream where he ripped it out of my hands and threw it out the window. I'd started having a dream where all my teeth fell out. I'd line them up on a table, little white soldiers, and then one by one I would put them back into my mouth, swallowing them down with a glass of water like they were Tylenol.

His reply eventually came when I was at the supermarket buying the ingredients for a stew. I opened my mail app out of habit and saw Arnold's name waiting at the top of my in-box. I had to sit on the back of my heels in front of the bread to read it, a knuckle of sourdough hovering in front of my face like a threat.

Hello, Roberta. It's lovely to hear from you, and thank you for reaching out. I wonder whether you might want to meet up at some point. Just for lunch or a cup of tea. Whatever suits. All best. A

I read it a few times over. Then I put my phone in my bag and went home. I cooked dinner, which Adnan and I ate on the sofa, dunking chunks of bread into a smoky lentil stew. After dinner I reorganized the drawer where we kept the tape and stray pieces of twine. Adnan asked if I wanted to watch an episode of *Parks and Recreation* before we went to bed, and so I sat and did that with him. I brushed my teeth, and then I joined him in bed, trying to relax each of my muscles one by one, the way they advise insomniacs to do. I didn't look at my phone until the next day, exercising the kind of manic discipline that comes from wanting to appear aloof. I started replying while walking to work. This made me feel like I was channeling an air of flippancy.

Hello, Arnold. Thanks for getting back to me. I'm afraid my weekends are all booked up at the moment, but perhaps one night after work?

I decided not to send it until I was at my desk, where I fiddled with the wording of the message for so long that words stopped being words and felt more like objects—objects I was arranging to determine my level of intelligence or where I fell on the autism spectrum. I waited two hours before pressing SEND. Arnold replied immediately.

> Thanks for getting back to me. I'm afraid weeknights are no good for me, as I'm prepping classes, have tutorials, research (etc etc). Are you sure you cannot fit me in at the weekend? A

I read the message. I had only said the thing about weekends to look busy and fulfilled. I felt myself grapple with how to undo it, to accommodate and make room. I could not believe he'd dealt me such a devastating blow, such a sharp calling of my bluff. I quickly replied in order to crisis-manage.

> Hello, Arnold. You know, I think I could fit you in at the weekend. I might have some time this weekend, actually.

As I pressed SEND, I immediately regretted not including a question. I remembered our messages at university, how I would carefully punctuate mine with questions, something for him to respond to—then, getting caught up, would forget myself and send him a message containing just a joke or an observation about my day and would not receive a reply until I fired up the conversation again. It was exhausting. I realized that even this brief exchange of messages had left me exhausted. I texted Adnan for some reprieve.

> What you up to?

He replied back immediately, Nothing, followed by a string of emojis. Cat with heart eyes. Yellow man having head massaged. Monkey with hands covering face. Feces.

Table Service

It was Arnold's birthday, and he wanted to go out for dinner. I was flattered that he had elected to spend it with me, even more so when I found out it was a Michelin-starred restaurant with bedrooms upstairs. He emailed me a link ahead of our visit, and I replied saying it looked very expensive. He wrote back that it certainly seemed like he would be picking up the bill, as usual, and so I didn't have to worry about that.

From the outside it looked like a little stone cottage, and I thought there was a haughtiness in its pointed simplicity. Inside, there were clean wooden tables and exposed-timber ceilings, a roaring open fire at the side. Arnold had booked us a table at the window so we could see out onto the river—and even though it was too dark to make out much, occasionally a scythe of light would catch where the moon hit the water. The sound of violins played perpetually from somewhere unseen, and flickering candlelight gave the evening a gothic feel. It felt both vivid and unreal: a diorama at Epcot, a cartoon hole painted onto a wall.

The waiter took our coats and pulled out my seat, confirming we'd ordered the tasting menu with wine. I'd bought a special dress for the occasion, scoop-necked and velvet. Arnold wore a slate-gray suit. When the waitress brought us our drinks, we pressed our glasses together. "Happy birthday to me," Arnold toasted wryly. To anyone glancing over, we might have looked like a perfectly normal couple.

The food was like nothing I'd ever seen—let alone something I'd eaten or enjoyed. Each dish was small and abstract. A separated yolk sitting solo: a bright yellow blob. Oysters whipped into macarons. Lamb cheek with fermented artichokes and smoked cream, a stringy mess of sweetness and earth. A burned-sugar-and-yogurt tart, all richness and crunch. Between each course we were served a small glass of wine, which had a more watery quality than the cheap wine I was used to. It didn't require that barbarous first sip, the first brutal jump into a swimming pool. It was like wading into warmth.

As the meal neared its end, I leaned back into my chair, noticing with some objectivity that I was drunk and not unhappy. The light was low and soft. The forestry of the interior and the thick pliancy of the tablecloths gave me a feeling of being swaddled. I felt padded, inside and out, full of food and cosseted in this lavishly cozy atmosphere.

I ate the last bite of my tart and, forgetting myself, made an emphatic sound, placing down my dessert fork, gratuitously patting my stomach. A waitress appeared over my left shoulder, elegantly removing the dish and fork, sweeping around to take Arnold's, too. As she walked away, I felt a strange twist in the atmosphere.

"I wasn't finished with that," Arnold said. I breathed through the shift in tone. It felt as if all the birds should be flying away, escaping something seismic.

Trying to avert the inevitable, I turned around to beckon the waitress back, but she was already away in the kitchen. I told Arnold we should say something, making my voice warm and supportive. I suggested we might get another (free!) dessert.

"I don't want another dessert," he replied after some time. "I want the base dignity of being able to finish what is in front of me."

"Maybe they'll knock something off the bill," I offered. "Or give us a round of free drinks."

I watched the ugly swell of indignation rising within him, something wild and untethered, all ego and entitlement. As the waitress approached the table, I tried to communicate to her with my eyes. Her white shirt clung efficiently to her slim frame. When I noticed how attractive she was, I thought, *You're on your own.*

"Can I get you any more drinks?" she asked. "Or would you like to see our cheeseboard?"

"What we would like is an apology for this abysmal level of service," Arnold replied. "Might you scamper back into the kitchen and get us that?"

I saw her flush with many things: the rot and humiliation of being an adult and being told off, the verisimilitude of understanding this is not the job you ever wanted and yet here you are, not being very good at it and actually caring.

"I'm so sorry," she began, summoning composure. "What seems to be the problem?"

"The problem," Arnold asserted, "is that I wonder whether you imagine I would like to eat the food you serve here or simply to gaze at it?"

"I'm not sure I understand."

"Oh, I am quite sure you do *not* understand."

I saw the small muscles in her hands flex at her sides. The sinews in her neck tighten. I watched as she twisted degradation into resolve. I wanted her to teach me those tricks.

"I am sorry if something has not been to your liking," she replied eventually. "I'm sure a small deduction to your bill can be arranged."

She quickly turned to leave. I admired her for not answering the question. I also resented her because I could see she was attracted to him.

After the meal we had aerobic and spirited sex. It occurred to me that my body was a stand-in for her body and I was being punished. But then my thoughts turned to the pale moon of my stomach and the bulging curve of my thighs. I wondered how I could possibly be beautiful to him. Full up and still wanting to be filled. The devourer and the devoured. How is a person supposed to be both things?

Later we lay naked with the sheets tangled around our feet. I was pleased to see the ridge of my hipbone, highlighted by a triangle of moonlight peeping through the curtains. I wanted to draw attention to it. I turned to look at Arnold and was struck by the grown man he was: the tired lines around his mouth, the weathered texture of the skin on his hands. He was so complete a person, and I was so incomplete, so tentative and transparent, a vapor floating over the mattress. I wanted to cling to his certain solidity as if it were something to be anchored by.

The next morning I soaked in a bath while Arnold packed our bags. I forced my big toe up the mouth of the tap, playing music from my phone. He had planned a ten-mile hike that I was not looking forward to, though I liked the image of us walking through the hills in the sunlight—the shimmy of my dress in the wind, his weathered hand right there where I could grab it.

"What's this?" he asked, peering around the bathroom door to better hear what music I was playing.

"Stars of the Lid," I replied, disheartened by his indifference to my naked body.

"I quite like it," he said, though I could tell he did not.

I patted myself dry as he went down to check us out. I applied my makeup in the mirror, looking at the reflection of my average and uninteresting face. I was undeserving of such a sumptuous hotel room. Switching on the television, I flicked idly through the channels as I waited for him to come back for me. My phone rang, and I was surprised to see it was Arnold. I answered it.

As I stared out the window, half contemplating the drop, I already knew I was going to do what he asked. The window was a large single pane with a side hinge. The catch opened easily enough, the frame swinging out so the window was flat up against the wall, ludicrously wide-open. It reminded me of myself.

In my dress and Doc Martens, I felt as adequately robed to climb out of a first-story window as ever I might. Hitching the hem of my dress over my knees and swinging my legs over the sill, I looked at the drop and realized I could jiggle halfway down the drainpipe before having to jump. I rolled over to lower myself, taking a final look at the tableau of the room: the artfully unmade bed, the fluffy white robes hanging against the open bathroom door, the television on mute. With each shuffle toward the ground, the scene lifted higher above me, and I realized I was leaving something behind.

It was trickier than I thought it would be, and the room was higher from the ground than I'd anticipated. I found a little nook in which to wedge my right foot and gripped the drainpiping while steadily lowering my other foot, feeling for somewhere to place it, resting it against a ridge in the brickwork. I lowered myself with my arms, removing my right foot from its nook and pressing against the side of the building, hoping the friction might hold me. Gradually inching my left off the ridge, I found that my right foot held. Maybe I could make it all the way to the ground like this? I moved my hand down the piping and steadied my leg, pressing it against the building, but as I moved, the grip of my foot suddenly weakened. I could feel it drag slowly down, burning the rubber soles of my boots, stretching my body out taut and painful. I tried to hold on with the other foot but panicked, losing friction, clinging on with just my hands, my body pressed against the brickwork. I'd gotten a fair way down, and my arms couldn't hold on any longer, so I released my grip and fell, landing with a painful crack and biting my tongue hard. I spit out blood and thought very calmly, *I've broken my ankle.* And then I howled.

I went home for five weeks. There were complications with the fracture after I developed compartment syndrome: the crushed muscles in my feet intermittently tingling and going numb. I needed surgery and had to walk with a crutch. It was a strange spell, spent dosed up on painkillers, moving around the house as if underwater. My mum was working a lot at the time, and so I was mostly left alone with Joan of Arc. I'd watch the funerals from the kitchen windows with a foggy detachment while she snored at my feet.

In the evenings my mum would cook me dinner, clicking back into a caregiving role with a mechanical grace, coolly rearranging her days around me. She'd make me meals from my adolescence: spaghetti Bolognese and shepherd's pie. I'd catch myself thinking, *The pasta is overcooked, the soup needs more seasoning,* but they were still some of the best meals I could remember having. Steaming and predicated on stodge. Cheese melted liberally on everything. Done with dinner, we'd watch television, plucking After Eights from the box that was a permanent fixture on the coffee table.

Joa slept with me every night, her moist and meaty breath on my face for the duration of my rest. Arnold and I spoke only after midnight, usually via email. I could feel him drifting away from me. I would imagine myself on top of a peak, witnessing him sliding slowly down the side and out of reach. But the panic I would previously have felt, the manic grab to keep him by any means necessary—all that had vanished, replaced with a sad sort of curiosity. I watched with a removed indifference as he went away, and although I was upset, it was the lingering sadness that comes in the silence after a good cry. A hangover of emotion before it is finally exorcised. And I did feel exorcised.

I remember watching a news segment about a woman who'd lost her horse. The horse was a cantankerous thing, prone to biting strangers and snatching apples so quickly she thought he would take one of her fingers off. One morning she woke to find he had vanished. She'd had him many years, and the fencing was higher than anything she'd ever seen him jump. There were no track marks. No horses had been seen roaming the surrounding area. It was a bit of a mystery.

"I suppose he could have just wandered off?" the interviewer asked.

The woman shook her head. "Oh no," she replied. "He's gone. I can feel it."

"What do you mean 'gone'?" the interviewer said.

"Gone," the woman said, clicking her fingers in the air. "Don't you understand? He's just gone."

That was how I felt about Arnold.

I went back to take an exam I had not studied for, despite having so much time on my hands. I sat in the room and felt anxious. It was not about the exam. It was about the plain fact of being in a room full of people. I stared at the page in front of me, feeling the thump of my heart tingling in my fingertips, the familiar, sick osmosis through my stomach, the seductive urge to stop resisting and just fall down into the reverberation of it. I drew a shallow breath and stood up from my desk, and I left the exam room without even filling in my name. I was done. I didn't want to be outside the circle looking in, and I didn't want to be inside the circle either. I didn't know what I wanted, but I knew it wasn't this.

I stayed at Arnold's, and he made me a couscous salad. There was something too light about it, too fragrant—all flavor and not filling. After, I lay hungry while we attempted to have sex, my still-throbbing foot pushed to the side. That night he clung to me, and I found the tacit need of his affection appalling.

Lying awake in his bed, I thought about the Lukas Moodysson film *A Hole in My Heart*. I'd been going to write about it in my exam as an example of withdrawal from the sensory world. The film is about amateur pornography makers in Soviet Russia; they are filming porn while one of their teenage sons sits in the next room listening to industrial metal. The son duct-tapes his own eyes, temporarily blinding himself to the situation that is his life. Much is made of his almost biblical act: the psychology of the unwatchable. I didn't feel much about that either way. What stuck with me was the moment when one of the male filmmakers vomits into the open mouth of the adult actress and she dutifully swallows it up. It made a lot of sense to me: the intolerable empty space, how you let people pour their stuff inside it, just to have it filled.

The following morning we had used up all our enthusiasm for reconnecting. He tapped at his laptop in bed while I got up and made myself a cup of tea. I took my time showering, receiving the warm baptism of the water, with my face tilted upward. I used all his expensive products, but none of them were enough to cleanse the sour filth of the night before, and each of the nights before that.

Wrapped in a bath towel, I teased the tangles from my wet hair with a languid patience. I rubbed his moisturizer into my skin. I used his tweezers to pluck my eyebrows. I looked in the mirror and saw the soft, supple face of a twenty-year-old, the dark bags beneath my eyes incongruous. All the while Arnold sat up in bed, not saying anything, just watching me move around the room. I selected a pair of socks from his sock drawer—fine, mustard socks—and stretched them over my feet. I blow-dried my hair so it was shiny and thick. I buttoned up my shirt with slow ease. I felt peculiarly powerful with his eyes upon me. "I feel like I am never going to see you again," he said, and I didn't respond, didn't even look in his direction. I left his flat without saying good-bye, just closing the door quietly behind me. I waited two hours before checking my phone to see if he'd sent me a message, but he had not. On the train home, I cried, mostly because I felt I should, like that was the correct course of action.

As I stepped onto the platform I was met with the brightness and heat of the day. I wanted to be outdoors somewhere vast, I thought. I wanted the feeling of enormity. I also thought, *I don't know what I'm going to do, I have absolutely no idea.* I remembered something Arnold had said to me early on in our relationship: *If you can't imagine a road, that's because there isn't one.* I understood now that he was talking about me.

Hunter's Stew

Fermentation is a process in which molecules are broken down anaerobically—that is, without oxygen. They metabolize themselves. It is quite a histrionic process.

Korea has a long tradition of fermenting foods. There's doenyang, a fermented soybean paste, used as a condiment for noodles or rice, and the Korean version of soy sauce. There's hongeo-hoe, fermented skate; the fish excretes uric acid through its skin, which breaks down into ammonia, helping to preserve the flesh and giving it a highly distinctive flavor. And there is kimchi, a side dish made from salted, spiced, and fermented vegetables. Kimchi comes in many varieties, from ponytail kimchi, which really does look like ponytails on the plate, to winter kimchi, made ahead of season using small, conker-shaped radishes from the autumn markets. But the easiest to make and the most popular is cabbage kimchi.

Begin with a napa cabbage. Slice it into five-centimeter-wide strips, then massage salt into the leaves until you feel them begin to soften. Be generous with the salting and take your time. Pack the leaves into a jar, cover with water, and leave for a couple of hours with the lid screwed on.

The kimchi's flavor comes mostly from its paste: garlic, ginger, sugar, and fish sauce, ground and stirred. Add chili if you want some heat. Drain the salted cabbage, rinse with fresh water, and carefully coat every leaf with your paste. Pack the kimchi tight into your jar. You may need to use a bit of muscle to wedge it in. Make up some brine, using half a cup of salt to four cups of water. Add a tablespoon of brown sugar, a sprig of fresh thyme, and two or three dried bay leaves for a more complex flavor. Pour it into the jar until the liquid rises above the cabbage, seal, and leave for around five days. Check daily, with a clean finger or a fork, to ensure that the cabbage is submerged in liquid, packing it back down as need be. After a week you might be tempted to try the kimchi, to serve and eat it, imagining it to be done. Be patient. The rot is still working its way through. It is much better after two or even three weeks.

I'd arranged to meet Arnold at a bland coffee shop. Exposed lightbulbs hung from the ceiling, and it was inhabited mostly by remote workers squinting at their laptops. I arrived early, needing the sense of control, the feeling of power. I sat myself down and reapplied my lipstick. I removed from my bag a copy of *Sleep Has His House* by Anna Kavan, a book I'd chosen specifically for this encounter, an exercise that had taken nearly a full hour. I sent him a message saying I'd found us a table at the back, then went about looking like I was engrossed.

Arnold arrived a few minutes later. I watched from the corner of my eye as he approached me, waiting until he was standing immediately above me before I made contact. I peered over the pages of my book, making my eyes large and doelike. "Hello, Arnold," I said, in what I hoped was a low and appealing register.

"Hello, Roberta," he replied, loudly clearing his throat.

Arnold was wearing a navy knitted sweater and fitted black jeans. He also wore a pair of glasses, something he'd rarely done when I knew him. He looked exactly ten years older.

He took a seat, and we both studied the plastic menu. I was struck by an urge to order something dainty and light. Something that would make me seem delicate. I eyed the superfood salad, trying to imagine the give of the butternut squash, the smush of the avocado, attempting to convince myself that's what I wanted. I could feel Arnold watching me. When I looked up, he looked down. I copied him.

"So your boyfriend doesn't mind us meeting?" he said, keeping his eyes on the menu. "I know if I had a partner, I wouldn't like the idea of her meeting up with her ex."

I put my menu down. "Adnan's very laid-back," I said. Then added, "Plus, there's obviously no threat."

I stifled a self-congratulatory smile, waiting for a reaction, but none came. Arnold said he'd go and order our food. I told him I'd take a latte and the watercress soup, watched him stride up to the counter and order. I couldn't stop comparing myself to the woman behind the counter. Was she prettier than me? Did she have a more attractive smile? I put on some lipstick before he came back.

I asked Arnold about his research cluster with Emmeline. He spoke for a long time about problems they'd been having in securing funding, the politics of how the work had been divided up. He then began talking about how many meetings he was required to attend, moving into a full deconstruction of "meeting culture" and how broadly damaging it was in terms of productivity and fostering a sense of professional autonomy. He outlined principles he would apply to all meetings. "I would put a clock at the head of the table," he said. "And when the half-hour mark arrived—I would just leave." He placed both his palms flat against the table and took a moment, as if he'd said something very profound.

I thought about how much time I had spent listening to Arnold talk. How readily an attentive smile had fixed itself on my face. How he made me feel like a little girl not the woman I was. I reached my hand down toward my ankle and rubbed the small, hard nub left in the once-broken bone, the size and shape of a fingernail. I thought about being collapsed on such an elegant lawn, my foot swelling to the size of a boot. I thought about how he had reminded me of every small, easy gesture. Every time he'd given me a lift because it was on his way. Every time he'd picked up the bill because he could afford it and I could not.

I started telling him about Supper Club. I wanted him to recognize that I had changed. I told him what we were initially trying to achieve but how that had become lost. I told him about Ashley and how Stevie no longer wanted to do it, which was why the project had lost momentum, though I knew this was not entirely true. I wanted to say more, to tell him how I was feeling vacant, that there was a gaping space where once I had this marvelous sisterhood—but I held back, clinging to the decorum of my attractive and grown-up projection.

He nodded his head slowly, like he was drinking it all in, sipping mindfully and metabolizing—but I wondered whether he was actually listening at all. On hearing the word "feminist," he shifted his gaze.

"You know," he said, "we've got to be very careful when we say 'feminist.'" I blinked at him. I was trying to determine whether this was part of a joke. He continued.

"Because there are many different iterations of feminism. I'm always saying this to my students. It's not a catchall term for those invested in gender parity, because different 'feminists' view equity as operating on often decidedly different platforms."

He paused a moment. I thought he was waiting to land the punch line. Perhaps even just to stop talking. But he started again.

"I worry," he said, "it's becoming a rather diluted term. You know, a second-wave feminist views the movement very differently to, say, a third- or even fourth-wave feminist. The feminists of my generation are very different to the feminists of your generation. A cultural feminist would not like to be lumped in with a poststructuralist feminist—let me tell you that!"

He took a large gulp of his coffee, and I watched it slightly pool at the corners of his mouth. He dabbed his face with a napkin, firm and determined blots.

"I just think we need to be more careful," he finished, "with labels." He squinted his eyes toward me the way a man at the Apple store once did when explaining why the volume on my phone had stopped working, why it would cost so much to fix. Like he was being very generous in the divulging.

I was relieved to see the waitress arrive with our food. I watched as Arnold subtly appraised her. She leaned over, and I found my face suddenly very close to her neck. She smelled like fresh carrots. When she left, I looked down at my watery green soup, the small roll of bread nestled beside it. Then I stared at Arnold's báhn mì. The oil had yellowed the bread. Cartoonishly red hot sauce crisscrossed juicy hunks of chicken. It was topped with shredded coriander, chopped chilies, and translucent slivers of onion. I lifted my spoon, and then I heard myself speak.

"Can I have that?" I put down my spoon and pointed at Arnold's sandwich.

"What?" Arnold replied.

"Your sandwich. Can we switch, please? I don't want this soup. I don't know why I asked for it."

I lifted up my bowl and handed it over. Arnold received it because he had no choice and watched as I lifted up his báhn mì and deposited it in front of myself. I wrapped both hands around it and took a large bite before he could protest. I felt the tiny slices of chili deliciously tingle my lips. I made a full-bodied sound to demonstrate my pleasure. Then, with my mouth full, I began to speak.

"You must be really embarrassed," I said. "You must be really embarrassed you just explained feminism to me."

When I laughed, a little bit of chicken flew out of my mouth and landed on the table. I wiped it away with my finger. I took a large and audible gulp of coffee, then went back to my sandwich. I watched Arnold gingerly sip his soup. I thought, *I hope it tastes like piss.*

I told Arnold about Adnan, though he hadn't asked about him. I told him Adnan and I were having problems but that I loved him more than I'd ever loved anyone, that I loved him more than I thought myself capable. I told him about Stevie. About how she was the greatest friend in the world. When he tried to tell me about some renovations he was having done to his home office, I said, "Oh, I don't think I'm interested in hearing about that." I carried on talking. I spoke all my unspoken thoughts and ideas. I spoke any notion that popped into my head. When I didn't think he was properly listening to me, I repeated myself. When he interrupted, I said, "I've not finished yet." When he told me something I already knew, I said, "Thank you, but I obviously already know that."

After we'd finished our food, I went to the counter and got two brownies bagged up, dropping them into my backpack. We said good-bye on the street, hugging for a few long seconds, and I thought, *I can feel every aching bone in your body.* Walking away, I realized it was possible to feel both light and full. I felt solid and grounded, and yet I felt I could will myself to float up and away like a helium balloon. I'd eaten both my brownies by the time I reached home.

Back at the flat, I felt silly and elated. I played Bruce Springsteen on my phone, chanting "U! S! A!" Adnan was watching television on the sofa, in a soft old T-shirt and shorts. I wrapped my arms around him, pushed up his top, slipping it over his head. I felt peculiarly powerful, being the one wearing more clothes. I wondered why it was always me who got undressed first. I pulled him to his feet and dragged down his shorts, stepping back to stare at him. His vital skin. The proud swell of his chest. He let me gaze, and I didn't determine whether he was enjoying it or not. After a while he smiled and stepped toward me. "Are we doing this?"

Sometime around midnight I reached for my phone. I'd been in bed for hours, watching Adnan sleeping, his heavy breathing as restorative as the sea. But still I felt restless and unsettled, a sense of something not yet resolved. Without thinking, or at least without following the thought through, I typed out a message and pressed SEND. Will you please meet me for lunch? Adnan reached over, woken by the glow of my screen. "What's the matter, love?" he asked, tucking his hand beneath my face, cupping it like a large piece of fruit. "What are you doing?"

"I'm messaging Stevie," I said. "I'm finally messaging Stevie."

He removed his hand from under my head and rolled all the way over. "That's a bad idea," he said, exhaling. "That's a really bad idea." Then, just as I thought he'd fallen back to sleep, "But it's not like you care what I think."

We arranged to meet at our old café, where we used to eat lunch together most days. Not speaking to Stevie, I'd realized how much I used to structure my day around this small window of time. It was a strange place, hard to pin down: half hipster diner, half families eating soup. The menus were waxy and tattered, containing far too many items to suggest that any one of them would be good. I got there first and found a table, gazing at the many variations of eggs. In my peripheral vision, I saw Stevie arrive, and I halfheartedly pretended I was too immersed in the menu to notice. When she was looming over me, I went to stand and hug her, but she'd sat down before I had the chance.

"Hi," she said, propping the menu in front of her, her brow furrowed to deep crevices between her eyes.

"Hi," I said back, and waited.

Quickly she placed the menu down again, announcing she was going to order the halloumi salad as if she were accusing me of a crime.

"That sounds nice," I offered.

"Don't be like that," she shot back.

"Okay," I said, and wondered whether my face had gone red. I went to say that I wasn't being like anything, but then she spoke over me, and instead we both abandoned our sentences midway. She kept scratching the left side of her nose. I couldn't tell if it was a nervous gesture or a legitimate itch.

The waitress came over and asked what we wanted. I ordered a cup of tea and scrambled eggs, and Stevie said she'd have the salad and whatever was the soup of the day. I was relieved by the momentary animation the waitress offered, but as she left, we resumed our silence, eyes fixed to the table between us. I felt myself getting hot, aware that I was coming across as particularly weird. I glanced at Stevie and imagined a thousand fireflies bobbing around my head, each representing something different to say, a gesture to demonstrate how much I'd missed her, how much she meant to me. But whenever I thought about committing to one from the swarm, I felt myself hesitate. Why this one? Why any? I picked up the menu again, just to give myself something to do.

"What's a cheeseburger toastie?" I asked, my gaze landing on the perplexing menu item, though I was certain we'd had this conversation before.

"I think it's just a cheeseburger with sliced bread," she said.

"Well, what's the point of that?"

"I have no idea."

I imagined that if I stared hard enough at the table, it might become imbued with all the things I needed to say to her. I wished we didn't have to say anything at all. I suddenly wondered whether I could move back in. Maybe Sash could live with Adnan, just for a bit? The whole thing was a total disaster, and it was all my fault. I had to say something, anything. "Stevie!" I blurted out. "I'm so sorry!"

Stevie's eyes remained on the table in front of her. There was a dark spot in the wood where it had been worn and stained.

"Don't say it like that. Nobody's got a gun to your head," she said. "Jesus."

"I don't know how else to say it," I said. "Please. Sorry. Please. I just want to get you to talk to me again. What words will do that? Tell me the words, and I'll say them."

"What are you even sorry for?" she asked. "Do you even know?"

"I'm sorry for how I treated you," I said. I felt like I'd popped a soap bubble sprung from the washing-up. Oh, that's right. Oh, of course.

"It wasn't fair to you," I continued. "I've been so selfish, and thoughtless, and—"

Stevie lowered her gaze further, now examining her hands.

"I totally love you," I said, and even as I said it, I thought about how saying "totally" made it seem less real. How I should have just said *I love you* but somehow could not. Perhaps that was the problem all along.

"You know," she said, "we used to share a bed nearly every night. You used to put your head on my chest in the mornings, and I'd stroke your hair. And suddenly that just stopped. Suddenly it was up to you to decide the parameters of our relationship, what was appropriate and what was not. And I kind of liked our weird gray area of a friendship. But as soon as Adnan came along, it was like I wasn't even allowed to allude to that."

Though I had been expecting an invocation of Adnan, I wasn't quite ready for my own fierce protectiveness in response. I wanted to squirrel away what we had, burying it in a small wooden box deep beneath the ground. Stevie had no right to look at it. I breathed and swallowed the impulse to slap her.

"I guess I just needed more," I offered. "Sometimes our friendship feels so intense it's like we might blow up the room. It's claustrophobic. And I'd never had a real relationship before, so yes, I got a little bit caught up in that. I feel so railroaded by you all the time. Like I'm just your shy sidekick. It's ironic, you saying that's how I am with Adnan, because that is how I feel with you. Always trying to be good enough or engaging enough. The whole time I was so scared of losing you, and now I basically have."

"But *you* didn't lose *me*. I'm still here. You went away, and now I don't know who you are. It's me who lost you."

We resumed staring at the table, a shared migraine of hyperemotion. When our food arrived, we ate it in silence. There was a horrible moment when I dropped my fork, slopping undercooked egg down my top, expecting an eye roll from Stevie, but she pretended not to notice. When we were finished, the bill arrived unasked for, and I thought, *This is it. I am never going to see this person again.* I pushed my arms into my coat and thought about how I would negotiate leaving. Stevie stopped me. "Come on," she said. "We need a drink."

So we went looking for a pub, turning down unfamiliar streets, wordlessly agreed that we couldn't go to any of our old places now. "We'll find one," Stevie said, a few paces in front of me. "There'll be one soon." We happened upon a place called the Crown Arms, and I could sense us both prickling at its novelty, feeling the place out. But it kind of helped, like having someone stamp on your foot so you forget about your toothache. We ordered our drinks separately, paid for them separately, then took a seat near the quiz machine. A guy in his early twenties was noisily playing a round, so we were forced to sit in silence, unable to talk over the electronic voice of the machine. By the time he bumbled away, having seemingly spent more than twenty pounds, the tension had somewhat dissipated and we were able to talk.

We talked about the first time we met. How we'd been dragged toward each other like the tide. We talked about moving in together, how natural and right it felt. We talked about Supper Club and what it meant to us now. We talked about sharing a bed together, its strange and comforting ache. We talked about Adnan and how that had changed things. It felt like a post-breakup debrief: examining our own narrative as if we'd entered a metaphase of our relationship. After our initial half-pints, we ordered a carafe of wine. We touched our glasses together gingerly for a toast.

Stevie asked how it was living with a boy, and I told her I was enjoying it but also sometimes hating it a bit. She told me I seemed happy and apologized for what she had said about how I acted meek and contrived around Adnan. "That's just what you're like," she said flippantly. The knowledge that it really was unraveled in my chest.

Stevie talked about her own anxieties, ordinarily closely guarded, about how she was wasting her life at our pointless company, never really doing anything with her art. She told me her parents had offered to pay for her to do a master's, maybe in gallery studies or arts management.

"I guess I'm trying to self-improve," she said defensively.

"That's great," I said. "I should do something, too. I am the worst."

"Ugh," she said, reaching over to squeeze my hands so hard they hurt. "This is it. This is the issue. You just make these blanket passive statements that mean you never have to be responsible. That mean you're never in control so you can't be held to account."

"Go on," I said, though I did not want her to, didn't want her to flip me over and examine my underside, the soft belly of a crab. I pulled my coat across my waist and hugged it under my clenched arms.

"I mean, why don't you do something else? What have you done since we quit Supper Club? Cooked a lot of dinners for Adnan. Watched a lot of TV. Read a lot of articles about the feminist credentials of said TV. What do you actually want from your life?"

I reached for my glass and finished the last of my wine. I felt drowsy and muted. Stevie went to the bar to get us another drink, and I watched her walk over. Her gigantic, unruly hair hanging like an industrial fishing net down her back. The wild colors of her clothes. It felt like a terrible injustice—that she might not become an artist, would not even try to be one. If not her, then who? As she came back, I grabbed her sleeve. "You should do it," I said, surprised by my slight slur. "You should go for it. With the art."

"Hmmm," she replied. "Perhaps I'll do an MA in fine art or something. You know I never go to the studio anymore? And I really should be doing something, if we're not going to do Supper Club. I can't just do nothing."

I tried to think about Supper Club—the gnawing absence it had left behind in the otherwise sensible thrum of my life with Adnan. But the wine had temporarily flattened my sense of those sharp wants and losses, and I felt only numbness, a placid lack of desire. All I could picture was the social-media management tool I used at work. It showed separate columns for all our channels, subcolumns displaying comments and replies, how many likes or retweets our posts had received. I stared at the columns within the columns all day long. They were the promise of order and sense. I began every day by staring at them.

"Oh, my God," I said to Stevie, grabbing her hands and wrenching them across the table. "We're supposed to be at work!"

Upon checking my phone, I found thirteen missed calls from Margaret, alongside several texts, all offering a variation of are you ok where have you gone do we need to call the police. I also had a number of messages from Adnan, all of the same content and tone. I'm fine, I replied. Sorry, lost track of time.

Stevie thought it would be a good idea to go back to the office. It was only just five o'clock, and most people would still be in. She said we could tell them she had come down with a terrible fever or a series of panic attacks and I had to take care of her. "You know I'm good at faking sick," she said. "Honestly, I'm a champ."

We walked in together, then separated. She went to the studio, and I went to my office. As I entered the room, Margaret dashed toward me. She was holding a pencil topped with pink bunny ears. Her imitation pearls had tangled up her hair. She wore not a scrap of makeup. I recognized her as my kin, somebody who existed in the negative space between things, forever trying to shuffle into this thing or that.

"Thank God! You're okay! You're okay!" It occurred to me that she was sincerely relieved to see me, that she had actually been concerned.

"I spoke to your boyfriend," she continued. "And he didn't know where you were either!"

"I was out with my friend from the studio," I explained, trying to recall the phrasing we'd agreed on. "And she was feverish. And having panic attacks. I don't know what was wrong with her, but I didn't have the chance to check my phone or get in touch."

I watched Margaret pause, boxing off what she would and would not believe. "Okay," she said after some time. "Okay. Well, as long as you're all right?"

"I am," I said. "Thanks."

She asked me if I wanted to go home, but I offered to stay and catch up on some things. She received this with a pitiful expression of mutual professional respect.

"Of course," she said. "Of course."

As soon as I was back at my desk, I wrote an email to Stevie.

ROBERTA: OH MY GODDDDDD!!!!!

STEVIE: I know. I've got an HR meeting on Thursday.

ROBERTA: Christ.

I stayed in the office until fifteen minutes after Margaret left. Adnan offered to come and pick me up, but I declined his offer and knew I'd done so out of a weird respect for Stevie and the life she'd chosen to live. I picked up McDonald's on the way home, two massive paper bags holding all the burgers, fries, chicken McNuggets, and apple pies I could carry. By the time I arrived at the flat, I'd sobered up, felt silly for having bought so much junk food. I plated it out on the dining table, hoping it might make the whole thing, might make me, more permissible.

"Let's just eat in front of the TV," Adnan said, grabbing a plate and walking through to put on an episode of *Mad Men*.

He went to bed earlier than me, and when I crept in later and tried to pull his arm around me, he rolled away very carefully. The next morning he wouldn't meet my eye.

"What?" I said eventually. "What is it?"

He held his coffee to his chest, a singular thermal comfort. "Do you have to ask?" he replied.

"Please tell me."

"You make up with Stevie for half a second and you what? Just forget to go to work?"

"I'm sorry," I offered automatically, wondering if I actually meant it. "I'm *sorry*."

"You're not a child," he said, moving past me with a pointed brusqueness, tipping the last of his coffee into the sink. "Stop acting like one."

As he left the flat, I saw that Stevie had sent me a video: a golden retriever trying to bite a shaft of light. I watched it a couple times, giggling against the kitchen sink. I was looking for a meme to send back when she messaged again. She wanted me to come round for dinner.

It was weird going to Stevie and Sash's. The house smelled sort of different on account of Sash's predilection for expensive scented candles, and they'd repainted the living room a rusty orange and put out new throws and paintings. I let myself in because Stevie never bothered with locks; she said leaving your door unlocked proved you believed in the best in people.

She and Sash were sitting at the kitchen table as I made my way into their home. They turned their heads outward to look at me. Their apparent intimacy felt compelling and staged, cameos in a museum about the Vikings. I found myself scrutinizing their interactions like I might Facebook photographs of an old boyfriend. They got on better than I'd imagined, better than I'd hoped they would. Sash was razor sharp, a fast talker, and she had seemingly seen every film ever made. They had in-jokes and shared references that I didn't recognize. They did this bit where Sash would put on a fake Home Counties accent and say, "I'd like a golden chicken nugget!" to which Stevie would reply, "If that's what the lady desires!" in the same voice, and then they would erupt into peals of laughter. It made me think, *I suppose this is why Adnan doesn't want to hang out with Stevie and me.*

Stevie had made macaroni and cheese. She insisted I sit down at the table while she poured me a glass of wine, and it occurred to me that she had never before cooked me dinner. I had eaten dinners she'd made, but always as one of many. I'd never been the guest of honor. She presented me with my drink and emptied a bag of sweet chili crisps into a large glass bowl in front of me. "Here," she said. "I know you get hungry waiting for the meal." I took a handful and thought, *You are my favorite person in the world.* When the pasta was ready, Sash exchanged a look with Stevie, then murmured that she had work to do and made for her room. I reached for her wrist. "Don't leave on account of me?"

Stevie jumped in. "Yeah, have something to eat with us."

Sash wavered, turning back to the table. "There isn't room for us all."

"It's fine," I said. "We'll just sit on the floor. We always used to do that. Indoor picnic."

We arranged cushions and blankets in the center of the living room, as we'd done many times before, and sat in a circle. Stevie placed the macaroni pot on a wooden chopping board, and we all helped ourselves to salty, steaming ladlesful, covering each mound with curls of Parmesan cheese. My eyes moved around the room as we spoke, noticing things I'd never seen before: a crack in the ceiling, a copy of *Infinite Jest*. I thought about the tumultuous momentum of things, how no one ever gets used to change, not really. Stevie put down her plate and looked suddenly serious. "Did you see the Supper Club email?" she asked.

"No," I replied. "I've not checked it in months."

"This woman in Berlin emailed. She wants to set one up. A Supper Club."

"Wow," I replied. "I mean . . . That must mean something? Right? What does that mean?!"

"It means," Sash offered, "it's becoming a movement. You two did that."

I blushed, then felt silly for it. Sitting with credit always made me self-conscious. I looked over at Stevie, who seemed surprisingly coy, too. She exchanged a coded glance with Sash. Then she fanned out all the fingers on both hands and presented them, palms up, to me.

"Listen," she said. "I've a proposition. And you're going to have to hear me out."

"Okay?"

"One more Supper Club."

I felt adrenaline pool in my gut like I was at the beginning of a race, suddenly tense and poised but not certain in which direction I was inclined to run. The thought of starting Supper Club again was invigorating, then immediately overwhelming. Aside from anything, I didn't think I had the energy. I imagined telling Adnan, the frost of his reaction, the prancing and pirouettes I would have to perform just to prove I still loved him, that this didn't detract from that, that it never had. How he would drag his feet and not meet my eye.

"I don't want to," I told Stevie eventually, imagining this to be as watertight a rebuttal as she would need. Where did I get an idea like that?

"You don't *want* to?" Stevie replied. "What do you mean, you don't want to?"

"I just don't want to," I said. "I don't. I'm sorry."

Stevie glanced over at Sash again, and I pretended not to notice. I could feel the threads of their communion like spider silk in the air. Sash's face saying, *I told you so.*

"Listen," Stevie said. "There's more."

I labored an exhale. I was listening, of course I was—I was the sensible one.

"Do you know what next month is?" Stevie asked. I stared at her, wondering what I could say to make her hear me, to make it stop, without ruining everything in a way that could never be fixed.

"It's your birthday. That's why we have to do it. Just one last time. The last Supper Club for your thirtieth birthday."

I thought about what a final Supper Club might mean. The hiatus we'd left it on was definitely an uncomfortable limbo. It might be good for me, for my relationship with Adnan, to put a proper full stop on it. Maybe then we could settle down. But none of this made the thought of telling him any easier. I thought about the sleepy happiness he embodied during the months I'd not been speaking to Stevie, the flinty worry he'd resumed in the days since we'd made up. How he would regard me—watching television, eating dinner, doing the washing-up—like I was a puzzle to be solved, like he was straining for the magic words that would make me stay.

Either way I was going to disappoint someone. But I got the feeling that if I were doing the same thing as Stevie, I would be somehow immune to the consequences. She always had that aura of invincibility—the hint of a promise that nothing could possibly go wrong. *Are we going to get away with this?* I wondered, and in that moment I had already made the decision.

Stevie grinned. "Come on, you know it's a great idea. Why *wouldn't* we?"

"Why would we?"

"Because we never said good-bye. Because if it's all going to be over—not just Supper Club but all of it—I want to go out with a bang."

Stevie's eyes went big. I couldn't tell if she was looking at me imploringly or instructively. Perhaps she was just looking at me.

"Fuck it," I said. "I'm in."

Roberta, hello.

How are you? Tip-top, I'm sure. I do hope you weren't too put out by me not being able to make it the other night. How long did you stay there for? Did they kick you off the table? I hope you got to eat some of that award-winning food at least!

You know, I once waited two hours for a co-worker to come meet me for supper at this little Greek deli on the corner of 7th and

58th. He'd told me this place is the best deli on 58th Street (high praise indeed). Anyway, I'm waiting there, ordering little bits off the menu, bit of souvlaki here, couple of stuffed vine leaves there, getting more and more annoyed, and finally he messages saying he's been waiting for me for two hours and where the fresh hell am I? I message back saying I'm here, too, where are you?! He tells me he's sitting in the window under the neon sign—and I am thinking, there ain't no neon sign on any of the windows here, pal, not that I can see anyway. Then, out of the corner of my eye, I spot a HUGE neon sign on the other side of the road, saying, I kid you not, *58TH STREET BEST DELI.* Well, I pay up and go join him, but by that time I've been grazing for two hours and can't eat another bite, so I don't get to try any of this so-called phenomenal food. We went out drinking after that, and I crawled in around two AM on a weeknight, but THAT is for another time.

Anyway, best go—writing this from the airport and just remembered I've run out of aftershave. The perfect opportunity to pick some up at duty-free! Always thrifty, me.

Hope you're looking after yourself.

All best,

Jim (Dad)

X

My thirtieth birthday began with a lurch. I'd read my dad's email late the night before, after leaving it unopened in my in-box for several days. When I finally looked, I felt very little; it contained more or less what I expected. But waking up the following morning,

I felt a swell of disappointment, followed by the dreary remembering. I was awake an hour ahead of my alarm, and I didn't bother trying to go back to sleep. I got out of bed and lay on the couch, dragging its felt throw over me, and I rang my mum.

"Happy birthday, darling!" She had probably been up for a couple of hours already.

"Thanks," I replied. "Adnan's taking me out for dinner."

"Well, that sounds lovely. Perfect birthday celebration. What sort of restaurant?"

"Turkish."

I pulled at a stitch in the throw lining, suddenly resisting the urge to cry.

"Is everything all right?" my mum asked after I'd been quiet awhile.

"I went to meet Dad."

"Right." She said it like I'd answered her question plus many more.

"Anyway, he didn't show up. And I waited for ages."

"Oh, love, I'm sorry."

"He didn't even apologize. He basically doesn't care at all. I feel like such an idiot."

"You're not! You're not an idiot. I don't know what to say. That's just who he is."

"I mean, I should have known that. I should have guessed this would happen."

My mum sighed noisily. "Well. The number of bloody times I made the same mistake. We'd arrange to meet, and he wouldn't show up—no word of explanation, just fresh air. I always wanted to believe he would change. Sometimes it was even funny, you know. I'll tell you those stories one day, and we'll have a good giggle."

I let myself feel the tiniest bit comforted.

"Listen, don't think about him. It's your birthday. You've got a brilliant day planned. Go and have fun, and call me again if you get the chance."

I lay on the sofa until my alarm went off, staring out the window. Adnan was still sleeping. I made us both a bacon sandwich and a coffee and placed them on the chest of drawers at the foot of our bed. When the smell hit him, he woke up, lazily rubbing his eyes.

"Shouldn't I be making you breakfast in bed, birthday girl?"

"It's okay," I said. "I was already awake."

I ate my sandwich cross-legged on top of the duvet, Adnan propped up with pillows in front of me. When we were finished, I took the plates and cups to the kitchen and gave them a rinse. I showered, dressed, then went to work.

I spent the morning reading articles about people with face blindness. Since I'd moved in with Adnan, I'd gotten lax at work, unable to summon the energy to affect even a simulacrum of diligence. Margaret would peek over at my monitor, and I wouldn't even bother minimizing my window of Internet shopping or herbal remedies for anxiety. I'd come in late, offering half-baked excuses like "I slept terribly" or "I had to buy something for breakfast." I'd sit at my desk and yawn.

Stevie sent me a "Happy Birthday" email. It said I would find a birthday treat in the staff kitchen, and I went through to discover a tall glass of hot chocolate topped with whipped cream and pale pink marshmallows. Tied to the base was a thin ribbon attached to a somewhat limp balloon, evidently fallen from the table and bobbing nervously at the floor. I took the drink back to my desk and sent her a string of heart-eye emojis. I ate the cream with the end of my pen, then sipped the hot chocolate, finding it absolutely lousy with booze.

By eleven thirty I was a little drunk, tired from the sugar crash, and already ready to go home. I invested the afternoon in a series of podcasts about bread. "We have been eating bread for hundreds of years," the host said. "And now suddenly it is what, unhealthy?" I admired his outrage.

At six o'clock I waited for Adnan on the corner outside the office. I watched him walk across the road as I might a handsome stranger, the softness of his steps and the pleasing symmetry of his features. Adnan had a habit of manifesting from nowhere; I'd rarely spot him approaching me or walking down the road. He would just appear, sturdy and rooted like street furniture, like he'd been there all along. He said hello and landed a kiss on the top of my head, where the part in my hair met my brow.

We held hands walking to the restaurant. The air was warm and heavy. When I stopped to smoke outside the restaurant, Adnan didn't complain, just leaned back against the wall, watching me. We'd booked a table at one of my favorite places. Adnan always wanted to take us somewhere fancier, sending me links to restaurants with decorative barren trees, furnished entirely in ecru, tokens to remind you not to overdo it, not to make a mess. But he'd allowed my choice this time—raising his eyebrows at the wait time and refraining from making a fuss.

A waitress saw us to our seats. We talked about our day. Adnan had forgotten what he was supposed to be saying in the middle of a presentation, making up something absurd about the film *Finding Dory*. I thought about everyone watching the presentation, witnessing his fumble, how they must have forgiven him immediately, had been rooting for him all along.

We smeared warm, floury flatbreads with hummus, sipped toosweet white wine while our meat grilled. We both had the lamb koftas, coupled with stewed zucchini and harissa-spiced potatoes. When I left to go to the bathroom, Adnan set down his knife and fork and waited for me to return, resuming eating only once I did. After we'd finished our mains, he inexpertly excused himself from the table to whisper to the waiters. A few minutes later, a sundae arrived at the table, complete with flaked chocolate, cocktail swizzle, and sparkler. Adnan sang me happy birthday along with the staff, properly singing it, singing it much louder than anyone else, to the horror and amusement of the other diners.

Over coffee we talked about our childhoods, the disastrous holidays and the stupid games we played. He used to play a game called Detective, in which he would be the detective and his brother would leave "clues." The brother would place socks, tissues, pieces of paper with a smear of ketchup, all around the house, and Adnan would have to solve whatever crime he'd cooked up. Adnan would come up with needlessly convoluted theories, and his brother would just agree with whatever he said. I told him how I used to sit beneath the bush at the bottom of my garden and watch people grieving at their dead relatives' graves. He scrunched up his face, and I regretted telling it—knowing it was not a fun story.

We went to a fancy bar for a drink afterward. The girls were considerably more attractive than me and an awful lot thinner. He kept his hand at my waist the whole time. I ordered a vodka and soda, and so he had the same, eschewing the strong German beers he preferred out of some strange celebratory gesture. We sipped our drinks staring at each other, the music too loud for us to be able to talk.

When we got home, he gave me my birthday presents: some books from my Amazon wishlist, a mermaid-tail blanket, a framed picture of an illustrated cat, and a gold pendant necklace, its disk engraved with my initials. We drank some of the prosecco we'd picked up from the Spar on the way home. We ate some of the fancy truffles my aunt had sent. We watched an episode of *The Office*. He tucked a cushion under my back and said he was worried about my posture, and I pulled it out and sprawled across him instead. We had a nightcap before bed, a splash of whiskey and a cube of ice. We drank it standing up in the kitchen, enjoying the heat.

That night we took our time having sex. As Adnan moved inside me, he said something in such a low whisper that I wasn't certain I had not imagined it. The next morning we lay in bed, not wanting to go to work, and I asked him what he'd said. He told me he'd said we could have such a nice life together.

We decided to cater the last Supper Club exclusively using food we'd foraged from bins or already had at home. Stevie and the others had been dumpster-diving all week. I hadn't joined them for fear of being told off by Adnan.

I'd considered not telling him about the final club at all. The option unfurling steadily in front of me: a tempting road to walk. It would be so easy not to say anything. To tell him I was staying at my mum's. To tell him I was sleeping over at Stevie's. He would never have to find out, and we would never have to fight. We could go back to sitting sleepily on the sofa. We could start to plan a life. But I knew that not telling him was antithetical to the purpose: twisting myself into a more pleasing shape to accommodate, to avoid giving offense.

I waited to tell him until the night before the party. I spent a full evening trying to do it, but I couldn't quite wrap my mouth around the words. So when Adnan was brushing his teeth, I followed him into the bathroom to perch on the toilet seat, a position calculated to emphasize the humbleness of my confession. I also remembered reading that it was impossible to cry when brushing your teeth, impossible to feel sad with your mouth forced into a smile.

"Adnan," I said, and he made an agreeable sound from the back of his throat, distorted by the hum of the toothbrush. "I need to tell you something."

He spit into the sink and dabbed his face with a towel. He would understand, I told myself. He would at least try to.

"Yes?" he said. I could see he was already lightly irritated by this rupture in his routine.

"We're doing another Supper Club," I said, my assertion only slightly wavering. "Just one more. This will be the last one. For my birthday. Also, it's tomorrow."

I surveyed his reflection in the mirror for a response. The small wrinkle that had dug its way into his chin appeared to wobble. His eyes seemed to change, but I couldn't determine how. He wrapped his hands around the lip of the sink, and I watched all his fingers turn white. For a moment I thought he might rip the basin from the wall. I thought about what a dreadful mess it would make. How we would have to call the landlady to have her fix it. I made mental calculations of the cost. He squeezed shut his eyes, and his mouth moved to meet them, his face terribly ugly all squished up, his back rounded and hunched. *Why is he like this?* I wondered miserably. *Why do I make people like this?* I wanted to peel off his angry, bitter skin and find the smooth, untarnished one underneath.

I moved to touch his arm, but he jerked viciously away from me, twisting his neck around, not to look at me but to demonstrate his contempt. I felt hungry for something soft.

"Say something, please."

"Are you fucking kidding me, Roberta?" He spoke very quietly, and I didn't know how to reply, what I was supposed to offer. I thought about apologizing, but I didn't want to. I thought, *This will be a fight, and then it will be over.* One week of discomfort, two at the most. Two weeks of penance and passive aggression.

He moved past me and went into the kitchen, pulling open the bottom drawer and seizing appliances: a waffle iron, a potato ricer, an egg pan. Gifts he had given me. Things he had picked up on the way home from work. *I am a bad person,* I thought. *I am the worst.*

"I am so supportive," he said. "I am a good boyfriend."

"I know! Of course I know that!"

"And I deserve better than you," he said, interrupting me. "Than this. I am trying to make you happy. But you insist on making me miserable. You act like a spoiled child."

I remained silent, staring at the floor.

"Do you remember what happened last time you did Supper Club? You think I don't know? What kind of maniac breaks into a shop and trashes it for no reason? Is that the sort of person I get to have as my girlfriend? Is it? Jesus Christ, you and *fucking Stevie.*"

"What about me and Stevie?" I shouted back, suddenly fired up. "What about us?"

Do it, I thought. *Do it if you dare.*

"It's fucking weird, okay?" he replied. "You trailing around after her. It's embarrassing."

"Embarrassing" was a term I'd heard him attribute to Stevie before. It was a word many people used, men under their breaths in neon-lit bars, girls picking at salads in the office canteen. What was it about her that made others feel embarrassed? That specific word, the idea of an audience, a stranger's exposure making you feel exposed. I wondered what Stevie exposed in Adnan. It made me want to be cruel.

"At least she's trying to have an interesting life! Not just sitting on the fucking sofa!"

"An interesting life? Okay. Let's look at Stevie's life. She doesn't have a real job. She's apparently an artist, but she doesn't make any art because she spends all her time sitting around telling *you* what to do—and you just run around after her, desperate for approval. She doesn't even care about you, Roberta! It's the most dysfunctional thing I've ever seen!"

I watched the heave of his chest as he drew breath, the muscles of his throat contract and expand. How much bigger his body was than my own. How much louder he could shout. I felt like I'd spent my life being yelled at by men in one way or another, learning how it warped and poisoned the air. How it forced you to crawl into the spaces outside it, no matter how small they were.

"You know what's dysfunctional, Adnan? Your pathological need for everything to be *nice* all the time. Not everything is nice, okay, and I'm *sorry* I'm never nice enough for you. I'm *sorry* I'm just not nice enough for your nice, unchallenging, pathetic little life."

A flicker of pain punctured his resolve, as if one of my arrows had finally hit, the pomp leaking out of him.

"Right," he said, making for the front door, pressing his hands to his body like he was checking for injuries, though clearly it was just to feel for the familiar bulge of wallet, phone, keys. I realized I'd been waiting for him to run away. That perhaps I'd been waiting for that right from the start. "I'm going to my brother's."

"Fine," I said. "Go."

"You have a choice to make, Roberta, and I'm fucking serious. You can't have it both ways. Why do you think you can have it both ways?"

He went for his jacket, though it was a warm evening, then pulled on his shoes, straining at the laces.

"This has to be over. I won't stand for it anymore."

He unlocked the door and stepped into the hallway. He lingered there in the half-light for what felt like a very long time, turned away from me. When he spoke, his voice was considered and flat. "Why is our life together not enough for you?"

I looked around at our home. How careful we had been in filling it. How there were still spaces on the walls where more pictures could go, gaps on the bookshelves for photos and plants. I looked at the teardrop-shaped stain where I'd spilled a cup of coffee. I thought about the drawer underneath the fridge where we'd found a beautifully carved wooden chess set and a black leather riding crop left behind by the last tenants. We knew all the secrets of this space. There was nothing left to learn. Sometimes I would lie on the bed and stare at the ceiling feeling a cavernous sense of yearning. But sometimes I would lie on the bed and feel that the room and the flat and Adnan fit me so perfectly that I could spend the rest of my life lying there and I wouldn't mind at all.

"It is," I said. "It is enough." But it was too late, and it came out sounding like a question, and he'd gone before I'd finished anyway.

Some mornings I wake up and the first thing I feel is terror. The idea of being singularly responsible for keeping myself alive is terrifying. That I have to get up and leave the flat and navigate the world protected only by my own skin. Like looking at an object and finding that it is fundamentally not fit for any purpose. Like feeling suddenly attuned to the flimsy metal box of the speeding car you're trapped within, recalling images of cars torn up in crashes, twisted and aflame. In those moments I feel certain I cannot breathe, do not understand the basic mechanics of breathing. The morning after

Adnan left, the morning of Supper Club, I felt that terror. I lay very still in bed until it passed.

We'd arranged to meet at Renni's flat and then have the club at a nearby park. The weather was glorious, and asserting ourselves in a public space seemed an apt way to end Supper Club. But that morning I had an idea. I rang Stevie and told her I wanted to do it here: I would host everyone at the flat.

"Um, will Adnan be thrilled about that?" she asked, and I told her I didn't know what he'd be. I was trying not to care.

I spent the rest of the day cleaning and tidying, getting the food ready. Stevie came round just before we were starting, and I stationed myself in the kitchen—letting her do the job of greeting all the others as they arrived. She had made a cheddar-and-parsley roulade. Lina had made a lentil goulash, plus almond-and-white-chocolate blondies. Emmeline had made two different types of risotto. Erin had made lamb-and-asparagus mini pies and a strawberry-and-spinach salad. Renni had made bread-and-butter pudding using chocolate croissants. Andrea had made a hearty beef goulash plus zucchini with feta and mint. Sash had made a giant pumpkin cheesecake. The kitchen was a kaleidoscope of smells.

We'd decided not to wear costumes or do a theme, and it was strange seeing them all arrive as themselves. Renni in a bright blue bandage dress. Sash in an oversize T-shirt and heels. Lina in a crepe skirt and sheer buttoned blouse. While everyone fussed with her food in the kitchen, I ducked out to pick something to wear. I found a floor-length white linen dress, something I'd bought in a charity shop months ago and never had the opportunity to use. I knew I would get it filthy before we'd even started eating. As I walked back into the kitchen, everyone whistled and whooped. I thought, *I am going to do a spin,* and then I did one.

I went to check on my dish, a hunter's stew made from dumpster-foraged vegetables and whatever else I had in the cupboards. I lifted the pot lid to stir it, left it simmering on the hob. Andrea came to loop her arms around me, pressing two pills into my hand. "We're starting now?" I asked.

"Might as well," she replied.

"What are they?" I asked, and she smiled and cocked her head. I clapped them to my mouth and swallowed.

We decided to push all the furniture back so we could eat on the living-room floor. There would be no courses this time; we laid everything out at once. I started with a spoonful of goulash and a side of salad, then had a handful of blondies, then went back for pie. Sash's pumpkin cheesecake was a hit, and everyone agreed Emmeline's beetroot-and-goat-cheese risotto was better than the one with sweet potato and chives. Stevie topped up everyone's wine many times, and we raised our plastic glasses and called cheers. We carried on eating and talking for a long time, but still much of the spread remained. Even the wine hadn't been finished. I wasn't sure if this was a victory or a failure. I just knew I felt full.

"I mean," Stevie said, casting her hand over the half-eaten buffet. "This is unlike us."

Sash tore off a piece of pita bread. "Don't appetite-shame me," she said, tossing the bread across the room toward Stevie. Stevie removed it from her dense tangle of hair and dunked it into the stew.

"Don't throw *dry* bread at me," she said, lobbing it back. "You monster."

It hit the shoulder of Sash's white T-shirt, leaving an oily red streak. Sash yanked down the sleeve of her top to inspect. "This is fucking Comme des Garçons!" she screeched. "*You're* the monster!" She dipped her hand deep into what was left of the beetroot risotto, squelching the fat pink rice between her fingers. Crawling over to Stevie, one arm suspended in the air, she wiped a sticky palmful across Stevie's face. "There, there," she said, in a mock-infant voice. "Hush now."

Stevie began rubbing it into her skin like a lotion. "Beetroot has excellent regenerative properties," she replied, picking off grains one by one and flicking them back at Sash.

I twisted round to see the white wall behind me flecked with beetroot. "Uh-oh," Stevie said, noticing me. "I'm sorry."

"No you're not!" I feigned outrage. "You're not sorry at all!" I picked up a couple of blondies, breaking them into chunks and volleying them at her one by one.

"Hey!" Emmeline called, standing up. "I think we all need to calm down!"

I saw Erin and Lina exchange a glance before tearing off custardy wedges of bread-and-butter pudding and hurling them at Emmeline's midriff. Emmeline's head dropped in sincere dismay as she contemplated the sticky, dripping mess that was her torso.

"The fuck," she said, wavering between outraged and willing. She picked up the metal salad bowl, emptying a glossy pool of dressing and dregs over Lina's head. Kicked the roulade toward Erin. She went to tip some goulash over Renni, then thought better of it.

"Hey!" Renni responded. "Don't leave me out!"

"We couldn't possibly!" Stevie called, and flung over a damp croissant, which landed on Renni's bare leg. Renni dipped her hand into the goulash and splattered it at Stevie, who responded with a handful of cheesecake and a handful of stew.

I plunged both my hands into the risotto, eager to get involved, but was immediately overwhelmed by the sensation of granular sludge. "This feels amazing!" I shouted, and Renni crawled over to join me. We lovingly worked the sweet potatoes between our fingers, then switched to the beetroot, whispering about the varying qualities of each texture.

Eventually we tired of the risotto and looked up. The room had descended into chaos around us. Emmeline and Lina were wrestling in the corner while Sash chased Andrea with the pot of stew. A steady hail of blondie shards flew in varying directions. I clambered up and pulled Renni to her feet, leading her through to the kitchen. Throwing open the cupboards, the fridge, we found more ammunition, returning to the fray with a packet of cornflakes, a carton of milk, and a large selection of soft fruits. We flung the food at the walls; we flung it at each other; we poured it over ourselves.

Catching my breath, I waded through the bodies to find my laptop, plugging it into the speakers and streaking the keyboard with grease.

"Hey!" I called over to Stevie. "Tell me a song to get us dancing."

"Wait!" she called, drawing out the word. Everyone turned to look at me, all ranged around the room, creaturely and grotesque and dripping in food.

"Before that, we have to do something else. We *might* have a surprise for you."

She staggered out to the hallway and returned with a large white book. Holding it out in front of her, she paraded toward me ceremonially. As she got closer, everyone began singing happy birthday. When she reached me, she dropped to one knee, ready to be knighted. "Your birthday present," she announced gravely, and I took the book from her.

"It's all our stories," Sash said, still breathless. "All our interviews."

I opened it up. Each page contained transcriptions, printed

testimonies signed by every member of Supper Club. Even Monica's and Ashley's interviews were in there. Or rather Rowena's.

"You know," Stevie said, "there are a couple of pages missing."

I stared at her, too happy to make a coherent sentence. "It's perfect. There's nothing missing. I love it."

"But there *is* something missing. We never interviewed each other."

I flipped to the back of the book—four blank pages, and the same prompt on each. *What are you afraid of?*

I looked at the flat white space. It seemed both too little and too much.

Stevie gave me a gentle nudge. "Now's your chance."

She handed me a pen.

I felt the weight of the book in my arms, imagined how I might cradle it in order to write, trying not to smear it with the filth on my hands. "I think I need some air," I said, and pushed through the gathered women, sliding open the balcony door. I heard Stevie follow me, then slide the door shut behind her. I leaned over the balcony, thinking about what I needed to say, the syntax of the sentence, the words I would use, the cadence. I couldn't find them. There were no words. There was no order that would make sense of it. The minutes weighed down on me. In the end I just said it.

"I was raped." I spoke the words into the wind, directing them away from the flat, away from my friends. "It was at university. Years ago. I didn't know you then."

Stevie stared at me. "I had no idea." She stepped closer, and I noticed that my hand was gripping the railing too tight for me to actually feel it. She placed hers on top of mine and squeezed it very hard. "I'm so sorry. I don't know what to say."

"It's okay. I know I can be weird about relationships, but, you know, it's hard for me to feel normal about them. I was with this older guy back then—he didn't assault me, that was someone else—but he was my lecturer. It seemed normal at the time, but I look back and think, 'What the fuck? What was he thinking? I was literally a teenager.'"

Stevie put both her arms around me, hugging me awkwardly from the side. I didn't cry, and I didn't feel better either—if anything, I felt worse for having said it all out loud. But I had said it, and that was something. When she released me, I spread my arms out across the balcony railing, leaning into the feeling of being a little bit too cold.

"Here," I said, gesturing for the book and pen.

What are you afraid of?

I sat cross-legged and started to write.

I am afraid of the dark. It seems silly to say, but it is true. I listen for noises: the moans and gives of the building, footsteps from upstairs, people making their way home, men and women shouting. I crawl the space for sounds.

Sometimes I think I hear someone outside my front door: the certain mass of a man shifting his weight. I hear the jangle of keys and the ratchet as they're pushed into the keyhole. I hear the quiet but insistent pressure of a body against the door. I hear the wood splintering and falling apart. I hear his footsteps down the corridor and across the kitchen. I hear his sight adjust to the dark. I hear him lay a hand on the doorknob. I hear him ease open the door and advance toward my bed. I hear the graze of his trousers against the swell of my duvet. His knees level with my prone body.

Or if not the front door, perhaps through the window over the cooker. Sometimes I think I hear that: his body heaving over the frame, landing with a dull thud. Sometimes I think I hear him pacing on the balcony. Sometimes I hear his breath, low and steady, as

he hides in the spaces between the walls. Sometimes I hear him easing out from under my bed, the slight friction of his clothes as he
crawls. I hear the *rub-rub-rub* as he drags himself out, and I listen
and listen, and I am certain he will be out soon, upright and looming
over me—but he never comes, and it is just the sound of my own
heart, beating into the mattress.

I am thirty years old, I thought. I handed the book back to
Stevie.

"Now you," I said. "Your turn. Not that I can imagine what you
could possibly be afraid of."

Stevie leaned with her back against the railing, staring at our
reflection, superimposed with the shapes of our friends dancing inside. She shook her head, looking suddenly teary and defiant.

"I'm afraid you're going to leave. I'm afraid you're going to realize
I'm not good for you. That I'm not good for anyone. I'm afraid everyone is going to leave when they figure that out."

She flipped round to face outward from the balcony. The streetlights below. Across the road another party.

"It's pathetic," she said. "Admit it. It's too pathetic even to write
down."

I looked at her carefully, the texture of her skin, prickled with
chill, all the hairs of her arms standing up. I had never seen Stevie
present herself as so uncompromisingly vulnerable, and I didn't quite
know what to do with it. The sheer courage it required. I was forever
impressed by her audacity, even now.

"Write it down," I said. "Write it down, and afterward we'll burn
it. We'll burn the whole fucking thing. We'll just set it on fire."

Stevie took the book from my hands, looking at me hesitantly,
and I nodded. I rested my gaze on the page, reading every word as
she wrote it down. When she was done, I slung my arm around her.

"You're weird," I said. "I thought I was the weird one, but it's definitely you."

We turned to watch the dancing indoors. Everyone seemed to be moving in a way that she hadn't before. There was a lot more energy. A lot more joy.

"Are we really going to burn it?" she asked.

I nodded. "But everyone should see this," I added. Stevie waited while I ducked back inside, persuading the others to come out, squashing everyone onto the balcony. By the time I returned, she had dragged Adnan's rusty old barbecue to the center of the gathered circle. She held out a yellow lighter to me, grinning like a maniac.

The flames caught at the bottom corner, then at the other pages, quickly engulfing the book. I held on to it until it almost burned my hand, then dropped it into the metal belly of the barbecue. It burned for longer than I expected, and people gradually quieted down, drifted back indoors. Stevie and I were the last on the balcony, watching the fire die, the pages turn to nothing, her fingers laced tightly through my own. "Come on," she said. "Tell me one song you want to dance to, and we're all going to dance to it. Everyone will dance to your song."

I thought for a few seconds and told her it was "Teen Age Riot" by Sonic Youth. I'd always wanted to dance to Sonic Youth with a group of friends. I didn't know why.

Stevie led me back inside and cued up the song, ordering everyone to dance: dance like it was the last song they would ever dance to, dance like their lives depended on it. And, to my surprise, everyone did. It didn't matter whether they knew the words or had heard it before or if it was one of their favorite songs of all time. Everyone danced the same.

After it finished, we went round the room and everyone chose her favorite song. Emmeline picked "Roadrunner" by Jonathan Richman. Renni's was "I Feel Love" by Donna Summer. We waited until the very end of every song before playing the next one, dancing with the same urgency and energy to them all.

"I know what my song is going to be!" Stevie announced, clambering toward the laptop as Donna Summer's voice pulsated and faded out. She made a show of pausing dramatically before finally hitting the spacebar: the room filling with "The Windmills of Your Mind."

"What the fuck is this?" yelped Emmeline.

I grinned at Stevie as she scrambled onto the couch. "It's Dusty Springfield!" She extended her hand to me, and I climbed up to join her. We wrapped our arms around each other, shifting our weight and trying to keep upright, slow-dancing on the sofa. I caught only flashes of her: a thick curl of hair, a small pink earlobe, the slope of her shoulder. *My Stevie,* I thought. *My brilliant Stevie.*

Erin took over, putting on the kind of high-octane dance track I didn't ordinarily enjoy, and we threw ourselves around the room as enthusiastically as ever. "What about the second before the second?" I shouted at Stevie, struggling to make myself heard over the music. "What about the moment before the moment? What about that?" She threw her hands in the air. "It doesn't matter," she shouted back. "Just keep dancing."

As I jumped up and down, the space around me seemed to dilate and contract, making calculations about how best to accommodate us. My dress was a mess of rioja and tomato sauce. Every time I moved, I slopped more wine onto the floor, interested to find I simply didn't care.

We stayed up until it started getting light, by which point we had danced ourselves to exhaustion. Sitting on the floor, Andrea rolled a joint, and we passed it around the room, lying on our backs to talk the way we'd done as children at sleepovers.

I lay between Renni and Lina. We teased Renni for blushing at the mention of her new boyfriend. Lina announced she was going to start trying for a baby. I imagined myself walking around the room, pausing to look closely at each woman. I wondered how much I would see of them after Supper Club came to an end. Not that much, I suspected. But it didn't matter. It wasn't something that was supposed to last forever, and that was kind of the point.

I felt the weight of myself press into the carpet. I thought about how I was carrying only that weight, how I was responsible for no weight other than my own. All I had to carry through life was myself. I wished someone had told me that sooner.

The conversation died down, and I thought about closing my eyes and falling asleep. I studied the stains on the walls: the streaks of beetroot and the oily drips of stew. I wondered what would come out and what wouldn't. I thought, *I will paint over it if I have to*. But it didn't matter. I felt a sense of existing authentically in the space and the moment I'd been allocated, of not stepping on anybody's toes. Existing because I had to. Existing because I didn't have any other choice. If you can't imagine a road, that's because there isn't one. They say when you're dying, hunger is the first thing to go.

Hunter's stew is also known as hunter's pot or perpetual stew. It is made in a large pot, and the ingredients are anything you can find. The idea is that it is never finished, never emptied all the way—instead it is topped up perpetually. It is a stew with an unending cycle. It is a stew that can last for years.

It dates back to medieval Poland, first made in cauldrons no one bothered to empty or wash. It began with the simmering of game meat—pigeon, hare, hen, pheasant, rabbit—just anything you could get your hands on. It would then be supplemented with foraged vegetables, seasoned with wild herbs. Sometimes spices or even wine would be added. Then, as time went by, additional food scraps and leftovers were thrown in—recently harvested produce, stale hunks of bread, newly slaughtered meat, or beans dried for the winter months. It would exist in perpetuity, always the same, always new.

Traditionally the stew has spicy, savory, and sour notes. An element of sourness is absolutely necessary to cut through the rich and intense flavor. It is said to improve with age.

ACKNOWLEDGMENTS

Thanks to Hermione Thompson for being the best editor in the game. It's been so wonderful collaborating with you and I feel a much better, more careful writer for having had the chance. Thanks to Sally Kim for your enthusiasm and wonderful insight, it's been great working with you, too.

Thanks to Becky Thomas for being completely brilliant always.

Thanks to Emma Brown, Elena Hershey, Gabriella Mongelli, Alexis Welby, and all at Penguin. Thanks to Annie Lee, Alžběta Ambrožová, and Maureen Sugden.

Thanks to Charlotte Greene, Danielle Jawando, and Jessica Treen for invaluable feedback. Thanks to Trans Media Watch.

Many thanks to the Society of Authors and the Authors' Foundation for a work-in-progress grant, which was so gratefully received and made a huge difference.

Thanks to my family for love, encouragement, and support. Thanks to my excellent friends. Thanks to Peet for everything.

Thanks to all the women in my life.